Sweet Love

Also by Sarah Strohmeyer

The Sleeping Beauty Proposal
The Cinderella Pact
The Secret Lives of Fortunate Wives
Bubbles Betrothed
Bubbles A Broad
Bubbles Ablaze
Bubbles in Trouble
Bubbles Unbound
Bubbles All the Way

Sweet Love

Sarah Strohmeyer

Dutton

DUTTON
Published by Penguin Group (USA) Inc.
375 Hudson Street, New York, New York 10014, U.S.A.
Penguin Group (Canada), 90 Eglinton Avenue East, Suite 700, Toronto, Ontario M4P 2Y3,
Canada (a division of Pearson Penguin Canada Inc.); Penguin Books Ltd, 80 Strand, London
WC2R 0RL, England; Penguin Ireland, 25 St Stephen's Green, Dublin 2, Ireland (a division of
Penguin Books Ltd); Penguin Group (Australia), 250 Camberwell Road, Camberwell, Victoria
3124, Australia (a division of Pearson Australia Group Pty Ltd); Penguin Books India Pvt Ltd,
11 Community Centre, Panchsheel Park, New Delhi—110 017, India; Penguin Group (NZ), 67
Apollo Drive, Rosedale, North Shore 0632, New Zealand (a division of Pearson New Zealand
Ltd); Penguin Books (South Africa) (Pty) Ltd, 24 Sturdee Avenue, Rosebank, Johannesburg
2196, South Africa

Penguin Books Ltd, Registered Offices: 80 Strand, London WC2R 0RL, England

Published by Dutton, a member of Penguin Group (USA) Inc.

First printing, June 2008
10 9 8 7 6 5 4 3 2 1

REGISTERED TRADEMARK—MARCA REGISTRADA

LIBRARY OF CONGRESS CATALOGING-IN-PUBLICATION DATA
Strohmeyer, Sarah.
Sweet love / Sarah Strohmeyer.
p. cm.
ISBN 978-0-525-95064-6
1. Single mothers—Fiction. 2. Mothers and daughters—Fiction. I. Title.
PS3569.T6972 S86
813'.54—dc22   2008015773

Printed in the United States of America
Set in Sabon

PUBLISHER'S NOTE
This book is a work of fiction. Names, characters, places, and incidents either are the product
of the author's imagination or are used fictitiously, and any resemblance to actual persons, living or dead, business establishments, events, or locales is entirely coincidental.

For my dear departed mother, Nancy,
who laid the path.

And

For my vivacious daughter, Anna,
who keeps me on it.

Sweet Love

Sonnet 56

BY WILLIAM SHAKESPEARE

Sweet love, renew thy force; be it not said
Thy edge should blunter be than appetite,
Which but to-day by feeding is allayed,
To-morrow sharpened in his former might:
So, love, be thou, although to-day thou fill
Thy hungry eyes, even till they wink with fulness,
To-morrow see again, and do not kill
The spirit of love, with a perpetual dulness.
Let this sad interim like the ocean be
Which parts the shore, where two contracted new
Come daily to the banks, that when they see
Return of love, more blest may be the view;
As call it winter, which being full of care,
Makes summer's welcome, thrice more wished, more rare.

"Stressed is desserts spelled backwards."
—Anonymous

Prologue

Love sought is good, but given unsought better.

—TWELFTH NIGHT, ACT III, SCENE 1

I can't help it. I'm worried about my daughter, Julie.

The way she works so hard and comes home exhausted every night, it doesn't seem like she has any fun in her life, no joie de vivre! No man, either. Not that men are any guarantee of happiness. (As anyone who's met Frank, my husband, knows, *ha, ha.*) But it would give me tremendous peace of mind if I could leave God's green Earth assured that my little girl had someone who made her laugh and took care of her. Someone who loves her as much as I do.

Because I don't have much time.

Not that I'm sick. Actually, I feel terrific. Old, yes, but I'm seventy-five for heaven's sake and I've already survived a bout of breast cancer. I won't be a Jack LaLanne pulling a boat at ninety, that's for sure, even if I do walk three miles a day and always take the stairs.

It's just that I've been dizzy lately and yesterday when I took down the cookbook to look up a recipe for Indian pudding—a recipe I used to know by heart—the words turned fuzzy. I had to sit at the kitchen table staring at the pages in order to make sense of them. Yet no matter how I squinted with or without my glasses, the blurring wouldn't stop.

I called out to Frank, "I think I've been hit!" And Frank, in the living room as always, told me to lie down and take it easy, that we didn't need dessert tonight.

That's when I knew my time was near. If I can't read, if I can't make a simple Indian pudding, then I don't see the point in living much more, really. Because aside from a good book and, perhaps, a fresh morning in a dew-covered garden, few things in life give me as much pleasure as the magic of making a truly spectacular dessert.

I'm a big believer in dessert. And let me tell you, if there were more dessert believers like me, this whole country would be a much nicer place. Certainly better than the nation of jittery, testy insomniacs we've become thanks to those damned Starbucks on every corner.

I swear this national caffeine addiction is what's making everyone so angry these days. Have you noticed? We're angry about the war, about debt, about politics, work, global warming, gas prices, the economy, our neighbors. But mostly, it seems to me, people are angry about not being more successful.

They're so busy getting ahead and not falling behind that they've forgotten the simple, inexpensive pleasures. Like eating fresh blueberry pie with vanilla ice cream outside on the picnic bench after a day of swimming and picking berries. Or gathering with friends in front of the fire on a snowy evening with hot buttery bread pudding and baked apples while outside a winter wind howls.

That's what dessert means to me: a dollop of sweet love in an otherwise cold world.

When the kids were growing and Frank was still in construction, I made sure all our meals ended with something sweet. Frank deserved it.

Sour cream brownies, banana pie made with vanilla wafers, lemon poppy-seed pound cake, strawberry shortcake, almond-scented tapioca, pecan blondies (oh . . . my . . . God, those are good), butter brickle ice cream with butterscotch, angel food cake with rhubarb compote, gingerbread with hard sauce, and on Saturday nights, peppermint ice cream sundaes topped with homemade hot fudge.

Homemade hot fudge is a snap to make on the stove with dark chocolate broken into heavy cream and corn syrup. It's a shame so many people buy that glop from the store. I tried to teach Julie how, but she'd have nothing of it. Julie hates to cook—because of me.

She's never said so to my face, naturally, but I know. I know she thinks I've been trapped in the kitchen, forced to serve her father the meat-and-three dinners he liked to have waiting for him as soon as he walked through the door. I can see that my life frightens her.

The thing is, she doesn't remember being a girl and helping me at the wooden board rolling out her little ball of pastry while I made pie. And how, all by herself, she delighted in folding her dough around a spoonful of raspberry jam. She forgets how she used to clap when it came out of the oven, her tiny pie, brown and sparkling with cinnamon sugar as it cooled next to my own.

I'd give anything to see her so happy again, especially since she's so alone these days and so wrapped up in her work she's forgotten to breathe, to live, to love.

Sometimes I fear it's my fault for standing in the way of the man who truly loved her. But what was a mother to do? She was seventeen, a baby, and he was twenty-one, a man. I saw the lascivious way he looked at her. I heard the scuttlebutt from my son. If I hadn't taken that young man aside and warned him in no uncertain terms to stay away, there's no telling what trouble she might have gotten herself into.

But now that I'm older and wiser and have learned youthful indiscretions heal quickly while broken hearts do not, I have to admit I might

have been wrong. I know for certain Julie's never felt that way about another man since—though she pretends to despise him. And I just bet he
isn't over her, either—though he acts as if he is.

The good news is that right when I decided it was too late for an old
lady to correct her mistake, I was offered a second chance to bring them
together in, of all places, a dessert class.

You never know, it just might work. Like the garlic mustard in my garden and the roses on my fence, love has a funny way of blooming after
years of being buried. If it's true love, then it will abide. If it was a fleeting
crush, then it will turn to dust.

Either way, the truth will out.

The Invitation

Congratulations!
You have received the exciting gift of
THREE (3) DESSERT TECHNIQUE classes taught by
CHEF RENE D'OURS at The Famous Boston Cooking School.
Have fun and meet new friends while learning professional secrets to
creating culinary classics sure to amaze your friends and family.

COURSE CURRICULUM FOR RECREATIONAL
DESSERT TECHNIQUES
CLASSES

WEEK ONE: Summer Abundance
    Almond-Infused Hot White Chocolate over Iced Berries
    Cold English Summer Pudding
    Fresh and Easy Strawberry Crème Brûlée
    Peach Cobbler D'Ours with Ginger Ice Cream
    Limoncello Sorbet and Wild Maine Blueberries

WEEK TWO: Simple Comforts
  Classic Tarte Tatin
  Warm Cherry Crisp with Vermont Maple Cream
  Almond Biscotti Tiramisu
  Old-Fashioned Gingerbread and Lemon Sauce
  Spiced Pear and Roquefort Flan

WEEK THREE: A Multiple Chocolate Orgasm
  Grand Marnier Chocolate Mousse
  Torta Caprese
  Chocolate-Dipped Strawberries
  Profiteroles with Dark Chocolate Kahlúa Sauce
  Quick Chocolate Soufflé

Where:

All classes are held at The Famous Boston Cooking School on New-bury Street between Dartmouth and Exeter.

When:

From 7 p.m. to 9:30 p.m. Fridays.

Requirements:

Students do not have to bring knives or other kitchen utensils. Aprons will be provided. However, cooking school policy politely requests students arrive in comfortable foot attire (flat shoes), skirts, pants, and shirts with sleeves. (This is a must for health reasons.)

Alcohol:

Will be served as an accompaniment to the desserts at tasting. Only students over the age of 21 will be permitted to partake.

Bon Appétit!

Chapter One

. . . we know what we are, but know not what we may be.

—HAMLET, ACT IV, SCENE 5

Ahh, the magic of an authentic chocolate chip cannolo made fresh in Boston's Italian North End.

Creamy sweet white ricotta center, crisply fried outside shell—not too thick, not too thin, never stale—the seductive, nay decadent, contribution of chocolate chips and a light dusting of powdered sugar to sweeten the lips.

This is what brings three generations of my family together for Mother's Day. Cannoli.

At Mike's Pastry, my mother, my teenage daughter, and I gather around our tiny round white table and dig in like pigs, inhaling the aroma of fresh cappuccino around us and savoring each crunch, every sweet, creamy mouthful. We are oblivious to the crowds of Sunday churchgoers who have forgotten their solemn prayers not to be led into temptation as they push their way to the front of the line and curse the cutters. Everyone's shouting like dockworkers in this crazy place, but not us.

We are silent in appreciation.

My father says the only way to muzzle a Mueller woman is to feed her. Very funny. Like he has room to talk. He's a man and what bonding experiences do men have? Football and hunting. Watching intellectually challenged mutants head butt each other back and forth down a field or pumping defenseless woodland creatures with shot. Really, it's sad. No wonder when it comes to making friends, men are as clueless as cavemen with cell phones.

"The floor is moving," says Em, my daughter, as she pushes away what's left of her cannolo and closes her eyes. "I might be drunk."

Like her grandmother and me, she has a promising sweet tooth, but without our experience lacks the crucial endurance. Which might be a good thing since too much sugar can steal a young woman's beauty. Already, her figure is rounding and softening—though that doesn't seem to put off the group of handsome dark Italian boys who've been eyeing her and her long blond hair.

"Fight you for it." Heartless, my mother points to what's left on Em's plate. "Can't just let it go to waste."

I sip my foamy cappuccino and tell Mom it's hers. "Happy Mother's Day."

"Aw, gee. You shouldn't have," she says, downing the morsel in one bite. "And now," she adds, opening her purse, "I have *your* present."

"*My* present?" I'm taken aback. "That's a switch. How thoughtful."

"Don't get too excited," Em says. "You're gonna hate it. Worst Mother's Day present ever."

"Watch it, kiddo. You're turning into a wise guy like your mother." Mom hands me a large white envelope. "Surprise."

A gift card to Neiman's, I hope. Or maybe a massage. Perhaps a whole spa visit. I'm dying for one of those. The stress at work has been killing me and those bags under my eyes! Doty, the makeup guru at WBOS, where I'm a TV reporter, has pulled every trick to get rid of them—tea bags, cucumbers, Preparation H—and only the Preparation H works (if you ignore the reek of cod liver oil and the trail of cats behind me).

But when I open the card, my heart falls to my full stomach. "Cooking classes?"

"Dessert," Mom corrects. "And don't be so ungrateful. It's rude."

Em mouths, "I told you so."

This, I suspect, is another one of my mother's sinister efforts to reel me into her world of hard-core domestication. Over the years she's given me oven mitts and aprons, a mini chopper, flexible cutting board (declared by Mom to be an "absolute godsend!"), a cherry pitter and a garlic press (neither of which I've ever used), and cookbooks galore, most with the word "Dummies" in the title.

Recently, she turned her attention to laundry, singing the praises of oxidizing bleach ("How did I ever live without it?") and iron-free shirts (polyester-coated cotton—why not just buy straight polyester for a quarter of the price?), though she never fully abandoned her core campaign to get me into the kitchen, as proven by this latest salvo:

You have received the exciting gift of
THREE (3) DESSERT TECHNIQUE classes taught by
CHEF RENE D'OURS at The Famous Boston Cooking School.

It's not that I don't want to learn how to cook, it's that I'm, well, afraid. Cooking reminds me too much of Mom's imprisonment in her Harvest Gold kitchen, chained to the stove in a dowdy pink quilted, zippered housecoat dicing, rolling, pounding, and mixing her dreams into an impossibility.

Dinner was Mom's raison d'être, her daily work product served promptly at six without fail. Though she rarely expanded beyond twenty rotated dishes, there was always a meat, starch, vegetable, and salad, with white bread in a plastic basket on the table next to a plate of rock-hard butter.

Two menus, however, were sacrosanct: Monday (meat loaf/mashed pota-toes/green beans) because she needed meat loaf sandwiches for school lunches, and Friday (fish/spinach/fried potatoes) because the Pope said so.

In between, it was a crapshoot—liver and onions once a month, ham to be recycled endlessly in hash, a Sunday roasted chicken that would mysteriously reappear as tetrazzini on Tuesday and then ground and mushed in those questionable croquets on Thursday. Spareribs with baked beans, brown bread, and applesauce on Saturday night. Spaghetti with ground beef, garlic bread, and salad on Wednesday.

I know Mom grew weary of making dinner, but she never tired of making dessert, the gooier the better. Even when European cheeseboards invaded America around the late '70s and doctors urged my father to in-crease his intake of fresh foods, my mother stood firm. If fruit had to be involved, then it would be baked to death in a cinnamon apple crisp and topped with artery-clogging whipped cream straight from the can as na-ture intended.

The truth was, 99 percent of her best desserts came off the backs of boxes—Hershey's fudge cake, banana pudding with NILLA wafers, ice-box cake made from Nabisco chocolate cookies—though on Saturday nights she'd make homemade dark chocolate sauce. I LOVE that fudge sauce, especially over peppermint ice cream.

But actually make it myself? No way. I don't care if it's as easy as my mother says. Once I start whipping up fudge sauce, I'll be on to brownies and cookies, slowly easing into the hard stuff like cakes, which require whole days to bake, cool, and frost. After that, can roasting a turkey and making tetrazzini with leftovers be far behind?

I shudder to think.

"Thank you sooo much," I coo, pecking her on the cheek and giving her a quick hug. "This is really, really nice."

"So . . . you'll go?" Mom asks doubtfully, her fading blue eyes questioning.

"Of course, I'll go. I'm looking forward to it. I'm actually very, very, very excited."

She sits back, satisfied. "Good. Because my guess is you'll be delighted by how much you'll like it. I've got a packet of information at home for you to read and even one of Chef Rene's cookbooks I bought on sale. Who knows, this might open a whole new world for you, Julie."

"Who knows?" I say, throwing up my hands in wonderment.

"Ha, ha," Em singsongs as we leave Mike's and head into a soaking May drizzle. "You have to go to school."

Yeah? That's what she thinks.

After Em cooks dinner (raspberry chicken *avec* Chambord/wild rice/ asparagus), she retreats to her room to do homework. Dad falls asleep as usual in the wing chair with the TV on low, and Mom and I? Well, what I had in mind was a relaxing evening on the couch with a book and maybe a teeny tiny slice of the baba rum cake we bought at Mike's. It is, after all, Mother's Day. The dishes can wait.

But not Mom.

Soon she's puttering around my kitchen, wrapping up food and quietly stacking plates. It's the quiet part that drives me nuts because it's so damn false. She *wants* me to hear so I'll feel guilty even though it's my house and as far as I'm concerned the dishes can sit until next year. Why can't she leave them be?

I try to read my book, but it's no good. I'm dealing with a pro here. She hums tunelessly. She drops cutlery. She goes "Ow!" if the water's too hot. And finally, when she groans as she bends down to put away a serving plate, I declare defeat.

"You should start with the glasses first." Victorious in her efforts, she happily dunks the Orrefors delicately in the fresh soapy water. "That way there's no greasy residue."

Thank you, Heloise, I think, waiting with a dish towel to dry and wondering when she's going to stop wearing those gawdawful T-shirts with the silk-screen prints: herbs, wildflowers, cardinals at the bird feeder.

Em and I have bought her other shirts, *normal* shirts worn by normal people, that she professes to adore. But the next day there she is going out to get the mail with a big grizzly bear stamped across her bosom and the word *Alaska* written in loopy cursive around her waist.

"This is the last dish in Aunt Charlotte's pattern," Mom says, handing me a rather hideous gold and green bowl. "All the rest she threw at Uncle Herbert."

I know this, of course, because Mom tells the exact same story every single time she sees that bowl. I can recite in my sleep how Aunt Charlotte trashed her entire set of wedding china when Uncle Herbert came home to announce that he'd blown all their savings in electric energy. And how Charlotte eventually admitted she'd been itching for an excuse to get rid of that pattern all along since Herbert's mother chose it and Charlotte, then a young bride-to-be, had reluctantly agreed simply to appease her future mother-in-law, who turned out to be a right witch who intentionally chose an ugly pattern.

Often my mother recounts these vignettes of family history when she's doing chores, yapping about Aunt Charlotte's plates or Uncle Herbert's basset hound, Pokey, who spent his days in Herbert's Laundromat where the steam zapped Pokey of his zing. Sometimes she incorporates cleaning tips, like how Nana used to spray the plastic shower curtain liners to keep them from molding (whereas my solution is to throw them out). Or how after the market crash of 1929, Great-Aunt Louise kept her family of five fed for two weeks on one ham thanks to an old-fashioned hand-crank meat grinder.

"You learned how to make the most of every last scrap during the Depression," Mom inevitably adds when retelling the Great-Aunt Louise Great Depression ham story. "Then again, I make the most of every last scrap, too. I'm not from your disposable generation."

Tonight, though, aside from the Aunt Charlotte comment, my mother grows taciturn, a word I learned when I studied for my SATs and I don't think I've used once since. She is pensive, moving methodically from good glasses to everyday glasses to good plates to not-so-good plates, to cutlery, her gray brows furrowing as she wipes and rinses.

I decide her sullenness is the fault of my brother, Paul, a playboy stockbroker in New York City who has forgotten to call on Mother's Day. An unforgivable sin in her book and one not easily atoned for with belated flowers or chocolate.

"It's not Paul," Mom says when I gleefully accuse him. "Anyway, he did send me a card and a pass to the Renew Day Spa in Waverly."

Damn. That's what I wanted.

"No, if there's any reason I'm off," she says with a pout, "it's because of you."

I dump the forks in the dishwasher, falsely accused again. "Me? What have I done now?"

"It's not what you've done. It's what you're going to do. Or, rather, *not* going to do. You're not going to go to those dessert classes I got. I just know it."

I find myself turning red as I attempt to sputter a lie. "That's not . . . not true. Of course, I'm . . ."

"Don't lie, Julie. I don't care if you skip the classes as much as I care that you tell the truth."

"Look, Mom. It's not that I don't appreciate the classes or your intention behind giving them. I do. It's just that . . ." What reason can I invent so I don't hurt her feelings? "I have to work on Friday nights and it might be hard for me to get away."

"Bull." Mom hands me the washed rice pot, suds still clinging to the handle. "You can change your schedule, it's far enough away, and you haven't even looked at your packet or cookbook. You've shown absolutely no interest in this gift whatsoever. I hate to sound crass, but those dessert classes weren't cheap, you know. Quite a bit of scratch for an old lady on a fixed income."

This is a new personal record for her. Gift guilt + daughter inconsideration + expense + the old lady + the "fixed income" line. One can't help but be impressed.

"Sorry, Mom. You're right. I'll go to the classes and enjoy them. In fact, I'll read over the packet tonight just to make you happy."

Mom goes, "Hmph." Though I can tell she's pleased.

But it's not until long after she's in bed and I'm flipping through the packet that I smell a skunk. My dear sweet mother's not eager to see me improve my culinary skills one bit.

For as I scan a list of fellow future classmates, I come to the bottom and stop short at the name in bold block letters.

MICHAEL SLAYTON.

The man I once loved to the depths of my soul.

The man whose career I once ruined.

Surely, this can be no coincidence.

Chapter Two

And giddy Fortune's furious fickle wheel,
That goddess blind,
That stands upon the rolling restless stone—

—HENRY V. ACT III, SCENE 6

On a blissfully sunny afternoon in June, which just so happens to be the day of the first dessert class, I take WBOS's star correspondent Valerie Zidane out to lunch at an outdoor café in Davis Square to give her a pep talk.

Kirk Bledsoe, our network's famous Washington bureau chief, is in town on a headhunting mission to snare new blood for his weary national election team. I applied and was promptly rejected in a form letter thanking me for my interest and years of service, blah, blah, blah. Valerie, however, got The Call. If she passes the interview with Kirk today, she's on the team.

This means months of flying with either the Democratic or Republican candidate on posh planes, sleeping in four-star hotels, hobnobbing with celebrities and, best of all, appearing nightly to 7.6 million viewers on the six-thirty news. Already Valerie's jumped the gun and bought a whole new wardrobe of St. John suits.

Sigh.

I'm trying to be a good sport about all this, but I'm ashamed to admit it's not easy. Valerie's ten years younger than I am and living a life of freedom, working as long and hard as her ambition dictates. I, on the other hand, am a single mother raising a teenager who sucks up time, money, and patience like a Hoover in black eyeliner.

Not that I'm complaining. Much.

"It's all screwed up," Valerie says, shaking a teeny amount of vinegar over her chicken salad, no dressing or, for that matter, chicken. "You should be their number one candidate. You've been here for ages."

Perhaps Valerie's heart is in the right place. Perhaps. But as I spear a forbidden French fry and study how her perky ski-jump nose wiggles adorably when she nibbles her endive, I can't help but suspect that like Boston Marathon cheater Rosie Ruiz, I never was in the running.

Valerie is an ideal eclectic mix of Algerian, Irish, French, and Puerto Rican descent with a thread of the British royal line. *And* she was raised in Thailand by missionary parents. Of course Kirk wants her. She's multicultural, multilingual, Columbia University educated, and absolutely yummy in her yellow-and-cream Akris Punto jacket and matching sheath.

Me? I'm so plain with my medium-length brown hair and brown eyes and pink suit from Macy's, strangers often mistake me for someone else. I am standard-issue middle American. Graduate of Boston University, middle of the class with a rubber-stamped degree in political science. If I were an appliance, my name would be Kenmore.

"It's okay," I tell her. "You and I both know how this business is, Val. After forty, the national desk doesn't want you, unless you're a halfway handsome man with a silver dye job. I say go for it while you have the chance."

She puts down her fork and cocks her head. "Thanks. You're sweet. It's so hard for me not to be overeager, you know. Raldo told me all the reporters who were chosen to work on the election team four years ago ended up with permanent assignments in the network."

"Is that so?" Raldo is our hypochondriac anchorman more famous for contracting imaginary deadly diseases than manning the hotline to network headquarters. His credibility on the non-disease front is generally very low.

"But I won't forget you when I'm in Washington and New York, I promise," Valerie says. "You've been a real mentor to me, Julie. I feel really fortunate to have a mature woman to turn to for advice."

My eyes involuntarily narrow. Who you calling mature?

"Which is why I put you down as my recommendation." Slapping her hands over her face, she says, "I know I should have asked first, but I felt awkward. What with you being here longer than me and . . . all."

I let out a polite laugh as I envision my manicured fingers around her throat. Let it go, I tell myself as I lay down my Visa. It's no crime to be middle-aged.

"I'd have used Arnie, but you know how he is. Sunny one day, stormy the next. Totally unpredictable. And besides, he told me I'm the best reporter here, so he has a vested interest in keeping me down on the farm. Whereas when I leave, you'll take my place as the best reporter, which means it's more likely you'll give me a better recommendation. Smart, huh?"

I say, "You were doing fine up until that last line."

"Too much?"

"You might at least try to feign some humility. Oddly enough, some people find it appealing."

Back at work I try to forget lunch by returning a couple of phone calls concerning Amy Michak, a nineteen-year-old college student from Somerville who went missing outside the Somerville Library last November.

I'm obsessed with this story, partly because I'm fairly certain Amy's dead and also because she is—was—the spitting image of my daughter, Em. I just can't imagine being Amy's mother, Rhonda. Months of waiting, hoping, fearing—I'd go insane.

Now, with the advent of summer, have come painful reports of random new sightings I'm obligated to confirm and, unfortunately, debunk. Amy spotted strolling along Revere Beach hand in hand with a tall dude sporting an army haircut. Amy fingering pink sheets at Linens'n Things at the Arsenal Mall. Bike riding by the Mystic Lakes. Standing in line to see *Indiana Jones.*

What amazes me about these reports is the assumption Amy would be so daft that she'd be out shopping and biking when across town her suffering mother creeps through life in agony, jumping at every ring of the phone, dreading every knock at the door lest it's the police with the news her daughter's body has been found.

Were she alive, surely this child would take a moment to put down the pink pillowcases and give her mother a ring from the Arsenal Mall pay phone, no?

After a morbid discussion with Detective Sinesky at the Somerville PD about Amy's suspected fate, I am in desperate need of chocolate fortification. Just a little something to satisfy my cravings, renew my spirits. Perhaps a bite-sized piece of Dove dark chocolate or a handful of M&M's. Checking the stash in my upper-right-hand drawer, I find, much to my joy, I have both! Hmm. Which to choose? Decisions, decisions.

Unwrapping the Dove, I think, cripes, I'm going to be a moose if I don't break this chocolate habit. After eating a piece—pieces—of Dove every day like this for years, Michael Slayton's going to wonder what happened to me. . . .

Okay, I have to stop focusing so much on Michael. Last night I spent two hours trying to choose which outfit to wear to dessert class, one that would meet Chef D'Ours's monastic requirements—covered arms; flat, closed shoes—and yet still be provocative. It was like being back in high school and trying to thwart the Our Lady of Miracles school uniforms by rolling down my kneesocks.

Not that I'm still interested in Michael that way. Be serious. The man despises me and just the idea of him makes me want to punch a pillow. My only objective is to walk into class looking *goooood*. Make him regret the tongue-lashing he left me with six years ago.

A "ratings-grubbing ice queen with no heart or soul or principles. A picture-perfect sellout." How dare he? What an arrogant, pompous prick of a . . .

"Here's a sorry state of affairs. The addict and her drug," a wiseass voice says behind me. "You know, there's help for that. BOS does offer free twelve-step programs."

It's Arnie Wolff, my short, bespectacled news director with whom I have a delightfully unorthodox relationship. He teases me and I annoy him and, together, we bug the whole newsroom.

"Want one?" I say, sticking out a Dove. "No, wait, I forgot. You like your sugar in strictly maltose form."

"Don't knock beer. It's the breakfast of champions. Anyway, I came to tell you that after you're done stuffing your face, Oompa Loompa, we're holding a meeting with you in the conference room."

"Mwe?" I ask, mouth full.

He winces in disgust. "It's such a pleasure to be around a true lady. Yes, you, Owen, me, and the Big Kahuna."

Owen Trumbull is our general manager, a blond, mostly harmless bureaucrat whose wetted finger is forever in the wind testing the political direction of the network. But who's the Big Kahuna?

I say, "Big Kahuna?"

Arnie glances sidewise at Valerie, who's all ears two desks away. "Don't make me spell it out."

He must mean . . . I mouth, *"Kirk Bledsoe?"*

Arnie slaps his forehead and motions me to follow him.

I have no idea what the famous Kirk Bledsoe would want from me until I pass Valerie, who hisses, "I'm counting on you!" and flashes me a big thumbs-up.

Oh, right. Her recommendation, nothing more.

Licking chocolate from my lips during the short march down the hall, I wrack my brain to list three positive attributes to pin to Val that would make her worthy of joining the national election team. All I can come up with is that she gets invites to sample sales like no one else and she's great at interior design, having done a brilliant job of choosing a couch to match my hideous flowered walls. Not exactly talents for grilling the next president of the United States, I suppose, unless the next president is Christopher Lowell.

In the conference room, Arnie and I are greeted by Owen's secretary, Eva, and none other than Kirk Bledsoe, *the* Washington bureau chief himself. It's positively thrilling. He's much taller than I'd have expected and grayer, especially with the trimmed white beard. I'm afraid to say he actually looks ancient.

Being naturally gifted under pressure, I, of course, manage to insult him right off by blubbering about how when I was a kid my parents used to watch him when he was a correspondent for WBOS in "the dark ages." Eva gives me a pointed look and Arnie whispers, "Nice move," though Kirk doesn't seem to mind. He says something about being loyal to WBOS ever since.

"I like to go back to my roots," he adds, pausing. "When choosing the person who will someday replace me."

"Like a salmon swimming home to spawn and die," I agree. Which is when Arnie kicks me under the table and I realize what I've said. "Sorry. I didn't mean it that way. I meant—"

Kirk holds up his hand. "You're exactly right and it's a beautiful image. No need to apologize."

"Yes, she does," Owen quips. "I'll make sure she writes fifty times that she must not offend the network's most famous correspondent."

We laugh nervously, relieved *that* disaster is over. Good thing I'm not the one up for the job. Whew.

"I'm sure you know why Kirk's here," Owen begins. "Especially if you went out to lunch with Valerie."

Kirk and Owen exchange knowing grins.

"I got the gist. If you want, I can jump right in and save us all a lot of time."

"First," Kirk says, "let's have a chat about you and where you're coming from. Nothing official. Just casual."

I've never been asked to give a live recommendation before, so I have no idea if this is standard operating procedure. "Okay," I say hesitantly. "Shoot."

"Owen tells me you're a single mother."

God. Is that all people talk about? Makes me sound like some blue-eye-shadowed tramp who got knocked up behind the Dairy Queen. "I'm divorced, yes. My ex-husband, Donald, lives in Newton, but I've mostly raised our daughter alone. He's, uh, on to his second family." Trophy wife, Jill, their spoiled son, Angus, piss-poor child support and zero alimony, for the record.

"Though you've had help from your mother, with whom you live."

I have to shift in my chair, partly because the conference room's high-voltage static electricity is hiking up my skirt and partly because I'm not sure I like this line of questioning. "Actually, I live above my parents in a double in Watertown. My father retired from the Watertown Public Works Department when he had a mild heart attack years and years ago. I bought the double shortly after the divorce so I could keep an eye on them and they could help out with Em, my daughter."

"Kind of a win-win situation," Kirk says.

"It has been. I mean, Em's a teenager now and about to graduate from

Newton South. Since Donald lives in Newton, she gets to go there. Great school, you know. She's very lucky."

Kirk nods, indicating I should get on with it.

"Anyway, these days it's less of Mom helping out with Em and more of me helping out Dad. You know, shoveling the walks, mowing the lawn. Mom went through a bout of breast cancer, so . . ." For heaven's sake, he's not interested in my life story. "Hold on. You don't need to know all that, do you?"

"I don't need to, but it helps. I've found that taking into account people's personal issues is the best way to ensure a happy, productive workplace," Kirk says.

How refreshingly progressive. "Well, Valerie's going to fit right in since she sure does have a lot of personal issues." And once again I catch myself too late. "Not that she has any serious personal issues, per se. I mean, not anymore." Another kick from Arnie under the table. "Shoot. I'm supposed to give her a glowing recommendation and that kind of blew it, huh?"

Indeed, Kirk stops writing and looks to Owen, who shakes his head.

"Julie," Owen says, leaning forward. "In case there's been a misunderstanding, we didn't bring you in here to discuss Valerie. We brought you in here to discuss . . . you."

Arnie says, "You're a candidate, too, you know."

"A pretty high up one," Kirk adds, smiling.

Okay, now I really wish I hadn't said that stuff about swimming upstream to spawn and die and that long monologue about my family life. Sitting up straight, I clasp my hands on the table, paste on an efficient smile, and say, "Wow. I had no idea I was still in the running. After getting that form letter . . ."

"You didn't get the memo?" Kirk asks.

"No. I did not get the memo."

Owen shoots a reproving look at Eva, who puts her head down and takes a note.

"Well, you should have," Kirk says. "I apologize. I realize we've given you no time to prepare for this interview."

Cripes. I can't believe I'm really up for consideration. It's just beginning to hit me. "That's fantastic," I gush. "I would be really excited to join the national election team. But, if you don't mind, why me?"

Kirk chuckles and tells Owen he'll handle this. "Easy. You've been here close to twenty years. You've covered a wide range of issues near and dear to the voters' hearts, such as health care reform, rising gas prices, the economy, and the outrageous cost of housing.

"I loved the profile you did last year on veterans returning from the Iraq War. It was a delicate issue you handled without pandering to either side. In addition, you've done a bang-up job covering several statewide campaigns, especially, of course, your award-winning exposé of Carlos FitzWilliams."

"Thank you." Though hearing FitzWilliams's name again reminds me of Michael's diatribe. *Ratings-grubbing ice queen with no heart or soul or principles. A picture-perfect sellout.*

Doesn't the fact that it might get me on the national election team prove his point?

"And, finally, your coverage of Amy Michak's disappearance is outstanding. Thorough, incisive without being exploitative. That's such a hard line to walk. By the way, I have a couple of theories about her abduction, if you've got the time."

"For you," I say, "anything." Because you, Kirk Bledsoe, are my new best friend.

"Then there's the matter of demographics. Indications are that this election could hinge on—if you pardon my bluntness—middle-aged women like you."

When he says that, I imagine frowning church ladies with blue hair and plastic purses. Certainly I'm not one of them . . . am I? I look to Arnie, who's stifling a laugh.

Now it's Kirk's turn to be shamefaced. "What I mean is, you share some of their concerns in your own personal life. Like them, you are feeling the burden of aging parents and, at the other end of the generational spectrum, teenagers who are testing the limits."

"I have no idea what you're talking about. Why, my seventeen-year-old is a perfect angel, does everything I ask, and is as neat as a pin."

Kirk smiles. "Sense of humor. Don't lose that. You're going to need it. Your life is going to be a roller coaster when you get on board August first."

August first. Right around the corner. Em will have to move in with Donald for the nonce, right when she'll be applying to colleges. By the time I get back, the applications will be in and I'll have missed so much. And what about Mom and Dad, if something happens to them? It's not like Paul's around to step in. They're my responsibility, Dad with his angina and Mom with her cancer woes.

Owen is saying something about keeping this under my hat until the background checks are completed.

Oh. I don't like the sound of that. "Background checks?"

"Precaution." Kirk waves this off as if a stranger prying into your most personal records is the most normal of circumstances. "Considering the fate of the world hangs on the next election, our new raft of reporters has got to be of the most impeccable character and totally clean. No drugs. No alcohol or sexual problems that might compromise their objectivity."

"No ethical issues," Arnie says, giving me a warning look.

What's he eyeing me for? "I don't have any ethical issues, Arnie."

"I'm sure you don't," Kirk says. "Still, it's better to wait until we've made a formal announcement. Already one of your colleagues, not necessarily at this station, has blown it by blabbing that he or she got the job when, actually, the background check turned up a tick."

Valerie, I think, shocked. What could she have done? *Paid too much for retail.*

For the next twenty minutes Kirk outlines my duties in case I'm chosen: how I should start reading everything ever written on both candidates, their campaign finance reports and voting histories, naturally, their speeches, archived articles in *The New York Times* and *Washington Post*, reports from watchdog groups and underground news sources. Chances are I'll get very little sleep in the upcoming weeks and may find myself in tricky situations that could try my sanity, once I'm on the road, he tells me.

"The national press corps is ruthless," Kirk says. "Hard-bitten and cynical. That's why we're looking for new blood, unjaded local reporters who can provide an authentic perspective more in tune with the average viewer's. It's not gonna be easy, Julie."

I tell him it sounds divine and, honestly, I'm so excited I feel like running to a mountaintop and twirling around in a crazy Julie Andrews kind of way. After believing that my years of slavery weren't going to get me anywhere, that I was too old to go to the network, my hard work is finally paying off. And right when Em has only one more year of high school, too. The timing couldn't be better!

"It's everything I ever wanted," I tell him. "Travel. National politics. A pivotal election. Nonstop action. Backroom ruthlessness." Suits. Heels. Limousines. White House press badge. Oh my God. I feel like I've just stepped into a Mitchum ad, it's so heady. "I mean, there's a fifty percent chance I'll be shoulder to shoulder with the next president of the United States."

Kirk says, "Talk to me in six months. Then we'll see how glamorous that is."

Eva comments on the time as Owen and Arnie excuse themselves to go to another meeting, leaving Kirk and me alone at last. Ominously, Kirk follows them and closes the door.

"There's just one last thing I want to ask before we wrap up," he says, sitting down.

Darn. I knew there had to be a catch. That's always the way it is with me. So close and yet so far.

"Going back to the Carlos FitzWilliams story, I heard your source on that was a guy you were dating—FitzWilliams's own campaign manager."

Involuntarily, I grip my armrest, Kirk's line about "impeccable character" still fresh in my mind. "You mean Michael Slayton?"

"Down in Washington, I paid extra attention to Slayton because he was from our hometown. As I recall, his star was rising and then, abruptly, it fell to Earth after your report aired."

Kirk is suddenly not so gray and avuncular. He's mean and suspicious as his gaze bores through me, right into my inner being. Not for nothing is he Washington bureau chief.

Willing my voice not to shake, I say evenly, "I've known Michael Slayton all my life. He grew up in our neighborhood. But I can honestly tell you that he and I have never had anything more than a platonic relationship."

"That's not what FitzWilliams told me." This comes out cold. "That's why he fired Slayton, for deceiving him, for falling in love with a reporter who was out to nail him."

I blanch. "FitzWilliams said that?" What a creep. To cover his own ass, he smeared Michael's and my reputation.

"Well, Kirk," I say. "If there's one thing I've learned being a reporter it's that every politician lies. There's not much I believe in this world unless I see it happen in front of my eyes."

"True," he agrees. "And that's what makes you an ideal choice to cover the presidential candidates. That said, FitzWilliams does raise a disturbing . . ."

"If you're asking who is my original source," I say, trying to keep my anger in check, "the one who led me to the women FitzWilliams hit on, it was . . ."

"I don't need to know that. . . ."

"It was my mother."

Kirk raises a brow. "Your mother?"

"At Mario's, the beauty parlor she goes to every Friday to have her hair washed and set. Her stylist was best friends with one of the girls and everyone was talking about what FitzWilliams was doing. It was a drop from heaven."

Kirk's shoulders slump in relief and he gives me a big grin. "Old-fashioned beauty parlor gossip. So there never was anything between you and Slayton."

Was there ever, I want to blurt. *I threw myself at him when I was seventeen and declared my love and he oh so gently turned me down, forever smashing my girlhood crush.* "Absolutely not. And there never will be."

"Good," Kirk says, nodding. "So I assume you'll have no problem if I ask him myself."

My gut twists into a clench. "No problem at all. You have free rein," I bluff, with forced cheer. "I am an open book." Though I wish I weren't. I wish I were closed and locked like my daughter's diary, safely tucked away for no one to read.

As my mother says, your forties are when you finally pay for your past mistakes, the cigarettes and sunburns, the Big Macs and smooth-talking men. She may be right. They may be gaining and getting closer. But I'm still in the lead.

And if I want this new job, I better start running, fast.

Chapter Three

I never tempted her with word too large;
But, as a brother to his sister, show'd
Bashful sincerity and comely love."

—MUCH ADO ABOUT NOTHING, ACT IV, SCENE 1

It's hard to remember when I didn't worship Michael Slayton.

Even now, despite our rocky history—or, rather, cataclysmic history—my instinctive reaction when I hear his name is to flush like I did when I was ten. Other girls might have swooned over the latest cover of *Tiger Beat*, but I was ga-ga for the boy next door.

The Slaytons (or "the crazy Slaytons," as my mother insisted on calling them) lived five doors down from our old house on Clark Street in a firetrap of peeling gray paint and untamed brambles.

They were an odd family, to put it mildly. I can't ever recall seeing Mrs. Slayton in something other than a breezy shift, and Michael's father was forever on the outs with various institutions such as the Newton police. Also, he reeked faintly of a chemical smell, something between rubbing alcohol and turpentine.

Understandably, my parents weren't overjoyed when Paul chose Michael to be his best friend. Michael was too wild with his unkempt jet-black hair and dirty jeans. But he was smart. Wicked smart. An unbeatable chess player and an expert on Shakespeare, able to quote complete soliloquies, much to the puzzlement of us neighborhood kids who had never heard of a nunnery. (How delighted we were to find it was another word for brothel!)

Elizabethan whoring aside, we didn't hang around Michael for his recitation of Hamlet's damnation of Ophelia. We hung around him because he was always building something. Usually something wonderfully dangerous—an elaborate tree house with trapdoors, go-carts with magnets in the noses, a pulley system to haul him (and Paul) from his front porch to the third-floor window. Javelins, rope swings, bottle rockets, homemade skateboard ramps fastened with rusty nails. There was no end to his inventive energy.

Miraculously, my brother and he never landed in the emergency room except for once, when Paul's foot fell through a rotted hole in the Slaytons' kitchen floor and his ankle snapped. That was the night my mother discovered the dirty truth about the Slaytons.

I was nine and Michael was thirteen, like Paul, and we were leaving the hospital on the fateful brisk October night with Paul on crutches, his ankle in a cast. Mom asked Michael if he would like to come to our house for dinner and his face went blank. He stood stock-still in the parking lot and said, "Dinner?" as if we had asked him to travel to Mars or swallow tacks.

"You do eat dinner, don't you, Michael?" Mom asked softly, smoothing down her homemade denim wrap skirt. She was no fan of the Slaytons, but she knew an underfed boy when she saw one.

"I eat dinner," he snapped. "I make myself a grilled cheese every night. And sometimes," he added proudly, "hot dogs."

That did it. Who were these "crazy Slaytons" who lived on grilled cheese and hot dogs and ripped holes in their kitchen floors? Magical people, I decided, feeling cramped by my mother's strictly enforced eight-thirty bedtime and warnings to stay off the parlor furniture.

From that point on, Mom assumed responsibility for Michael's basic needs. Without ever so much as hinting that he wasn't the most loved and adored child, she got him to fork over his dirty clothes and take showers and eat at our table five nights out of the week, never sending him home without a late-night snack of banana cake or tapioca pudding in Tupperware. Gentle reminders that comfort and order were never far away.

It also got so she routinely added an extra lunch for Michael in Paul's backpack, pushed him into a barber's chair, and even took him to our dentist. Paul and I pretended not to notice and Michael's parents never objected.

"So sad," my mother said, clucking her tongue. "It's like they just don't care."

But I cared. I cared a lot. To have the enchanting Michael Slayton at our house taking a shower—naked!—in our bathroom, to sit right across the table from him almost every night was some sort of miracle.

I began to think of Michael as mine. My destiny. We had a special bond, a sweet bond. With a wink, he'd sneak me cookies under the table and teach me the Ruy Lopez opening in chess, his long fingers gracefully moving his pawn to d4. Someday, I vowed, those artistic fingers of his would clasp mine and on bended knee he'd ask me to be his wife. His Heathcliff to my Catherine.

Thirty years later I get chills remembering that, still.

I don't know if Michael was aware of my desperate crush. If he suspected, he was too considerate to point it out. As for me, I suffered in silence until he left for Princeton on full scholarship, returning during school holidays and summer breaks with one beautiful, perfect girlfriend after another.

Bad enough they were long-legged and clear-skinned with shiny thick hair and impossibly athletic bodies. They also spoke fluent French or obscure dialects of Cantonese, understood particle physics and the history of the Franco-Prussian Empire. Plus, they adored him so much they didn't mind his mother prancing about in her nightgown or the piles of garbage on the back porch. It added to his mystery.

Clearly, I, with my awkward teenage mannerisms, didn't stand a chance. And neither did they.

No matter how pretty or smart the girl, she never returned for the next break. It was as if Michael were searching for the unreachable ideal, the utopian woman who didn't exist. That was until he came home from college senior year smitten by a New Jersey senatorial candidate reputed to be the next John F. Kennedy. Finally, he had found his true love: politics.

But, geesh, the phrases he used—"man of the people" and "visionary"— were so naïve that even in my high school innocence they sounded silly. No one's really a man of the people, I scoffed. Certainly not someone with a mansion near Jackie O and a stable or two of prize Thoroughbreds.

Mom's theory was that though Michael had been raised—if you could use that word—to pursue his intellect, he'd grown up in a house free of necessary discernment. (Translation? Free of henpecking gossip, the bailiwick of my mother and her sister, Aunt Charlotte, Queens of Schadenfreude.) He did not know, as I did, that politicians were all hot air and bluster, that campaign promises weren't worth the paper they were printed on. Michael honestly bought the propaganda that one good person could change the world.

Absurd.

I had to hand it to him, though. He never lost faith. When I last bumped into him six years ago he was working as the tireless campaign manager for Carlos FitzWilliams, a long-shot candidate to represent the Eleventh Congressional District in Massachusetts. By that time, Michael had achieved a reputation in Washington for sending underdogs to the Beltway, and no wonder. The guy was on fire.

It was baffling. Here he was in his forties and still he *believed*. He believed FitzWilliams was the Eleventh District's one and only answer, the Second Coming who could clean up Congress and save the district's downtowns. It was like he was sixteen, ecstatic over the zip-line he'd strung from his bedroom window to the garage, gushing about speed and friction.

Except he wasn't sixteen. Nor was he—to my chagrin—available. Two years before, he'd eloped with a Virginia debutante named Cassie who, according to Paul, was the kind of pearl-wearing sex kitten most prepper boys dreamed of marrying. Pretty, blond, athletic, super teeth, and a devoted sister of "Pi Phi."

In other words, so not Michael's type.

Not that his new marriage had anything to do with the vigorous way I plunged into investigating Carlos FitzWilliams. Yes, I was divorced by then and I couldn't help feeling slightly depressed and rejected that Michael had married another woman without ever once considering me.

But we were adults now, professionals, and FitzWilliams, I discovered, was a letch with a penchant for young campaign staffers. There was no choice, I had to out him and in so doing, ruin Michael's career.

He never forgave me for not holding the story until he could finish his own inquiries, as he requested. And I never forgave him for asking. After his venomous diatribe chastising me for "selling out," all communication between us ceased.

I haven't spoken to him for six years.

As for the night I declared my undying love when I was a tender seventeen? That's why I have to talk to my best friend, Liza, the only other person who knows my awful secret. Besides Michael, of course.

He, I pray, will forget.

"You set me up!"

"I did not. That's a blatant lie and you know it," Liza declares when she answers the door half dressed in a white terry cloth robe, her flowing hair dripping wet and curly.

She's one of those sexy big-boned women whose breasts are so generous and brown eyes so smoky most men don't notice she is, according to those stiffs in the insurance industry, fat.

"By the way," she asks. "What are we talking about?"

"You know perfectly well what we're talking about." I step over a suitcase and make my way into her incredible apartment with its twelve-foot ceilings, fireplaces, and view overlooking Commonwealth Avenue. "Your sneaky dessert class."

"Oh, that," she says. "Yeah. You're right. But I got more important things to worry about right now, kiddo. My life is over. Walk with me."

I follow Liza down the carpeted hallway, past her massive red and white kitchen, where Marisol, her assistant, a plucked weasel with hair yanked so tightly into a ponytail the veins on her forehead throb nervously, is furiously thumbing a BlackBerry while simultaneously barking into a cell phone something about hotel reservations in Skopje.

Tonight Liza leaves for a monthlong pilgrimage to search for authentic recipes in the old Yugoslavia and Romania. Serbia and Bosnia are the dernier cri cuisines on the horizon, according to her, and so easy to modify with shortcuts.

Whenever she says this, I picture yak smothered in Campbell's Creamy Mushroom and nearly barf.

This is Liza's forte: writing The Hot Cook's Guide to Haute Cuisine series on how to make international dishes with six cheap ingredients, no more—for people who just don't give a damn.

Think Chateaubriand served with a Lipton's Onion Soup mix demiglace or, as in the case of Liza's last mega best seller *Hot Haute Indian!*, chana dal made with chickpeas and a can of tomato rice.

I know, disgusting, but the woman sells by the truckload. She's the Queen of Costco, where her cookbooks are stacked by the foot next to a large cardboard cutout of her (trimmed down) proudly displaying a can of creamy celery soup—her favorite standby.

"My tenth trip in two years and you'd think it was our first, we're so disorganized," Liza says, scurrying into her bedroom and into her all-white master bath. Slamming the door, she adds breathlessly, "I'm so glad you're here. You can be a witness."

"To what?"

"To me firing Marisol."

Oh, no. Here we go again. Liza going nuts before one of these recipe excursions.

Partly it's the stress of packing up and going abroad for weeks and weeks. Partly it's the fact that for all her traveling, Liza is the worst flier alive. Passengers in first class have been known to volunteer to sit in coach after an hour of my best friend yelling, "We're going to die!" at the top of her voice and clutching the hand rests so fiercely, she once broke one on British Airways.

"You're not going to fire Marisol. She's your right-hand woman." I drop the toilet seat and push Liza onto it. "Where's your Valium?"

"You don't know. She completely screwed up the Budva end. We were supposed to meet with Herzy in Montenegro on the second and it turns out he'll be in Paris and there's no way we can get together now. The most cutting-edge chef in all of Serbia and I'll be stuck in the Riviera. I can't take Valium. I've got too much to do. Our flight leaves at ten."

"Okay." I spy the Valium bottle by the sink and pop it open. "Do you want one or two?"

She holds up a finger and I tuck a little V tablet under her tongue. Psychosomatically it does the trick. Liza instantly chills.

"Thank you," she says.

"You're welcome."

"I won't fire Marisol. You're right. She's a doll."

"Good girl." I pat her on her wet head. "That's wise."

Then, as if just registering my complaint, she says, "How'd you find out I arranged the dessert class?"

"I'm a reporter. I got instincts. One of them being that no way would Mom have chosen the high-falutin' Boston Cooking School on her own. Then, when I checked online and saw the price for three classes was two hundred and fifty dollars, my suspicions really took off."

Liza hops up and digs into her makeup bag, slapping on moisturizer, dotting on foundation, running sticks around her eyes, and lining her lips in bright red as I go on.

"A few calls, a few emails, and lo and behold I discover Our Lady of Miracles raffled off Boston Cooking School dessert classes last month to raise capital to remodel the parish kitchen and who should be head of the fund-raising committee? My oldest and dearest friend, Liza Librecz, she the descendant of traveling, deceiving Gypsies."

Liza flicks on the blow-dryer and shouts, "So your mom won the classes for fifty bucks. Big deal. Doesn't mean she can't give them as a gift. It was a good cause."

"You're missing my point," I shout back. "I know you rigged that raffle, Liza, and not because you were desperate for me to learn how to make cherry flambé. As always, there's a man involved."

"Hah! How true."

"So you admit it."

"Sure." She turns off the blow-dryer and fluffs her hair, frowning at her reflection in the mirror. "I like him. I think he's drop-dead sexy and eminently fuckable. Is that a crime?"

"You haven't seen him in . . ." I have to count back to the last time Liza would have run in to Michael. Probably the night I attacked him. "In thirty years. You have no idea if he's eminently fuckable."

"For your information, I ran in to him last week, right after I taught my last recreational class at the cooking school. Six-Ingredient Meals Under an Hour."

"What was Michael doing at the cooking school?"

"Michael?" Liza wrinkles her nose. "I was talking about Chef Rene D'Ours. You know, your instructor? The father of my future children?"

I'm flummoxed. Throughout my entire rant we've been talking about two different men.

"Have you ever seen Chef Rene?" Liza bubbles, skipping over our misunderstanding. "The spitting image of Fabio except he likes real butter, not the fake stuff, being that he's French."

"An I-Can't-Believe-He's-Not-Fabio."

"Exactly. Better yet, he just broke up with his girlfriend, an obnoxious Italian prima donna with a spoiled little dog. This is my window of opportunity and you're the woman to push me through it. When you take that class, talk me up to Rene, make me sound dangerous and sexy so he'll ask me out, okay?"

Hold on. Hold on. I have to press my fingers to my temples to stop the whirring within. "This is not what I came here for," I say, sitting on the edge of her Jacuzzi. "I came to chew you out for setting me up with Michael at a time when I need to distance myself from him as far as possible."

Liza blinks and says, "Why?"

"Aha!" I snap an accusatory finger. "So you knew Michael was taking the class."

"Of course I knew. I sold him the raffle ticket."

"You did?"

Twirling up a lipstick she goes, "Uh-huh. Hunted him down at his consulting headquarters and everything."

She's amazing. Where does she find the time? "And then you rigged the result so he'd win the class and I would, too."

"Duh. You think you two ended up in that class by chance?" She caps the lipstick and tosses it back into the bag. "It's Our Lady of Miracles, Julie, not Our Lady of the Ridiculous Statistical Coincidences."

Even for Liza, who's legendary for throwing surprise parties and playing pranks, this is a topper. Still, something's off. I haven't spoken of Michael in years and while she must remember him from our childhood, I doubt she would have gone out of the way to track him down at his office and sell him tickets to a church raffle without the prodding of another party.

"Someone put you up to it," I say. "Who?"

"Uh . . ." Biting her lip and ruining her fresh lipstick, she says hesitantly, "That's a secret. I'm under strict orders not to reveal his or her identity."

"I'm going to kill you."

"Don't. You can go to jail for that. Come on." Throwing open the bathroom door, she marches into her climate-controlled walk-in closet with its electronic coat hangers and luscious cedar shelves. "All I can tell you is that the person who asked me to set you up had your best interests at heart."

While she figures out which of the one hundred black pants to change into, I try to figure out who could have been behind such a scheme. Not Em. Not Donald. Not Paul because, well, he's an idiot. Not anyone at work. And then it hits me—the most obvious choice.

"Mom. This was her idea."

Liza throws off her robe to reveal blindingly pink lace underwear. "Your mother? Get real. You know how she felt about you going after Michael back in the day. She was dead set against it."

"Yeah, but that was years ago when she called me a tramp and said he'd never respect me if I threw myself at him, that I should keep a safe distance whenever he was around. Maybe she's changed her mind."

Liza snorts and steps into a pair of Nanette Lepore striped trousers. "Betty Mueller change her mind? She's always had a bee in her bonnet about Michael, admit it. Anything Slayton was never good enough for her daughter. She wanted you to marry a doctor from an old Boston family, not the wild offspring of the neighborhood drunks."

"And look where that marriage got me." Donald was a big baby of a man who got freaked out by fatherhood. "Nowhere."

"It got you Em, don't forget," she says quietly.

"Touché." I'm dutifully humbled.

"Your problem," she goes on, flipping between white silk blouses that, from where I'm sitting on a bench, seem perfectly identical, "is that you are still lugging around a case of sour grapes because Michael rejected you when you were seventeen and then had the audacity to marry another woman, even though they have been divorced for years now."

"That's absurd. I do so not have sour grapes."

Yanking a blouse off a hanger, she says, "Possibly not. But you know that's what Michael thinks. You told me so yourself."

"It was only a theory."

"Have you ever asked him?"

"Would have been hard to do considering we're on nonspeaking terms." There's a tag hanging off her sleeve that's bugging me. Opening my purse, I search for my nail scissors to cut it. "The only thing I'm going to ask Michael is to keep his trap shut when they do my background check." Aha. Found it.

She stops buttoning the blouse halfway. "Background check?"

Clipping off the tag, I say, even though I shouldn't, "I'm up for the national election team. The *network*, Liza."

Squealing, she nearly impales herself on my nail scissors in the course of giving me a huge hug. "Congratulations! That's so exciting."

"Thanks." I steal a glimpse of my watch and realize if I don't get moving I'm going to be really late for class.

"You know what's so great about this?" she says, back to buttoning. "Is that it happened to you in your forties, right when you're beginning to wonder if life is over."

"It hasn't happened *yet*, Liza."

She ignores this as she rustles through her jewelry collection. "The beautiful thing about being our age is that you start to focus on what's really important instead of getting distracted by men and kids."

This is kind of funny coming from Liza, considering she has neither men nor kids.

There's a knock at the door and without waiting for an answer, Marisol pops in. "It's six-thirty. You said I was supposed to get you."

Liza checks her own watch. "Already? Okay, I'm almost ready. Just tell the car to wait."

Marisol goes blank. "Car?"

"The car." Liza plugs in one more earring. "Remember? It's supposed to pick us up at six-thirty."

The poor girl throws her arms over her head like she's ducking a hailstorm. "Oh, geesh. I forgot to call for one. Please don't kill me."

Liza slowly turns, her purple eyes shooting darts. "Marisol. You had one task this afternoon, to make sure we had a car to the airport. It's an international flight with tons of security. We can't be late."

"I know. I know." She's hopping up and down. "Just that I got so caught up in the Skopje reservations, I forgot."

Liza says to me, "*Now* can I murder her?"

"No." Getting up, I pat Marisol reassuringly and tell Liza I will take the two of them to the airport on my way to dessert class. Never mind that Logan Airport is across town and on the waterfront while the Boston Cooking School is two blocks away, this is what friends do.

"Thank you," Marisol blurts. "Thank you, thank you, thank you. I'll never make a mistake like this again. I promise."

As we exit her apartment, Liza says to me. "If she's this bad in Boston, what's she going to be like in the outskirts of Bucharest?"

"It depends," I say. "How well does she network with goats?"

Chapter Four

O, beware, my lord, of jealousy;
It is the green-eyed monster which doth mock
The meat it feeds on

—OTHELLO, ACT III, SCENE 3

On the way to the airport, Liza and I hashed out a strategy for dealing
with Michael and now I'm much more relaxed. This is going to be a piece
of cake. Not to pun.

All I have to do is go to this one dessert class, pretend to be fascinated
by the nuances of flaky pie crust, and somehow get Michael alone so I can
convince him to play dumb should he receive a call from Kirk Bledsoe
concerning our relationship during the FitzWilliams debacle.

Simple, no?

Of course, there is always the possibility he might refuse since I ruined
his career so why shouldn't he ruin mine. To which I'll have to choose
Plan B: my mother.

Michael adores Mom, the woman who fed him and clothed him and comforted him while his own mother lay in bed entertaining "fantasies." There's nothing he wouldn't do for her.

But lie? Hmm. That's a toughie. Michael has an annoying loyalty to the truth. How he managed to survive all those years in Washington is a mystery.

After dropping off Liza and Marisol at Logan, I find a parking spot a mile from the cooking school and dash down Newbury Street, red faced and hair flying in my mandated closed-toe shoes (pink ballet flats) and flowered cotton dress with sleeves. The flowered cotton dress is a definite mistake, I decide as I catch my reflection in Bergdorf's window. This is not the effect I was looking for, preteen bride of Utah polygamist Warren Jeffs.

Too late now, I think, snaking among the cluster of culinary students enjoying cigarette breaks in the warm summer evening. Quickly, I climb a flight of stairs to Kitchen 2B. The hallway outside smells of warm yeast and melting chocolate and my adrenaline spikes as I catch the vague drone of a lecture followed by the sound of clanking pans and laughter within the classroom. So what if Michael's here? We're adults. *Breathe, Julie.*

Quietly, I turn the handle and open the door. It's a much smaller kitchen than I would have expected. A wall of stainless-steel stoves and sinks, one refrigerator, and lots of hanging pots and evil utensils dangling over a raised counter around which my classmates sit on stools. All laughter and conversation stops as they turn to look at me.

Not *too* awkward.

There's a Japanese couple, two nuns in full habits (do they still wear those?), a fat, balding man and a violently orange-haired woman, a suburban mother in a riotous Lilly Pulitzer skirt (here to get away from the kids, no doubt), and a deformed creature of blond perfection rising to a swan neck with tanned, toned arms and Valentino jewel thongs. Blatant violations of the cooking school guidelines, I might add.

Naturally, Michael's smack next to her. He is so predictable.

Our gazes click and he gives me a wry smile, as if he had money on me being the last one to class. He's still gorgeous by conventional, middle-aged women's standards. Tall, dark. There's a little more gray at the temples and he's sporting wire-rims, but he's got his hair and—damn him—he's able to pull off a gray T-shirt and faded jeans like he's in college. Grow up, I think. Get a gut.

That my heart does a double beat is inconsequential, nothing more than a muscle twitch. Adoration in its death throes.

Smiling back defiantly, I let him know I have as much a right to be in this class as he, though inwardly I curse my mother. This is all her fault. If she hadn't guilted me into going, I could be somewhere else, at a movie with Em or out to drinks with Arnie and the guys from work. But as I have no other choice than to be in the same room with *him*, I'll be damned if I'm going to let him act superior.

All I have to keep in mind is that I have done nothing wrong. It was Michael who was wrong, asking me to hold off on the story, berating me for doing my job. I was right. *Remember that, Julie.*

"You must be the one remaining student?" Chef D'Ours says. "Julie Mueller."

As he steps down from around the raised cooking area, he diminishes to about my height, with high cheekbones and sandy blond hair pulled into a ponytail. What's Liza talking about? He's a shrimp.

"So sorry I'm late," I say. "I had to drive a friend to the airport and Friday night traffic and there's absolutely no parking anywhere." I'm only making things worse. "I mean . . . sorry."

He lets out a pained sigh and drags another stool to the far end of the counter, away from You Know Who. "You can wash your hands and grab an apron while I continue my demonstration. Next time, please try to be punctual."

Is it just me, or is it frosty in here? Waving my hand under the water, I tie on a green BOSTON COOKING SCHOOL apron, maintaining my happy face as I go to my stool. Everyone has a glass of champagne except me.

I try catching the eye of a woman with a nose ring and purple bangs cut straight across who seems to be D'Ours's assistant, but it's no use. She's too busy slicing fresh strawberries to be bothered filling my glass.

Willing myself not to sneak a peek at Michael, I concentrate on what D'Ours is saying about strawberry crème brûlée being a dish that sounds elegant but is actually so simple we can make it for guests between dinner and dessert. Easy for him to say. It'd take me an hour just to slice the strawberries, not like Purple Bangs, who works rapid fast, dealing the strawberry slices into cobalt-blue ramekins like she's working the black-jack table in Vegas.

The strawberry, he informs us, is a member of the rose family and its botanical name, *Fragaria*, means "fragrance." And while most people know it is the only fruit with seeds on the outside, it is actually not fruit at all but swollen stems. It is one of the few fruits to contain *ellagic acid,* a compound believed to prevent healthy cells from turning into carcino-genic ones.

My classmates cluck their tongues at this.

"And the best way to cook the *fraises,*" he says in his distinct fresh ac-cent, "is to barely cook them at all. Which is why my strawberry crème brûlée is so fantastic. Quick to make, delicious, and the texture of the berry remains firm."

Combining strawberries in rum, sour cream, and cream plus a dash of fresh lemon juice in a bowl, he tosses the mixture and spoons it into ra-mekins. Ideally, he says, the strawberry mixture should be refrigerated for several hours to meld the flavors. However, since we're on a time crunch, he sprinkles each with brown sugar before sliding them under the broiler so the tops turn a crusty caramel in seconds.

Everyone goes, "Ooh," the kind of "ooh" I might utter if George Cloo-ney had appeared to me naked in a hot bubble bath, raring to go.

The orange-haired woman asks if she can substitute no-fat sour cream and skim milk, seeing as she's on a diet. D'Ours does everything except roll his eyes. "Dessert is to be eaten in small amounts, as they do in my native France," he says petulantly. "If Americans didn't chow down on huge slices of Chocolate Peanut Butter Pie at T.G.I. Friday's you wouldn't have the need for artificial entities such as no-fat sour cream."

He's right, but that doesn't make him *right*. Chastised, she bites her lip and slinks back. Her husband the bald man pats her hand and says, "Chris has lost sixty-two pounds."

I applaud, to give her a boost. "Sixty-two pounds. That's fabulous." Everyone else claps, too.

D'Ours says dryly, "Bravo."

Good choice, Liza. Super-fun guy. Love the ones without senses of humor.

We each get a ramekin to taste. Tapping my spoon against the brittle caramel shell, I am rewarded with the satisfying crunch that distinguishes the great brûlée. Underneath, the slightly tart strawberries remain red, fresh, and firm, bursting with flavor enhanced by the sweet rum and cream. So simple and light and, yet, so rich.

I could linger forever, but already we are on to the next lesson: almond-infused hot white chocolate over iced berries. How bizarre.

"Very popular in England," D'Ours observes, a tad derisively.

I find myself strangely mesmerized by the melting of white chocolate chunks into heavy cream, a slight almond fragrance emanating as the mixture swirls and warms in the double boiler. I've never been a fan of white chocolate. I've never seen the point of chocolate without, well, *chocolate*. But I have a feeling I'm about to be converted.

The frowning Angela distributes bowls with red and blue frozen berries slightly thawed. From a little pot, she pours the hot white chocolate sauce over them and it thickens immediately on contact. To top it off, she sprinkles on a few chopped almonds.

"Bon appétit," she snaps, filling my glass of champagne.

Okay, I may have just passed dying and stepped directly into heaven. This is, hands down, the most fabulous thing I've ever eaten. It should be illegal, it's so good. And the weird thing is, it doesn't even taste like white chocolate over frozen berries. It's sweet and perfumed and something else entirely. It's gooey.

Michael is staring at me with the oddest expression.

He is about to mouth something when the anorexic blonde next to him leans over and whispers in his ear.

They came together. *Naturellement!* Probably he was too afraid of me to come to class alone. Hah.

We are barely done with the berries when Angela whisks away our dishes and we go for a break. I studiously avoid Michael by washing the sugar off my hands with as much thoroughness as Lady Macbeth used to clean off blood. He's not paying attention to me, anyway. He's too enraptured by his ex-wife's stand-in.

When we return to our stools, D'Ours is thickly slicing a huge brioche while Angela is laboring over a pot from which rises the heady aroma of cooking berries and some liquor.

We are making cold summer pudding, another English classic, D'Ours says, punctuating his disapproval with another snort. The beauty of cold summer pudding is that the thick slices of brioche are soaked in a soup of berries and Chambord and compressed so the result is an intense berry dessert that's both comforting and cool since, unlike most bread puddings, it does not involve baking.

Chris's husband, apparently not quite over the Chocolate Peanut Butter Pie crack, says, "Another English dish? I thought their food was crap."

"Did I imply that?" D'Ours asks as he layers the brioche in a purple sauce of simmered raspberries and blueberries. "Well, it would be relative, no? If, for example, meat pasties and bubble and squeak are your idea of delicate cuisine, if sheep bladders seduce your palate, then by all means, dig in!"

I've drunk a glass of champagne, so my mind is a bit fuzzy. Sheep bladders? I look to Michael for a clue, but he's snuggling up to the blonde, her practically sitting on his lap.

Which raises this question: If he's not here to learn about desserts, then why did he bother coming to class in the first place? He was under no obligation to show. He could have blown it off and avoided me altogether.

The blonde erupts in a peal of laughter and Michael throws his head back, joining her silently.

"Get a room already," D'Ours mutters. "Why do I even bother?"

I want to reach out and say, *You and me both. You and me both.*

Done layering the slices of soaked bread with spoonfuls of sauces, D'Ours explains the next step is to compress the pudding by weighing it down with a pan and two heavy cans. Then it is refrigerated overnight.

From the refrigerator he removes a premade one and carefully inverts it over a plate. Out falls an expertly formed pinkish-red pudding. Again, a trick I'd never be able to achieve. Mine would stick to the pan and mush on the plate.

I'm beginning to get an inkling of what Liza sees in this French dough boy. Every move of D'Ours's hand is artful, the way he slices the pudding and dollops it with crème fraîche (heavy cream plus buttermilk, easy). How he circles the slice with more fresh berries and tops it with a sprig of mint. A man who devotes himself so wholeheartedly to making food magic can't be all bad.

My fork cuts into the thick, chilled bread oozing berry juice onto the plate. The pudding is refreshingly tart with just enough sweetness to be satisfying. Definitely benefits from the crème fraîche, which adds oomph to the berries without oversweetening the dessert. I can't wait for my mother to try this.

We clear our plates and it's on to peach cobbler D'Ours with ginger ice cream.

"And now," D'Ours says, taking a swig of champagne, "class participation. Half of you will make ginger ice cream with Angela." He chops his hand down between the nuns and the Japanese. "And the other half, a peach cobbler with me. In the end we'll put them together for a spectacular dish."

I am on the peach cobbler side with Chris, her husband the bald man, and the nuns. The Japanese, Michael, his girlfriend the human Barbie, and Lilly Pulitzer are on ice cream duty. Clearly ice cream duty is the hip crowd. Peach cobbler is so frumpy.

Michael and his girlfriend linger some more, talking. I turn my back to them and join D'Ours as he tosses sliced peaches with brown sugar, tapioca, and—his brainstorm—a touch of balsamic vinegar, to offset the cloying sweetness of most cobblers. Our job is to cut cold butter into a mixture of flour, baking powder, salt, brown sugar, and a half cup of heavy cream, and then to roll it out for the crust.

This is the hard part. I've never been any good at rolling out pastry and the cobbler top is no exception. Chris is a pro and the nuns have no problem, but me? When it comes to my turn the dough rolls up on the pin and sticks, splitting the crust and turning it to shreds. This is why I hate cooking. I swear I'm jinxed.

"Julie. Don't fight it," D'Ours says, coming behind me, sliding his arms around my waist and placing his hands over mine. Soon he's rolling the pin methodically as his body rhythmically presses against mine. Roll. Pound. Roll. Pound.

It's the closest I've come to sex since a regrettable night at a conference in Phoenix and I might just faint.

"There," he whispers, practically nuzzling my ear. "You've got to let go and *feel* the dough, Julie. Let the pin take over. That perfume of yours . . ." He inhales deeply. "What is it?"

"*Wha min,*" I say, meaning, White Linen.

"That's not the way Father Tom taught me how to roll out pastry," one of the nuns, Sister Martha, quips as we pinch the pastry crust to seal the edges. "Maybe since I wasn't wearing *Wha Min* perfume at the time."

Everyone's a comedian these days, even the bride of Christ.

The nuns weren't the only ones watching us, though. As we line up to wash our hands and get ready for the grand finale, the bald man warns me to be careful, that D'Ours has a reputation as a lady-killer. This is bad news for Liza. And for him. She has a way of dealing with lady-killers that can leave them very messy.

From across the room D'Ours flashes me a sly wink.

Liza's right. He *does* look like Fabio.

"Making new friends?"

All of a sudden Michael's by my side and he's gazing down at me with his dark, smoldering eyes. I'd forgotten how tall he was.

"Hello," I manage, nearly coughing on my peach cobbler. (Juicy peaches in a comforting syrup baked in a buttery, flaky crust. Yum!) "Fancy meeting you here."

"I was just about to say the same thing." Slicing into his cobbler, he says, "When I saw your name on the list, I was trying to figure out if you joined the class to expand your already accomplished culinary skills or if you were looking for a way to bump into me so you could finally apologize."

"Apologize?" The hairs on the back of my neck bristle. "As if."

"As if, what? As if had you given me a chance to find out if there was any basis for your lies, we might have a decent man in office instead of an incompetent rube who brutally slashes federally funded health care for children? That kind of *as if*?"

All right. I know I have to be nice to him so he'll do me a favor. Still, he's going too far. It's not my fault FitzWilliams lost. I wasn't the one going around hitting on volunteers. "It was six years ago, Michael. How about we bury the hatchet."

"I think you already did. In my back."

I wince. "*Soooo* dramatic. Looks like your Shakespearean background is coming in handy. *Et tu, Brute?*"

Michael smiles reassuringly at his date, who's eyeing us with concern. "Look. I didn't come over to get in a fight with you. Believe me, I never wished for this to happen, to be on the outs with you, of all people. Hell, what you did almost killed my thirty-year friendship with Paul."

What I did. What *I* did. "Then why *did* you come over? You could have just ignored me, like I was doing to you."

"Oh, right." He laughs. "If by ignoring you mean constantly checking me out."

"You egotist." I put my plate down and the fork clatters to the table. "I was so not checking you out."

"When you walked in you zeroed in on me. You were just begging me to talk to you. It's your guilt, Julie. You can't ignore it. You'd have to have the hard heart of Lady Macbeth not to feel at least some regret."

This is so outrageous I don't know how to respond other than, "Yeah, well, what's done is done."

Michael nods. "A direct quote from Lady Macbeth herself. I'm impressed."

Excuse me?

I'm about to ask what he means by that when Michael's girlfriend pops up and regards me with red pursed collagen-filled lips. God. How can he go out with such a poseur?

"This is Carol," he says, taking her elbow. "A close friend. Carol, this is Julie Mueller. An *old* friend."

"*Love* the dress," she says, looking me up and down. "Is it vintage?"

My dress. I forgot about that. Glancing down at the floral pink and green print, I can summon no defense except, "Don't I wish. My mother made it for a wedding."

"Julie's mother is a fantastic woman," Michael tells Carol. "Giving. Warm. Loving. Generous. Odd, how traits skip a generation."

Very funny.

"So you two have a history?" Carol regards me with fresh appreciation.

"Michael grew up five doors down from us. He was an urchin."

To which Michael says, "And Julie was the TV reporter who aired that report about FitzWilliams. The one I was telling you about."

"Ohh," Carol says. "The erroneous one."

Erroneous? That's such a crock of . . .

"Though I guess she's finally getting her reward," he continues, not giving me an inch. "I got a call this afternoon from the Washington bureau chief at WBOS. Apparently my old friend here's being promoted to the network."

He got the call already? I try to read Michael's expression, but he's a blank slate. There's nothing written to indicate how the conversation went, if he told or didn't. I want to jump up and down or shake him until he spills.

"Interesting," Carol says, meaning the opposite. "I came to remind you, Michael, we better get going. We were supposed to meet up with Jan and Mark a half hour ago."

With a casual "nice to meet you" she leaves and I grab Michael's wrist before he can escape. "What happened? What did you say?"

"About what?"

"*You* know. The WBOS call."

"Oh, that." He squints, pretending like it's all a fog. "My memory's a bit fuzzy. Why don't you give me a ring next week and maybe by then it'll come back to me."

"But . . ."

"Monday morning," he says, pressing a business card into my hand. "Surely you can wait two days, just like I did."

I have no idea what he's referring to until I remember how I refused to show him a tape of our FitzWilliams exposé ahead of airing—standard journalism procedure. To do otherwise would have violated WBOS protocol and gotten me fired on the spot.

However, that meant Michael had to wait two days for my report, with no indication of what evidence I had. Thinking back, he must have been tortured over whether it would end FitzWilliams's campaign or not. How could I have done that to him?

Because there are rules, I tell myself. And rules are there for a reason. Like Arnie's always complaining, so many journalists these days consider themselves exceptions—inserting their personal opinions into straight news reports, striking deals with their sources, paying their sources, *sleeping* with their sources.

Well, not me. I have always adhered to the highest standards. And though I'm sorry I caused Michael pain by sticking to protocol, it was worth it in the end because I'm going to the network.

However no matter how often I tell myself that, it doesn't make me feel better in the least.

Chapter Five

From women's eyes this doctrine I derive:
They are the ground, the books, the academes
From whence doth spring the true Promethean fire.

—LOVE'S LABOUR'S LOST, ACT IV, SCENE 3

"A bread pudding you don't bake?" Mom hulls a strawberry and frowns with disapproval. "I never heard of such a thing."

"Every bread pudding I've ever made," chimes in Lois, who's at the stove stirring the strawberries, "is three eggs and a loaf of bread and milk baked at 350 for fifty minutes."

"If you don't bake it, you'll get worms," adds Teenie.

Who knew an offhand remark about dessert class would explode into such a cultural breakdown. I'm like a *National Geographic* photographer explaining cameras to a clan of tree-living Indonesian Pygmies.

"There are no eggs. Just strawberries and other berries and bread that you soak and put in the refrigerator." Grabbing a handful of hulled strawberries, I toss them into Lois's simmering jam. "Plus some sort of alcohol for flavoring, like Chambord."

"Now you're talking," says Teenie, who's at the kitchen table, sorting berries. "Though when you bake it, all the alcohol will burn off. I've always found that to be such an unfortunate side effect."

She's still not getting it. "You know what this reminds me of?" I say.

Mom pulls off a stem. "What?"

"That time you made baked Alaska for Nana. She liked it so much, she asked for the recipe so she could make it for her bridge club. Only she insisted on baking it for thirty minutes at 350 degrees because that's how she always baked cakes and she refused to change. Which is why it turned into soup."

"Bread pudding is in no way, shape, or form like baked Alaska," Mom says. "Hey, we've got to get moving. If we don't can these strawberries by tonight, they'll be rotted tomorrow."

They're already rotted, I think, checking the clock for the umpteenth time. Four p.m., Sunday, only seventeen more hours until I can call Michael. The wait is killing me. *Killing* me. What did he tell Kirk? Does it matter if I hit on Michael when I was seventeen? Would Kirk consider it a lie that I told him Michael and I had nothing more than a platonic relationship? I'm so antsy I could climb the walls. My whole future, all my aspirations, hinge on what he said.

It's impossible for me to sit still. Yesterday, I took the recyclables to the dump, hoed Mom's garden, weeded, mulched it, and repaired a gap in the chicken wire. Then I repainted the door to Em's room, went for a five-mile run, and read an entire mystery until collapsing somewhere between one and six a.m., when I bolted upright and decided what we had to do, simply must do, was pick the last bumper crop of strawberries at a farm in Danvers.

Now we've got more strawberries than we know what to do with and Teenie and Lois are stubbornly refusing to consider alternatives to jam, unless it's strawberry shortcake. Or maybe an easy strawberry cream tart—graham cracker crust into which a whipped filling of sour cream,

cream cheese, lemon juice, sugar, and almond flavoring is poured. Top that with fresh whole hulled strawberries, and brush over it seedless raspberry jam liquefied in the microwave. Chill for four hours minimum.

Not bad.

My problem is I'm dealing with three old ladies who are like spiders when it comes to fresh fruit. Their first instinct is to kill it, wrap it up, and store it away.

"Strawberries are too precious to waste," Lois says, proving my point. "Better to boil them down and put them by to save."

Lois, also known as "Poor Lois," is a hulking woman with a cereal bowl haircut and a fondness for macramé along with the color brown. Mom befriended her ages ago in the peanut butter aisle of the Star Market when she found her sobbing over her Smuckers grape jelly. It wasn't really the grape jelly making her cry; it was her husband and that he never liked grape jelly until he fell for their eighteen-year-old babysitter with whom he was having a scandalous affair.

Just a whiff of peanut butter and jelly can trigger a rant from Lois about promiscuous teenagers and the dangers of free love.

Teenie, on the other hand, is crazy for free love. In her heyday she was the town slut. Well, that's not entirely accurate. She was *rumored* to be the town slut because of the way she dressed. Unlike Lois, who's given to hand-knit bulky sweaters and tweed pants, Teenie never quite abandoned the golden age of Pussy Galore.

Tight colorful capris, pointy padded bras, a bouffant of spun white-blond hair, etched-on brows, blue eye shadow, and fabulously pink lips. That was—and still is—Teenie's getup. Only, she's eighty now and as shriveled as a shrunken head, so all her Pussy clothes hang on her like potato sacks. You can't but admire her, though, for keeping up the fight.

It's heartening to see that despite their differences, Teenie, Lois, and Mom click and hum in perfect synchrony like an antique glockenspiel that's never a minute off. I've been thinking about that all day because we're celebrating a monumental milestone in their relationship—the anniversary of the summer Lois and Teenie saved my mother's life.

It was five years ago when Dad called me at work to say Mom had breast cancer and had already undergone a lumpectomy. After that, he didn't want to talk about it. Not a peep. He also didn't want to visit her in the hospital or discuss her "female problems." It was no business of his.

"Every woman in your mother's family gets *this thing*," he said, unable to say the words "breast cancer." "Her mother. Her grandmother. Her sister. They all had it. It's no more than a toothache to them." And then he went off to see what dinner my mother had left for him in the refrigerator.

Meanwhile, I was left holding the phone, shaking with anger, and debating whether to remind him that Mom's older sister, the bossy but loving Aunt Charlotte, procurer of the ugly green china, had *died* of breast cancer. A bit more than a toothache, in my book.

Looking back, I'm ashamed of how grumpy I was during that whole ordeal. First I was mad at Mom for not telling me she'd found a lump. (Though, in all fairness, she didn't tell anyone except Lois and Teenie.) Then I was mad she went into surgery without telling me. Then I was mad at Dad for being pig ignorant and selfish. But that wasn't all.

My anger grew delicate shoots that flared up at the least little slight.

I was mad at other drivers on the road, people in the grocery store who blocked the aisles, the mailman for dropping a letter in the mud, Mrs. Crebbin, whose dog, Brutus, regularly defecated on our lawn. I was daily peeved at all my friends and family members. There seemed to be no end to the potential sources of my aggravation. My fists were balled 24/7.

Finally, Lois took me aside and slapped some sense into me. "Look, Julie, your mother didn't want anyone to know about the cancer because she didn't want you all to worry until she knew how bad it was. So why don't you snap out of it and stop causing her more distress by acting like a petulant child."

"I'm not a petulant child," I said, acting like, well, a petulant child. "My father is. He's not even visiting her in the hospital."

"So what, your father can't deal. *You're* not married to him."

That shut me up. For a day.

"Men are weird," Mom once observed when Lois and I were waiting for Mom's last radiation treatment, yet again without Dad. "When their loved ones get sick, they see it as a personal affront to their abilities as protectors. Men hate to be helpless."

"That's no excuse," I said. "Dad's a—"

"Ahem." Lois cleared her throat and gazed at me sternly. "Your mother knows what your father is, Julie."

"He's my hero." Mom took a stitch in her needlework, a small pillow of a butterfly she worked on only during radiation days.

"He's your hero?" I could have gone off on that, but I was too cowed by Lois to try.

"Your father loves me very much in ways that you don't know and never will," she said quietly, concentrating on each stitch. "It's not for you to say what he does or doesn't do is right or wrong. Yes. To me, he's my hero."

Hmph. Mom might believe her own hype, but I knew who the real heroes were. The real heroes were Teenie and Lois.

On the days I couldn't drive Mom to radiation, Lois or Teenie did. Afterward, they took her home and fed her tea and homemade thin ginger cookies to settle her stomach.

Then they'd draw her a nice hot bath with lavender bubbles and put her to bed in crisp, clean sheets. If she wasn't too tired, they watched old movies with Bogart and Bacall, Tracy and Hepburn, or those goofy On the Road flicks with Bob Hope and Bing Crosby.

They laughed. They ate tapioca pudding and Jell-O and held Mom's head when she threw up. And when the movies were over and/or when Mom was too tired, they lay on the bed with her and traded secrets like schoolgirls. Secrets to which I could never be privy. They let her cry. They let her vent and probably let her swear up a blue streak. (Though Mom never ever swears in front of me or Em.) They held the pillow while she punched it.

They held *her*.

My father, meanwhile, continued to pretend as if Mom had gone to Arizona to visit her cousin Justine. He moved to Paul's tiny apartment in New York and made it his mission to make my brother's life a living hell until Mom's own hell was in remission.

To this day I'm convinced that while the nurses, surgeons, radiation, and chemo drugs killed my mother's rapidly multiplying cancer cells, it was Lois and Teenie who *cured* her. Had they not been there to hold her hand, to clean her house, and drive her back and forth to radiation, she would not be here hulling strawberries today.

"How's the job going, Julie?" Lois asks as I line up sterilized jelly jars on a bleached kitchen towel. "Any new developments?"

I freeze, my hand clutching the tongs in midair. How does Lois know? I haven't said a word to Mom, since her idea of keeping a secret is confiding in a close circle of friends. That wouldn't be a problem except the close circle of friends includes every patron of Mario's salon and anyone who happens to be standing behind her in the checkout aisle at Shaw's.

"The job's fine," I say, pulling out another jar from the top of the dishwasher. "Nothing big."

"That's too bad. We were hoping you'd get that national election assignment. Did they give it to the young girl?"

"Young-*er*." Geesh. How come everyone keeps making that mistake? "And, no, I don't think they've made up their minds. Not definitely." There. I didn't lie.

"Well, take heart, Julie. Maybe this TV journalism gig has run its course. There's nothing wrong with slowing down and becoming a school librarian, you know."

The image of me in a long black skirt surrounded by clamoring children sends pains up my arm. "Er, yes. That might be worth looking into."

"Summers off and school holidays, too. You could plant a garden. Go to Europe in July. That's the life."

Actually, that could have its appeal, now that I think of it.

"Okay, we got the fire started," Em announces, tromping up the back stairs with her friend Nadia—she of big hair and very little brain. "And we did it without lighter fluid because we're environmentally friendly."

"Well, you two are a couple of vestal virgins, aren't you?" Lois says, turning off the stove.

Em and Nadia exchange quick looks. "Vestal *what*?" Nadia asks.

"If they still offered Latin, they'd know this," says Mom.

"Virgins," I tell them. "A distant memory for you, I'm sure. Vestal virgins were even more distant, a group of women in ancient Rome considered priests who maintained the fire of the goddess Vesta. Very highly regarded, except if they were found to have had sex. Then they were buried alive."

"Harsh," Nadia says. "When my mom found out I'd had sex, she just took me to the doctor for Norplant."

Oh, I wish she hadn't said that in the presence of my mother.

Mom frowns and shakes her head. "Call me old-fashioned, but this day and age of friends with benefits is cheating you girls out of real love. Boys are growing up into men who don't respect women, and girls are growing up into women who don't respect themselves. And I thought it was bad when Julie was coming of age. Heck, this generation's three times worse."

Here it comes, I think, removing another jar, a tirade against the "MTV generation."

"It's MTV, that's the real culprit here," says Lois, going to the sink to wash her mannish hands. "I've only seen it once or twice, but what I've seen turns my stomach. All that bump and grind and half-naked dancing. It's so *demeaning*."

Shaking a paring knife at Em, Mom says, "I was strict with your mother, stricter than she is with you when it comes to sex. And thanks be to God. Who knows what trouble she could have gotten into if I hadn't seen to it that certain *temptations* did not present themselves."

She's referring to Michael, of course. How did we get on this touchy subject, anyway? "That fire's not going to stay hot forever," I say, trying to get off topic. "We should strike now."

"It's not as if this generation of girls invented sex," Teenie adds, either ignoring or not hearing me to begin with. "Think of what it was like during World War II with all those brave men going off to war and marrying any girl they could get their hands on."

"The operative word being 'marry,' " notes Mom.

"Oh, I don't know about that." Teenie's expression is turning misty. "There was one soldier I remember in particular, Harry Fordham. Ooh, was he handsome and smart. And he sacrificed so much for our country. Was it so wrong that on one snowy winter evening the night before he was to be shipped off, I tried to show him my gratitude by letting him . . ."

Nadia and Em are hanging on her every word.

"Ahem." Mom pushes back from the table. "That's enough, Teenie. Julie's right. That fire won't stay lit forever."

Em says, "What did you let him do, Teenie?"

"It sounds so romantic," says Nadia.

"I just . . ." Teenie glances cautiously at Mom. "I better tell you later."

Later, when it's just the two of us and I'm helping her down the stairs to the outside, where Em, Nadia, and Lois are waiting, Teenie tells me the rest. "It was an incredible night," she whispers. "What those girls don't know is that I offered him my all, body and soul. And . . ."

"And?" I'm riveted.

"He turned me down." She shakes her head, remembering. "He said, Teenie Dawson, tonight would be an incredible night for both of us. But tomorrow, I'll be gone overseas and I don't know if I'll ever be back, and for me to abandon you that way would be incredibly unfair."

Looking off, she adds, "His plane was shot down two months later."

"Oh, Teenie," I gasp, imagining the sacrifice on both their parts and then the irreconcilable pain. "I'm so sorry."

"Not a day goes by that I don't think of him," she says, her rheumy eyes getting watery. "They don't make men like that anymore, Julie. Harry Fordham was moral, brave, and principled. He was the kind of man worth waiting for."

Like Michael, I think, catching myself. Why Michael?

"I'm going to go get Mom," I announce, rushing back upstairs, my heart fluttering. *Like Michael.*

When I get to the kitchen, I find my mother leaning against the refrigerator and clutching a plain plywood box. "I got a bit dizzy," she says, straightening. "Lost my balance for a second."

The day picking berries has been too much for her. We were up awfully early. "Do you need to sit down?"

"No. I'm okay now. I got up too fast, was all." She pauses to brush a tear from her cheek. "Five years is the benchmark, but it doesn't mean I'm cured. The cancer could come back."

"It could," I say, trying to keep my own emotion in check. "But it won't."

"I might need this, though."

"My ass. Let me have one last look."

Mom opens the box and hands it to me. There lies the tiny pillow with the butterfly half finished, only the orange wings and one green leaf done, the needle with yarn still stuck in the matt. The sight of it brings a lump to my throat. "The pillow you worked on when you were going for radiation treatments. You never finished it."

"Oh, I finished it several times. Just kept ripping it out, like Penelope. It wasn't the suitors I was holding off, though. It was death."

The final suitor, I think, closing the box and handing it to her. "Let's burn this sucker."

"But I . . . ?"

"When you burn it," I tell her, "you're celebrating your victory over cancer. You conquered it, Mom. You destroyed it before it could destroy you."

Mom nods, agreeing. "That's what I did, didn't I?"

"Come on, Betty!" Lois shouts from the backyard. "Quit yapping."

"You're right. It's time," Mom says, taking the stairs slowly, her arthritic knees not what they used to be.

From the back porch, I watch Mom, flanked by Teenie and Lois, place the box on the fire in our rusted suburban grill with its caked-on hamburger grease and spilled barbecue sauce. In seconds, it bursts into flames and the last symbol of the scourge that threatened to take my mother from us shrivels and turns to ash at the hands of three old crones and two vestal virgins.

The power of women united, I am again reminded, is an invincible thing.

Chapter Six

Love all, trust a few,
Do wrong to none

—ALL'S WELL THAT ENDS WELL, ACT I, SCENE 2

On my way to work Monday, I grab a *New York Times*, a *Washington Post*, this week's *Economist*, and the *Wall Street Journal*—enough boring, stuffy reading material to knock out the most hyper insomniac. As a precaution, I pick up a triple-shot espresso to counter the effects. As if.

I've got no other choice. Kirk told me to start reading all the major newspapers every morning in preparation for the national election team, and that doesn't include the mounds of background material I'll have to consume in order to catch up, the voting records and lobbying reports. Oh, God. The lobbying reports.

Still, there could be worse situations, like finding the national election post was given to someone else—a panicky possibility that crosses my mind as I walk into the newsroom and see Valerie being interviewed by Kirk in Arnie's glass-walled office.

Uh-oh.

Dolores Poultney, Arnie's rotund secretary, lifts her gaze from this morning's sudoku lying next to a heaping quart of pick-your-own strawberries. Seems like I wasn't the only one with the bright idea. "Take a number, Julie. Arnie told me not to disturb those two unless it's an emergency."

"I have a great recipe for those," I say, pointing to the berries. "Freeze them on a cookie sheet maybe with some raspberries and blueberries. Then melt a good quality white chocolate in cream." Dolores makes me hold off until she gets a slip of paper so she can write it down. We agree that it's ideal for warm days like this one. No one wants to heat up the kitchen in summer by baking shortbread.

We go on and on about wild berries versus cultivated ones, about what constitutes good white chocolate and if it matters what kind of butter you use. According to Dolores, butter with low moisture and high butterfat makes all the difference. She suggests Amish block butter or something called Plugrá, a bastardization of the French phrase *plus gras*, meaning "more fat."

Only the French, I think, would add fat to their butter.

I can't believe I care about butter. Before cooking class I wouldn't have given a tinker's dam, yet here I am wondering whether I can sneak over to Whole Foods to buy some for tonight. Dolores says it's fantastic on French bread, with a good Pinot Noir.

"Ooh," I hiss, licking my lip. Then the awful truth hits me.

I have become a foodie!

"What am I doing? I can't stand around here talking about butter, not when I'm up to my eyeballs in work." *Not when I'm in the running for my dream job.*

Dolores slumps her shoulders and goes back to her sudoku. "I should have known. All anyone wants from me is gossip about what's going on in Arnie's office, why Kirk Bledsoe brought in Raldo, then Valerie. Who's going to get sent to the election team."

Raldo?

"Reporters are so hopeless. Can't have a conversation with you people without you always angling."

This is so not true. I want her to know that I didn't go off on the butter tangent simply to eke out information about why Valerie's in with Kirk. But how do you tell a person something like that? *Because you like to eat, Dolores, and eat a lot, so I thought I'd tell you about the berries.*

Instead, I say, "I can't wait to try the Plugrá."

"Uh-huh." And she writes down a 9 in the upper-right quadrant.

Raldo?

I dump the papers on my desk and get Michael's card from my purse. Raldo's at his computer intensely typing, probably looking up some rare disease with few symptoms that causes instant death. I try to picture him on the national election team and come up with him moderating the presidential debate in a head-to-toe white hazmat suit.

Why would Kirk even consider him?

Wary of Dolores's sensitive feelings, I pretend I have no interest in finding out as I punch in Michael's number at Slayton Consulting. Michael as a consultant, now there's a twist. All that spark and inventiveness and this is the way he spends his life, advising other people how to live theirs.

Michael's not in, so I leave a message about getting together for lunch. Then I hang up and turn my attention to *The New York Times*, a front-page article about the Republican candidate's economic platform and an analysis of thirty years of tax policy.

I am going to need way more caffeine. I am going to need intravenous amphetamines.

Halfway into the article I realize a) I really, really want to get my hands on some of that Plugrá and b) I'm going to have to read this guy's autobiography—only to find out he's written five. (Five autobiographies? Just how many lives has he been leading?) I also notice Valerie's still talking to Kirk. Dolores is away from her desk and Raldo's furiously typing.

Time to take a break.

"Hey, Raldo," I say casually. "Whatcha doing?"

He flinches and tries to click out of the site. Too late. I've caught him Googling *flesh-eating disease symptoms*.

"Are you kidding?" It's all I can do to stifle a giggle. "What are you doing that for?"

He points to a paper cut on his finger that's slightly red. "Doesn't this look bad? That's how necrotizing fasciitis starts, you know. A cut. A little redness and before nightfall your whole body's eaten by bacteria." He logs off and runs a hand through his feathered silvered hair.

Despite his Viagra ad style, Raldo's about my age. He dyes his hair silver to add a touch of respectability since he's not a reporter's reporter, he's a highly paid teleprompter reader. Thankfully, he's harmless, aside from his bizarre hypochondria and addiction to Lysol.

Perching on the corner of his desk, I start off with a jovial inquiry into his family life. "How's mini Raldo? Looking forward to graduation?"

This grabs his attention and he brightens immediately, always eager to brag about his son, a strapping captain of Exeter's lacrosse team. "Spending the summer checking out colleges. Is Em doing the grand tour? You know, Harvard, Brown, Yale, Princeton, Vassar."

"Sure," I say, though this is a lie.

Em's nowhere near that level, a fact that—rightly or wrongly—makes me feel like a failure as a parent. If Donald and I hadn't gotten divorced . . . If I'd been able to stay at home and fill Em's days with trips to the science museum and Suzuki violin lessons and library story hours and Waldorf Nursery School . . . If I'd been able to afford to send her to Exeter like Raldo, Jr., would she be on a "grand tour" this summer instead of digging out mint chocolate chip at Brigham's?

Then again, while I care what school Em goes to, she's shown absolutely no interest. She's perfectly happy drifting along, hanging with her friends, and dreaming her days away reading romance novels or watching endless reruns of *Buffy*.

Don't get me wrong: Em is a joy to have around—loving, smart, funny, and, as far as teenagers go, wash and wear. But not much has changed since she was born two weeks late and the doctor had to suck her out with a vacuum. She prefers to operate on low frequency.

Raldo and I chat some more about our kids and then I get down to business. "My lord," I say, acting surprised. "Valerie's been in with Kirk a long time."

He cranes his neck to check Arnie's office. "Poor girl. Kirk's got a lot of ideas about how she should handle her new assignment and he's giving her an earful." Then, as if just remembering me, he adds, "I hope you're not upset by that."

Panic zips through my sternum. *I've lost the promotion.*

"Uh, no. Valerie's a terrific reporter. She'll do a great job." Though now that I've grasped the brass ring, no matter how briefly, I'm not all that willing to let go. Valerie's a terrific reporter for her experience level, but I'm better overall. There's got to be a way to change Kirk's mind.

"That's what I think, too." His thin lips form an avuncular smile. "It's always nice to see the next generation sprout up, don't you think? Gives you hope that the news biz will plow on despite us."

"Uh-huh," I say, biting my nail, curious as to what, exactly, Michael told Kirk when he called.

"It's a young man's game, Julie. Pretty soon you and I will be forgotten dinosaurs."

Over my dead body.

The door to Arnie's office opens and Valerie emerges all smiles and shaking hands with Kirk. Then she turns and makes a beeline for my desk.

The newspapers! *The New York Times* and *Washington Post* and *The Economist*. They'll tip her off that I'm up for the post, too. I've got to ditch them before Valerie gets her gossiptrometer going.

Mumbling something about a phone call, I leave Raldo with his Google hypochondria and rush to my desk, where Valerie's already waiting, staring at the *Economist* curiously. "You actually read this?" she asks as I snatch *The New York Times* and the *Post*.

"Occasionally. You might want to try it. I mean . . . now that you've got the job." *Thunk*. The papers fall into the wastebasket in violation of WBOS's recycling mandates.

"So you heard already."

"Word gets around. It is, you know, a *newsroom*." I stick out my hand. "Congratulations."

She lets out a sigh and shakes it. "I'm so relieved you're not upset. I know how much this story means to you."

Her use of the word "story" triggers a thought. *She's not talking about the national election team.*

"Arnie told me to ask you for your notes and contacts . . . if that's okay."

What can she possibly mean by "story"?

"You know, the detectives' numbers and Rhonda Michak's unlisted home phone." She blinks. "Are you following me?"

Rhonda Michak, the mother of Amy Michak who disappeared last November. Oh, no. I'm getting a bad feeling.

"Why do you need to talk to Rhonda?" I ask, not sure I want to hear the answer.

"Because she's a suspect, that's why. Not officially, but that's where I'm leaning. Kirk thinks it's a hot lead."

The room feels like it's spinning, I'm so confused. Somehow we've gone from Valerie landing a spot on the national election team to Rhonda Michak being a suspect in her own daughter's disappearance.

No wonder Raldo asked if I was bothered. This is *my* story, one I covered better than any other reporter in the Boston area. I've held countless interviews with Rhonda and Amy Michak's friends. I've retraced Amy's steps that night, combed the woods, pestered the detectives, unsealed police reports. And never, *never*, has her mother been considered a suspect.

For one thing, Rhonda was cleaning up tables at the Brown Derby at the very moment police believe her daughter was abducted. It was physically impossible for her to have been directly involved. Though, I suppose, that doesn't rule out indirectly.

"Did the police tell you this?" I ask.

"No. But Kirk says the mother as murderer twist is the kind of juicy tidbit the cops would intentionally keep from reporters to throw us off track. And now that they've found Amy's body . . ."

My peripheral vision goes black. It's as if I'm staring down a long, dark tunnel. *They found Amy's body.* "She's dead?"

"I thought you heard."

"No. That's horrible!"

Of course, in the back of my mind I'd assumed Amy was dead. Girls don't go missing for months because they need to get away from it all, especially young women like her. Amy was generally at peace with herself. She had a boyfriend, a new car, was studying to become an occupational therapist, had plans to travel with her girlfriends to Mexico over winter break.

I'd always held on to a sliver of hope. The improbable *what if* . . .

"A hiker found her pretty decomposed up by Walden Pond, wrapped in a black garbage bag under a bunch of leaves and wood." Valerie is rattling off the gruesome specifics with as much breeziness as when I was talking to Dolores. "The coroner's office is there now and Jason's at the scene doing the shoot. He says the word among all the other cameramen is she's probably been there for months."

"Since the night of her abduction."

"That's what Jason says. She was killed right away."

Raped. Murdered. Terrified. Instantly, my thoughts turn to Em and I check the clock. It's eleven and she should be off to Brigham's. Please may she arrive safely today and every day, I pray.

"You okay, Julie? You look a bit shaken."

I have to take a deep, cleansing breath to compose myself. "I'm okay. It's the similarities that get to me. Amy and my daughter, Em, are—*were*—so much alike. Blond and flighty. I can't imagine being in Rhonda's position. How do you go on after something like this?"

"I know." Valerie regards me with something approaching pity. "It must be hard. That's why I'm better able to handle this story now, psychologically. I don't carry the, uh, baggage, you do of being a single mother—like she is."

Give me a break. I might be sympathetic, but I've been a professional reporter longer than you've had the caps on your teeth, kiddo.

"You're off the mark about Rhonda being the suspect," I say, setting her straight. "There are others the police have pegged as persons of interest: the local drifters who use the public library bathroom, perhaps a man she met online, even her boyfriend. Not her mom."

"Oh, really?" Valerie has a hand on her hip. "Is this inside information you've got or what?"

"Experience. Mothers don't generally rape and strangle their daughters and leave their bodies in garbage bags by Walden Pond." Valerie's corrupted by *CSI* and *Law & Order.* "If you'd covered crime for as long as I have, you'd know that."

A comment of this order would have completely deflated me at Valerie's age. I would have found it humiliating for a veteran reporter to have knocked me down a peg. But Valerie's a different breed, part of this new crop of women remarkable in both their lack of introspection and their hyperconfidence.

"Well, I'm sorry you feel that way. But that's your opinion. Only your opinion. And, really, I guess the only person who knows for sure and who's still alive to tell is . . . Rhonda."

"Maybe," I say, giving her the benefit of the doubt. "But if the cops have crossed her off their suspects list, what are you going to do?"

"Ask her myself. That's why I need her number. Though, on second thought, it's probably better if I go straight to her home and confront her when she comes back from the morgue. She won't be able to hang up on me then."

"You're going to confront her when she comes home from the morgue?" Smacking my head in disbelief, I say, "You can't do that! You can't ask Rhonda if she killed her own daughter."

"Why not?" Valerie flips her head. "The first rule of journalism is that there are no wrong questions, just bad ones."

Unbelievable. If Valerie had a teenage daughter like I do, she wouldn't think of asking such a thing, especially not on the day Amy's body was found.

"Have you told Arnie you're going to do this?"

"Uh . . . kind of."

"And he's fine with it?"

She shrugs. "It's not his story." Then, dropping her voice, she adds, "It's not yours, either, Julie. I just came over here to get a few phone numbers—you can hold your opinion."

None too eager to engage in a catfight in the middle of the newsroom, I say in an equally low voice, "You're making a huge mistake, Val. For one thing, you're wrong. For another, you are going to further hurt a woman who's living her worst nightmare. Think about that."

"See? This is your basic problem," she replies in a sweet girly-girl voice. "You're innately biased, Julie. And I'm not the only one who thinks that. Arnie does, too. And . . . Kirk."

"Kirk?" He would never have said that about me. Just the other day he was singing my praises.

As if I were a child, she continues. "Honey, that's why you're not going to the network—because you're too subjective. If you can't bring yourself to look Rhonda Michak, a regular waitress, in the eye and ask her if she had a hand in the murder of her own daughter, how do you expect to ask the presidential candidates under what circumstances they'd start a nuclear war? Now you think about *that*."

She's hit my soft spot, my long-standing suspicion that no matter how hard or how long I duke it out in this business, I simply lack the balls. If I didn't, I wouldn't still be earning close to minimum salary at an O&O (owned and operated) television station in Somerville, Massachusetts. I'd be Candy Crowley or Katie Couric. I'd be *someone*.

This is why the national election team means so much. Not because I'll get to travel and be up close and personal with high-stakes politics, but because it will prove, once and for all, that the past two decades have not been one long professional mistake. That my life counted.

Gathering myself, I say, "Okay. Like you said, it's your story and it'll be Rhonda Michak's grief."

Valerie shifts her gaze to the notebook in her hand and says, "You can email me your contacts. You know the address." Then she goes off. Perhaps chastised. More likely, not.

Crap. The orange message light on my phone is blinking. The papers must have been covering it, I think, hurriedly punching in the code. The first message is from Michael asking if instead of lunch we can meet outside the Davis Square T station at eleven—in half an hour. Unless he hears from me otherwise, he'll be waiting right by the entrance.

The second is from Detective Sinesky calling in an overdue tip that Amy's body has been found. "As you might have guessed, Rhonda's a mess and so is Ray," he grumbles, referring to Rhonda's live-in-boyfriend. "We all knew it was coming but, damn, for her to have to identify her daughter's remains . . . I gotta go."

That's it. I have to do something about Valerie. Or Rhonda. Or maybe both.

But right now I have to see Michael and find out just what he said to Kirk that deep-sixed my career.

Chapter Seven

I do desire we may be better strangers.

—AS YOU LIKE IT, ACT III, SCENE 2

It doesn't register until I'm outside that it is actually a pleasant morning. The warm, slightly moist air and the bright sunshine remind me of being a kid in summer camp weaving God's eyes on Popsicle sticks and taking swimming lessons in the over-chlorinated waters of the town pool. Ahh, that was the life.

I've never quite gotten used to working during the summers. Just because we're grown-ups shouldn't mean we have to imprison ourselves in dark offices while around us children are diving and skateboarding and biking for ice cream. It's not fair. We've earned the right to be soaking up the rays, too.

Like Michael. He's leaning against the wall of the Davis Square T station, eyes closed, a slight smile as he faces the sun. At first it seems he's dozing, but as I get closer I see he's listening. Listening to the homeless man crouched at his feet.

I know this guy. Everyone who rides the T to Davis Square knows him and his constant "Spare change for coffee, if you don't mind." Mac or Mick or something. Normally, I ignore him and try not to make eye contact, though that's not exactly easy since he reeks like a Parisian *pissotière* and he often insists on holding open the door and being paid for it.

I'm not eager to join their conversation, not after the morning I've had, so I give a shout from the opposite corner. But Michael, being Michael, waves me over.

"Hey, Julie, I want you to meet a friend of mine. This is Max."

Max. *That's* his name. "Hello."

He sticks up a dirty hand and challenges me to shake it, which I do, if only to show Michael I'm not afraid of his little tests.

Max says, "You come in on the 9:45, dontcha? Leave on the 7:50."

Okay, that's creepy to have a homeless man monitoring my exact schedule.

Michael, though, is intrigued. "The trains have times?" he says in a gee-whiz voice. "I thought they were random. First come, first served."

"No, sir. There's a whole bunch of machinations going on, you have no idea. Schedules. Safety switches. Alarms. Antiterrorism devices. Cameras galore. That's Big Brother's hideout, the T."

Next he'll be going on about the UFO sighted over the Mystic Lakes.

"Julie might be interested in that. She's a news reporter at WBOS up the road," Michael tells him, though I wish he wouldn't because now there's a chance Max will show up at work wanting me to investigate the Davis Square T as CIA hangout conspiracy. "Take a good look at her," he says, slightly teasing. "She's determined to be famous someday. Could even be delivering the six-thirty national news."

Fat chance.

"Bahh. TV news. Garbage." Max waves his hand in disgust. "I don't own a TV."

I don't take this personally because he clearly doesn't own anything, except for that ratty coat and shoes held together with duct tape, the poor man. Perfectly fine for sunny weather like this, but what about winter, when the temperatures dip into the twenties and snow whips through the square?

Michael says, "Max was reciting 'Tintern Abbey'—"

"Actually," Max cuts in, "its authentic title is 'Lines Composed a Few Miles Above Tintern Abbey.' "

"By Wordsworth," Michael finishes. "Start all over, Max."

Max squints his yellowy eyes and, in deep dramatic tones, begins. "Five years have passed; five summers, with the length / of five long winters! and again I hear / these waters, rolling from their mountain-springs / with a soft inland murmur. . . ."

It's a lengthy poem, that much I remember. "I hate to butt in. By the way, wonderful, Max. . . ."

He bows his head.

"However, we do have to get going, Michael. You have a lunch date and I've got a kind of crisis at work."

"Right." Pulling out his wallet, he slips Max a ten. "But make sure you come back and ask him to finish it. When he gets to the part about the Friend, I guarantee you'll choke up."

Max holds out his other hand to me and I, somewhat reluctantly, give him a five. Michael may have shamed me into giving him some money, but a ten is ridiculous.

"He used to be an investment banker, you know," Michael begins, walking at such a brisk pace I have to double-step to keep up. "Then one day, he got out of bed and said fuck it. Left behind a huge fortune and a town house in Back Bay."

This is the sweet, if terribly naïve, side of Michael's personality—his gullibility—and I can't help but tweak him for it. "Oh, I'm sure. Those million-dollar bonuses and summer homes on Nantucket are so done."

"It's true. I know you don't believe me, but he's legit. Max told me all he wanted to do was read. Isn't that fantastic? The guy reads everything. Last week it was Plutarch's Lives and this week it's all of Wordsworth's poetry. Took him no time at all to memorize 'Tintern Abbey.' He's probably the most well read person I know."

"You're gushing," I say, smiling, as we abruptly hook a right and head down an all-too-familiar block. And though Michael's eagerness to believe in the magic of ordinary humans is endearing, I have to remind myself that it's this very trait that got him into trouble with Carlos FitzWilliams. If he'd been less idealistic, more cynical, he might have seen before I had to point it out that FitzWilliams was a sleaze.

"You know what your problem is?" Michael asks.

"If you ask Valerie Zidane, I'm biased."

Michael stops in front of the Storybook Café, my absolutely favorite place in the world. "What did you say?"

"Nothing. What do *you* think my problem is?"

"That you don't gush enough. If you did, you'd be a much happier person." He swings open the white picket gate. "After you."

Right. Like I'm going to buy that a homeless man's really Warren Buffett on a literary lark. And who's to say I'm not happy, anyway?

Inside, we are confronted with a devilish array of cookies, candy, muffins, scones, cakes, tarts, *tartelettes*, cannoli, and cupcakes. *Now* I'm happy.

"This place is out of this world," Michael says, surveying the glass case. "Have you been here before?"

A vision of Carol, super-thin Carol, with her long neck and toned arms, pops to mind. These are the women Michael prefers, women who nibble celery and shop for skinny jeans, size 0 petite.

"Oh," I say, "once or twice."

"Julie!" A cry goes up from the kitchen as Tony emerges, wiping his hands on his apron. "My favorite customer."

Tony is what you'd call "larger than life." A huge dockworker of a man with a tattoo of Mom on one arm, his dog on the other, and a crooked black toupee on his head to top it off. "Second visit in one morning. To what do I owe this honor?"

Michael grins and murmurs, "Didn't think you meant once or twice a *day*." Then he blows out his cheeks and looks exactly like he did when he was sixteen making faces at me from across the dining room table.

I elbow him hard and tell Tony I'll stick with coffee, thanks.

"Nonsense. I just finished the cupcakes. And we know how you like my cupcakes."

I feign puzzlement. *What are these things you call cupcakes?*

"A piece of advice, my good man." Tony throws his huge arms over the counter. "You like this girl? You want her to be your girlfriend? You bring her here and keep her filled up with sweets. I'll tell you which ones." Then, ticking off on his fingers, he lists my many weaknesses. "Blueberry scone. Chocolate croissant. Bear claw." Eyeing Michael, he adds with a wink, "That one she really, really likes."

I am going bright red, Tony so has my number. Those bear claws with the flaky pastry and gooey almond filling oozing out between the "toes." That and a latte on a Saturday morning with a good book is the ideal way to start a weekend. I don't care if it's like a gazillion calories. They're worth it to maintain basic mental health.

Tony hasn't stopped yet. ". . . flourless chocolate cake, macaroon, cupcakes. Those she'll do anything for . . ."

"I'll take a half dozen," Michael says, laughing. "I don't care. Any flavor."

"Okay, but watch out. A half dozen cupcakes and she could be trouble." He goes back to the kitchen, folding a white pastry box along the way.

When he's out of earshot, I say, "I'm really not that much of a pig."

"Julie. I grew up with you. I've seen you eat an entire bowl of raw chocolate chip cookie dough in one sitting. And just last Friday I watched as you inhaled five different desserts. You don't have to pretend with me."

"But I'm not pretending." My stomach growls, as if to object. "It's just that . . ."

"Frankly, I'm glad to feed your addiction. It's the only time you smile, when you're eating something sweet. Did you know that?"

"No." He's not right. I smile all the time. And to prove it, I make a big effort to raise the sides of my mouth, like a clown."See?" I say through gritted teeth.

"Here we go." Tony plunks the box on the case. "And I threw an extra one in for the dumpling."

I quit smiling. Granted, it's been a while since I stepped on the scale, but . . . could I be that big?

"Don't look so sad, prima donna," Tony says. "I meant I put in another cupcake for your daughter."

Twenty minutes and two cupcakes later, Michael and I are sitting side by side on a bench outside Storybook enjoying our sugar high and savoring what's left of our coffee.

We've discussed Em and my brother, Paul, and whether he'll ever marry Scooter, his fiancée for the past eight years. We've gone over why Michael moved back to Boston. (Washington's too cynical, he claims, thereby raising the obvious question, "And Boston isn't?") We touched briefly on his ex-wife, Cassie the Virginia debutante, though Michael wasn't too eager to trash her and for that I admire him. In turn, I was equally reserved in updating him about my ex, Donald, the self-centered psychiatrist. We even debated the Red Sox's chances of winning the pennant again.

We've talked about everything but the reason we're here.

"So," Michael begins, balling up his paper napkin. "What's all this about you heading to the big time?"

I'm as clueless as you are, I'm tempted to quip. "It depends on what you told Kirk Bledsoe."

"Was that his name? I didn't quite catch it."

"He's only the most famous reporter the network has. I'm sure you watch *Noon Newshour with Kirk Bledsoe*."

"Yeah, that's what I do. I sit around my office watching TV in the middle of the day."

It must be a sugar low, because he's turning difficult. Or maybe it's that we're talking about the news business—not exactly his cup of tea.

"I guess what I'm asking is, is this what you really want?" He turns to me, his dark brown eyes concerned. "Washington is a town of cutthroats, Julie. Trust me. Everyone's out for themselves and how much power they can soak up from the people around them. You can't be invited to a party without wondering why you were asked and what your hosts want from you."

"I'm all grown up, Michael. I'm not Paul's little sister anymore. I can take it."

"I know you can take it. The question is, why should you have to?"

"Because it's exciting." Isn't that obvious? "I've been cooped up in this same sixty square miles all my life. I would have gone to Washington or New York when I was younger, except I got knocked up when I was twenty-three and all of a sudden my dreams weren't a priority anymore."

"*Ohhhh.* Are we having a pity party?"

I could slap him for that. He'd never had children, he was never that courageous. "Until you've raised a child, I don't think you're in any position to criticize me."

"Sorry. You're right. I was out of line." He leans on his knees and looks off.

Sitting back, I study a flock of gray pigeons eating up our crumbs and try to gather my thoughts. "Why do you care, anyway? It's not like you and I are friends anymore."

"And whose fault is that?" He holds up his hands. "Sorry *again*. Didn't mean to go there."

"Yes, let's not." My shoulder aches, a sure sign of stress and a reminder of what's waiting for me back at the office. Valerie's persecution of Rhonda Michak. "I'm sorry, too. You're not entirely to blame for my snapping. I had a supremely lousy morning."

Without going into too many details, I give him the lowdown and Michael does a commendable job of listening without offering his unsolicited opinion. This might come from being a consultant where no opinion is offered without establishing a hefty retainer first.

The more I think about Valerie's course of attack—and attack is definitely the right word—the more I'm bothered. I can't help but put myself in Rhonda's position. What if Em went missing for a year and then turned up dead, likely having been kidnapped, raped, and strangled? How would I feel if some young reporter eager to make brownie points with her superiors raised the unfounded issue that I'd been responsible for Em's death?

Valerie's intended line of questioning is unfair and cruel and, most important, an abuse of her power as a TV reporter. It's wrong and she needs to be stopped. The question is . . . how.

Michael looks at me as if I'm a changed woman. "She called you biased? That's the most hopeful thing I've heard about you in years."

"Oh, please." I snort and look off, desperate to hear what he has to say. "That's ridiculous."

"Are you kidding? It shows you have a soul, that you care about that woman. You're not an automaton."

"You can be unbiased without being an automaton."

"How? Humans have opinions, that's the way we're built. There's nothing wrong with that when it comes to journalism—it's just that you guys need to recognize your unavoidable biases and go on."

"Try telling that to my news director, Arnie. He despises any form of emotion. Unless it's swearing. That's fine. Especially if you're swearing at the Sox."

"I'm serious." Michael leaps up, energized, the wheels in his brain whirring. This is the man I'm used to, the excited, motivated, inspired Michael on whom I once had a maddening schoolgirl crush. "In fact, I think you've got a great opportunity here, Julie."

The sun's in my eyes, so I can't really see the expression on his face. "Do I?"

"You have a chance to show viewers that objectivity is an illusion, that you have feelings, too. Maybe you could do a Point-Counterpoint thing with this other reporter on why this woman deserves our sympathy."

"Oh, Michael. That's just . . . impossible." I could cite him chapter and verse out of the WBOS code and any other boilerplate journalism ethics policy that strictly forbids showing favor. "Acting like a fellow human being could get me fired. Or worse."

"You sound like a Nazi, some sort of goose-stepping, Brownshirted flunky."

"*Jawohl, mein Herr.*" And I begin gathering my stuff, annoyed and tired. "I'd love to kick back and plan the Fourth Reich, but I've been insulted enough for one day. So, if you don't mind, I think I'll head to the office, where at least I'm paid to be abused."

Idiot that he is, he blocks the gate and refuses to let me pass. "Do you know that Frank Zappa song, 'What's the Ugliest Part of Your Body?' "

"Yeah, your mind. Apology accepted. Okay now . . ."

"In your case, Julie, the most beautiful part of your body has always been your heart."

I swallow. That's actually very touching—even if it is supremely goofy. "When did you get so sappy all of a sudden?"

"Look, I remember when you were a little girl and used to sing and dance as if no one were watching. You were adorable. You brought me joy, Julie, and gave me hope. I used to think, how bad can life be if this little girl is belting 'A Spoonful of Sugar' at the top of her voice? Seeing you smile, hearing you sing helped make my childhood not so miserable."

A lump comes to my throat. I had no idea he thought of his childhood as miserable. He always came off as so cavalier, as if he enjoyed growing up with a drunken father and a mother who slept. Period. Just slept. "Well, it was sugar I was singing about, after all," I say. "You know me."

"Then what happened?" He's close to me now, intense, as if our years of animosity have simply disappeared. "You don't sing anymore. Or, rarely. I don't think it's your divorce or family obligations that are weighing you down. It's that you're immersed in a profession where you have to hide your best part, your beautiful heart."

Those words "beautiful heart" hang between us, draining me of snappy comebacks. I feel as if I've been given a serious, important gift I never asked for and don't particularly want.

"Is that what you said to Kirk? That I had a beautiful heart and it shouldn't be hidden? Because if you did, he must have burst out laughing."

"Actually, when I returned his call this morning I was much more erudite."

Putting his hands on my shoulders and looking deep into my eyes, he says slowly, "I told him it was no business of his what my personal relationships were and that he could take his obnoxious question and shove it up his own ass."

Oh, God. I feel sick. "That's erudite, all right."

"Yes," he says, standing by and finally letting me go. "I thought so, too."

Chapter Eight

Rumor is a pipe
Blown by surmises, jealousies, conjectures, . . .

—HENRY IV, PART TWO, INDUCTION

Perhaps Kirk didn't take offense. Maybe this is the way men banter with one another, lots of swearing and ass jamming. In fact, out of all the answers Michael could have given, this wasn't so bad, I decide. It didn't conflict with my statement that Michael and I had had only a platonic relationship and Michael didn't have to lie.

In retrospect, what he said was pretty darn brilliant.

And then I sit down at my computer, log in, and find this cryptic note highlighted in my inbox.

FROM: Kirk.Bledsoe@ubcnews.com

TO: Julie.Mueller@wbostvnews.com

RE: Michael Slayton

Julie----

Busy in meetings all morning and didn't get a chance to talk to you
before I left to catch my flight back to D.C. Touched base with
Michael Slayton an hour ago. Some disturbing issues we need to
discuss in person.

Will try to call you tomorrow when I get back. Or sometime this
week.

Kirk

Disturbing issues? Why would he have disturbing issues? All Michael
did was tell him to take his question and shove it up his own ass. How
disturbing is that? Answer: *very* disturbing.

Okay, calm down, Julie. The way to get a handle on anxiety is to focus
only on that which you can control. In this case, nothing.

Michael has—upon deep reconsideration—*rudely* and crudely told my
future superior to do an unmentionable act. But what's done is done and
I can't undo it until I talk to Kirk. Though I'm not sure what magic words
I can summon to soften the blow.

Man, I wish I hadn't drunk all that coffee. I'm sweating like a pig and
my heart is racing so fast, I might be one of those statistical flukes, a
woman in her early forties who drops dead of a massive myocardial in-
farction at her desk.

Where's Valerie? If I ask whether Kirk interviewed her for the national
election team this morning, she won't hesitate to brag. Then I'll know for
sure if I'm cooked.

Valerie is nowhere to be found. Raldo, who's heading out to lunch,
says she's off with Jason for the noon news conference on Amy Michak
and then she's going to stake out Rhonda, which means she might not return until after the evening report.

No. This can't happen. Just when I'm about to call him and ask if he has a minute to discuss this, up pops another email. Speak of the devil.

FROM: Arnold.Wolff@wbostvnews.com

TO: Julie.Mueller@wbostvnews.com

RE: Campaign finance reports addendum

J--

My calendar says the deadline for filing addendums to the campaign finance reports is today. I'm not expecting much, but we have to check in with the secretary of state's office just in case.

If you have any questions about this, see me. Otherwise stay far away. Word in the newsroom is you're in a mood.

A

Arnie ducks when I burst into his office a minute later.

"A mood? That better not be a PMS crack. I don't know if you've noticed that men have moods, too. And not every twenty-eight days, either," I tell him. "Twenty-four seven."

He winces. "Did you have to come in here? I nicely asked you not to."

"With an email like that, yeah, I'm coming in."

"But I wanna eat my lunch." He points to a hot dog with sauerkraut and chili sauce sitting on the foil wrapper. "And you might make me sick."

"Well, if I don't, then that rancid vendor food will. But go ahead. Help yourself to a healthy dose of bacteria. I'll wait here." Throwing myself into his red chair, I clasp my hands and stare him down.

Arnie is my news director and like most news directors, he loathes his job. He's short, tidy, with Coke-bottle glasses and a receding hairline. You'd never know that inside thrives a big kid, as evidenced by his white sneakers and extensive collection of Red Sox bobbleheads.

The problem is Arnie's been in the business too long. He's burned out on ratings wars and pushy general managers and vain anchors and whiny reporters. I am the exception because I take him out for beers and shrug off his occasional acerbic banter and, on my better days, can return a few volleys of my own.

He's often remarked I would make a great dog, if dogs could run tabs.

Mostly Arnie lives for the Red Sox. The walls that aren't glass in his office are papered ceiling to floor with Red Sox paraphernalia. Posters of Kurt Schilling's bloody ankle when he pitched the sixth game in the 2004 play-offs against the Yankees, pennants, a team roster, a signed picture of David Ortiz, framed headlines of major wins, souvenir trash. He should have stayed a sportscaster. He was never happier.

"Dolores tells me you're taking dessert classes," he says, licking chili off his lips.

My, such housewifey gossip from a sports nut. "Yeah. That's why I asked for my Friday night schedule to be changed."

"Oh." He slurps his Coke. "I wish you wouldn't do that."

"Not take off Friday nights? Geesh, Arnie, aren't we becoming quite the taskmaster."

"No. I wish you wouldn't give Dolores more ideas for more food. I'm worried about her heart. By the way, when you were walking across the newsroom the other day I noticed you could afford to lose a few."

"Like snarky news directors. I could lose a few of those."

He shrugs and opens his chips. "Just performing a helpful service. Butt monitoring. But I bet that's not why you're bothering me on my lunch hour, is it?"

"Nope. I came to harass you about Valerie." Stealing a commemorative baseball off its nerdy glass stand, I roll it between my hands to bug him.

"That is signed by Papelbon the god. It is not for you mere mortals," he snaps, snatching it back.

"That signature's forged and you know it." I gesture to the red spot on his tie. "Got some chili sauce there."

"Shit." He reaches for his dirty napkin and brushes at his tie furiously, only driving in the stain more and adding grease from his fingers. "I knew you'd throw a fit over Valerie getting the Michak murder. I should have told Dolores not to let you in."

"This is not a fit. A fit you'll see tomorrow if Valerie goes over to Rhonda's tonight and asks her why she murdered her own daughter."

He quits wiping his tie. "You don't like that, huh?"

"Of course not. Do you?"

Hook-shooting the napkin into a wastepaper basket, he says, "Hell, no. I almost resigned when she told me that. But then I remembered my kids' college tuition and the more practical part of me wised up."

"Then why are you letting her get away with this?" I ask, sitting up.

"Not my decision. It's Owen's. He's the one who wanted to test her on this Michak story to see if she had the balls to handle the sharks in D.C. and now you're seeing the result. Our precious Valerie is trying out her brand-new sharp teeth. Ouch."

I knew this aggressive line of questioning was somehow connected to the national election team. "Which means Valerie's the number one candidate for Kirk's team, isn't she?"

Arnie gives me a sheepish look. "I'm sorry, Julie."

Damn. Worst fear confirmed. And why? All because of an unconfirmed rumor. If Kirk weren't in the air right now I'd call him myself and tell him what a mistake he's making in Valerie and why he's wrong about me.

"It's not your fault, though," Arnie adds, taking my silence for sulking. "Not directly. If you want my opinion, your boyfriend really screwed you over."

I have to roll my eyes. "Michael Slayton's not my boyfriend and you know it. Never has been, never will be."

"Right. And it's perfectly normal for ex-managers of a campaign that fell in the toilet six years ago to rip Kirk apart for asking a standard background check question." He shakes his head. "You can't help it, you two were in love. But you shouldn't have lied to Kirk."

Love. That's so quaint of Arnie to use that term.

"I didn't lie. And if we were in love, Arnie, then, logically, I would have helped Michael by *ignoring* rumors of FitzWilliams's sexual harassment instead of undercutting him by exposing his candidate."

"Unless Michael rejected you. In which case, your FitzWilliams exposé would have been pure retaliation." Dumping the rest of the chips directly in his mouth, he adds, "That's FitzWilliams's spin on it, anyway. The old 'hell hath no fury like a woman scorned.' "

"More Shakespeare. He's everywhere."

Arnie flips up a finger. "Aha! Not Shakespeare. Everyone thinks that, but they're wrong. It's actually William Congreve."

Who? "I don't care. It's meaningless. Long ago I had a schoolgirl crush on Michael, nothing more. And Michael has never shown any interest in me other than that of a big brother. We're barely acquaintances, which is fine because, personally, the guy's a bit of a flake. He honestly fell for it when a homeless guy spun the old scam about being an investment banker who sacrificed all material pleasures for the comfort of a good book. Michael's like a child."

"Boy. For an *acquaintance* you certainly can wax rhapsodic about the guy. Hate to see what you're like if you were a full-fledged friend."

Time to switch subjects. "Let's get to the point. Am I definitely disqualified for the national election team?"

Linking his hands behind his head, Arnie leans back and considers this. "I don't think so. After Kirk calms down, I'll explain Slayton's being a prick who's still nursing a grudge against the station." He picks up the baseball and rolls it around, studying Papelbon's bogus scrawl. "You've got to see the situation from Kirk's point of view, Julie. He has to be assured you're not some black widow who goes around sleeping with campaign workers and biting their heads off. That could ruin a network's reputation forever."

"But I never slept with Michael."

"You say that and I believe you. But just saying you don't love him doesn't make it so."

Arnie and I sit in silence as he studies the ball and I study the poster of Johnny Damon onto which some joker from sports has drawn devil's horns and a goatee. Did Johnny Damon think with his heart or his head when he traitored out to the Yankees? *He thought with his wallet.*

"What do I do in the meantime?" I ask at last. "Between now and when you talk to Kirk."

He replaces the ball on its stand and goes back to examining the ceiling on which a giant red sock has been painted. "Put your nose down. Keep your mouth shut. Read all you can and, most important, stay out of trouble."

"Sounds dull."

"Then why don't you go home and make those desserts. That's how they used to keep women busy in the old days, rolling piecrusts and stuff."

"I bet you'd love it if we women got out of the workplace and back to the kitchen in our flowered aprons and pearls—like the 1950s."

"Please, not the 50s. That was the worst decade in Red Sox history. Ted Williams and his Seven Dwarfs. A nightmare."

"Is there any situation that you don't turn into a baseball analogy?" I ask.

Arnie frowns and says, "Sex. It's impossible to think about sex and baseball at the same time. It's too damn distracting."

The sad thing is, I bet baseball distracts him from sex—not the other way around.

Chapter Nine

I understand you not: my griefs are double.
Honest plain words best pierce the ear of grief. . . .

—LOVE'S LABOUR'S LOST ACT V, SCENE 2

I love my mother. No, I really do. It's just that . . . she has the absolute worst timing.

Here I am trying to make sense of this recipe for peach cobbler D'Ours, so immersed in how to cut butter into flour that I don't notice the front door open and Mom sneaking in until I feel a tap on my shoulder and jump back wicked fast. Boom! Off the counter go all my perfect New Jersey peaches, the prize first crop.

"My word, Julie. Chill out." Mom bends down to fetch a peach, but I beat her to it. I can't have my seventy-five-year-old mother picking up after me.

"What's wrong with you? You've been so jumpy lately. At night I hear you stomping around in the kitchen when it's way after two a.m. Are you not sleeping?"

"Got a lot on my mind, Mom." I reach to retrieve the last peach stuck way under the table. It's covered with dust and a plastic tie from a bread bag.

"It could be menopause. I hate to say it, but I was about your age when it started."

Nice try, but she's not roping me into that one. So far I've been able to stiff-arm Mom on the "menopause discussion" and I have no intention of losing ground. Reminds me of when I was a kid and she tried to trap me in her bedroom to have a mother-daughter chat about "a wonderful cycle a woman goes through each month that perfectly prepares her body for a baby."

That is not the kind of shop talk a ten-year-old girl wants to hear. Trust me. Much better to get the lowdown from your friends who have absolutely no idea what's going on. (Don't even ask where Liza was sure the fallopian tubes were located.)

"I am not going through menopause," I say, carving out a blossoming bruise on the last peach.

"Perimenopause, then."

"Is perimenopause related to Perry Como? Because, if so, that could be a helluva act in Vegas."

"Ha, ha." Mom thrusts out a metal box in the shape of a barn, complete with worn yellow chickens and rusting cows raised on the sides. "Now that you're taking dessert class and actually cooking for once, I thought you might appreciate this."

It's familiar, a relic from my childhood. Mom kept it in a cabinet above the oven next to her Crock-Pot and the wok she never used. "Is this a . . ."

"Recipe box. My very own." She rocks on her heels, proud. "There are fifty years of recipes in that box, I'll have you know. Recipes you can't find anymore if you tried."

And there's a reason for that.

Salmon aspic. Oxtail soup. Holiday cottage cheese log. Curried chicken salad with hard-boiled eggs. Lamb rice balls. Baked stuffed onions. Plus that favorite standby: Jell-O. Jell-O with pineapples. Jell-O with marshmallows. Celery Jell-O ring with tomato. And, for when company came, the always miraculous triple-layered Jell-O fruit parfait.

"Thank you, Mom. That's so sweet."

"They're treasures. I clipped and pasted them over the years. *Woman's Day. Family Circle. Reader's Digest.*"

Depressed Housewife Monthly.

"I will *use* this," I gush. "Definitely."

"Really?"

"Absolutely."

"Great." Mom glances sideways to the flour, sugar, and peaches sprawled across the counter. "Shouldn't you be at work instead of cooking? I heard on the radio they found Amy Michak's body. I was going to call you, but I know how you hate to be bothered when there's a breaking news story."

What my mother's not saying is, *This is your big story, Julie. Why aren't you on the scene?*

"Arnie took me off the story. He assigned it to Valerie." And I go back to mutilating the peach with an apple peeler and having a dickens of a time. The skin comes off in hard strips, if at all, or it mushes the valuable orange insides, leaving my fingers sticky and slippery.

"There's an easier way to do that, you know." She fetches a pot from under the sink and fills it with water. "Drop the peaches into boiling water, boil for one minute. Then remove with a slotted spoon and dunk in ice water. They slide right off."

I can't do anything right. I can't even peel a peach.

Mom turns on the heat and says, "You having work problems, hon?"

"Nope."

I'd like to confide in her, honestly I would, but I can't. It's not only that she'll blab to any stranger who crosses her line of vision. ("Hey, you, gas station attendant. Let me tell you about my loser daughter who blew her chance at being on the national election team.")

It's also because she worries too much about my financial future. Yes, I've got a piddly IRA and, aside from this house, a thin savings account. T. Rowe Price isn't going to feature me in a commercial, boating on a misty lake to my massive retirement waterfront home anytime soon. But I'll get by. Somehow. I don't need her prying into how much I'm socking away each month or if I've considered annuities.

But what I really dread are her platitudes when things don't work out. That tomorrow is another day, that everything happens for a reason, and God has plans and is opening doors and closing windows . . . or is it closing doors and opening windows? I forget.

I can tell Mom is desperate for me to confide and discuss. That's what she did with her sister, Charlotte, with her own mother, Nana, what she does with Lois and Teenie. Share, bitch, cry, soothe in a never-ending loop of tears and tea.

Well, I'm sorry. I just won't give her the satisfaction. I'm a forty-something woman and it's time I stood on my own. I do not need a live-in therapist.

"I'm . . . a . . . failure!" I hear myself moan. And before I can get a grip, the peach slips out of my hands, bounces into the sink, and Mom has her arms around me. "I'm a complete and utter fuckup."

"No, you're not. No, you're not," she coos, leading me to the kitchen table. "Sit down and I'll get you some water." She gets me the water and then settles in across from me for a good gossip fest. "Now tell me what this is about and don't spare me any details. I can take them."

I don't spill about the national election team since Kirk told me to keep it under my hat. But I do my fair share of wheedling and whining about how I'm mediocre at best. A straight-B student of life.

"That's not so," Mom says, getting up and dropping the peaches into the boiling water. "Look how much you've accomplished. You have a beautiful daughter who is a delight to be around. A house. A car. An exciting, glamorous job."

"Hah! I spent half the day sitting in the musty basement of the secretary of state's office going through campaign finance reports. How glamorous is that?"

"To some people it might seem very glamorous."

She needs an ice bath for those peaches. Going to the freezer, I point out that while I may have a house, a daughter, and a job, I also have a divorce, no savings, and a stagnating career.

"More than I had at your age," she says, poking at a peach with the spoon.

"At my age you had a husband, two kids, and a house that ran like a Mussolini train station. Sheets white and crisply folded. Living room dusted and decorated with heavy damask curtains and matching furniture. Dinner on the table at five-thirty every night without fail complete with two vegetables, a meat, and dessert." I run water into the bowl of ice and help take out the peaches. "Em is lucky if I remember to stop by Whole Foods on my way home from work. Otherwise it's Chinese takeout, straight out of the box eaten in front of the TV at nine."

I throw in the last peach and turn off the stove. "Twenty years of perfecting my skills as a journalist and I'm no better than when I was twenty-three. In fact, I'm worse. Too biased, according to Arnie, and not biased enough, according to Michael."

Mom squeezes off a skin. "Michael who?"

"Michael Slayton." I try following her example but, naturally, my skin sticks. "We had coffee this morning. He told me I've changed, lost my joy or whatever, because I don't follow my heart. Which, if you ask me, sounds like something off a Hallmark card or a Nicholas Sparks novel."

Mom is stuck on one track, though. "Why were you having coffee with Michael Slayton?"

"Kirk Bledsoe called him. . . ." Oops! I almost told her.

She holds up a peach, stunned. "Kirk Bledsoe from *Noon Newshour with Kirk Bledsoe? That* Kirk Bledsoe?"

Now I've done it. She'll never let this go. "Yeah, uh, he was in town to visit family over the weekend."

"Why was he calling Michael? Was he calling about you?"

God, she's good. How does she do it? "Uh . . ."

"What is it you're not telling me, Julie? What's really . . . ooh." She teeters and swings, bumping the bowl of ice water and gripping the counter for support.

"Mom!" I cry, steadying her. "Are you all right?"

"Just woozy all of a sudden." She puts her finger to her temple and closes her eyes, an image that seems disturbingly familiar. Just the other day this happened, no?

"You want me to call the doctor?" I say, leading her back to the chair.

"The doctor?" she scoffs. "No, Julie. I don't need a *doctor*." As if I'd offered to summon the friendly neighborhood voodoo witch. "This is called getting old. It'll happen to you one day, too."

It's not called getting old. Getting old means your joints don't always do what you tell them to and that your skin loses its elasticity. This is something else. But what?

The phone rings, startling both of us. Caller ID says unknown, which means it's a telemarketer interrupting an important moment. Have those people no shame?

It's not a telemarketer, though. It's Ray, and for a second I have to place who he is.

"I'm sorry for bothering you at home," he begins hesitantly. "But this is an emergency—kinda—and I was told you wouldn't mind."

Right. Ray is Ray Schmuler, Rhonda's live-in boyfriend. A gentle, practically illiterate garbage hauler who's tirelessly tacked up posters and accumulated reward money for anyone with information about his girl-friend's kid.

"Are you kidding? You can call me whenever, Ray. I'm so, so sorry about the turn of events."

Ray says, "Yeah?" Though he sounds skeptical. "I'm not going to keep you. I just wondered . . . You know, I don't even know if you can, but . . ."

All of a sudden, Ray gets off and there's much muffled noise in the background. Mom mouths, "What's going on?" And I shrug.

"Julie?" The voice at the other end is a woman's, thick with emotion.

Oh, God. It's Rhonda herself. "Rhonda," I say, not knowing where to start. "I'm so, so sorry. I had hope."

"Me too."

"I've been putting myself in your shoes all day and I can't imagine how you're holding up. I know how close you and Amy were."

What follows is the most wrenching sound in the universe, a mother breaking down over her dead child. "It's been . . ." She catches herself and gulps. "I wouldn't have had Ray call you except that . . . these lies. It's so painful, Julie. The pain. The pain is overwhelming. Every part of me hurts."

Closing my eyes, I wish I were anywhere but here right now. I want to help Rhonda and yet I can't. I'm *forbidden*. Even so, I ask, "Is there anything I can do?"

"Make her stop." Rhonda's breath rattles as she tries to compose herself. "Make her stop saying that about me and Amy. I never would have laid a finger on her. She was my *baby*, Julie. I carried her for nine months. I sewed her dress-up clothes. I stayed up all night with her when she was sick. Julie . . . she was my best friend!"

No. No. I can't listen to any more of this. It's hitting too close to home. "Rhonda, I'm coming over," I hear myself say. "I don't know if there's anything I can do, but I'm coming over."

"Okay," Rhonda says, though it's not really a confirmation. It's more like a declaration of surrender. "Okay."

We hang up and I find Mom already assembling the cobbler without me, dotting the peaches with dough balls in place of a fancy rolled-out pastry like D'Ours's. The bottle of balsamic vinegar—D'Ours's secret ingredient—is on the counter still sealed.

"But I haven't added the vinegar yet."

Mom wrinkles her nose in disgust. "Thank heavens. When I read that on the recipe I figured it must have been a mistake. Who adds vinegar to cobbler? Cinnamon. Sugar. A squeeze of lemon, perhaps. But not vinegar. That's for salads."

Ugh. This is going to be the same ol', same ol'. Right off the back of the Bisquick box.

"Anyway, I couldn't wait for you," she says, popping it in the oven. "You might have been on the phone forever."

"Why the rush? It's only for Em and she won't get off work until eleven."

"Because if you're going to go over to Rhonda Michak's then you can't go empty-handed. You've got to bring something, Julie. And to make you feel better, I'll go with you, too, for support."

My mother and I and a cobbler are going to join the side of Rhonda Michak in her fresh battle with my news station and a colleague who sits two desks away from mine.

Clearly, I'm about to cross a very dangerous line.

Chapter Ten

. . . Never shame to hear
What you have nobly done.

—CORIOLANUS, ACT II, SCENE 2

What a horrible night!

It wasn't just finding Rhonda so overcome with despair she couldn't lift her head off the couch. It was also that Ray chose me to be the target of his boiling anger and frustration. As I stood trapped in his cramped kitchen awkwardly holding my cobbler, he went off on the useless news media, cursing it for exploiting, not helping, Amy and being positively worthless when it came to finding her killer—at large now for nine months.

"There are two tragedies," he kept saying. "Two tragedies. Some creep killed Amy, but it was you people who killed Rhonda. Look at her! Look at her! She's dead."

Indeed, I had to agree. Rhonda wasn't dead, but she wasn't living, either. It was an awful thought to think the people I worked with and for had had a hand in that.

There was nothing I could do, no way to reply, no way to escape even, since around us crowded equally angry friends and family. Meanwhile, a throng of news media was camped on the lawn, their idling white satellite trucks filling the air with fumes, their blinding klieg lights and constant chatter invading Rhonda's front windows.

Why don't you take your rage out on them? I wanted to tell Ray. I'm one of the good guys. Why me?

Instead, when he was done and his face began subsiding from a fiery red to a moist pink and the onlookers began to slink away, I handed him the cobbler and said, "Here. It's all I had to bring," and went outside to find Mom and Valerie.

Mom seemed to be thoroughly enjoying herself among the grief junkies. She was intensely chatting with some reporter as I pushed through the crowd to find Valerie primping for her next shot.

"Julie? What are you doing here?" she exclaimed, keeping her lips parted so as not to smudge her latest coat of gloss.

"I wish it had been you instead of me in there with Ray five minutes ago. I just got an earful about what we've done to Rhonda."

She cocked her head in that way of hers and, totally missing the point, said, "What were you doing with Ray Schmuler? This is my story."

"I wasn't there as a reporter. I was there as a human being. You might want to try it sometime." Then I huffed off, got Mom, and sped away.

Later that night, after Em got off work from Brigham's, she and I made another cobbler using the leftover peaches. As so often happens with cooking, we settled into a rhythmic conversation about my decision to go to Rhonda's even though it violated WBOS's conflict-of-interest policy. This led to a debate about when rules should be followed and when conscience dictates they must be ignored—a subject about which most teenagers can go on endlessly.

As Em rolled out the pastry and I tossed the peaches with sugar and D'Ours's touch of balsamic vinegar, I decided with satisfaction that this was one of those rare moments when I was really parenting—not by lecturing, but by modeling. Em was proud of me for my choice and there's something about your children's pride that's better than all the promotions and pay raises in the world.

Well, depending on how big the raise. Let's be real.

This is on my mind, life choices, as I climb the stairs of the Davis Square T station and find Max the homeless man waiting for me at the door. Bummer.

"Ready for the rest of 'Tintern Abbey'?" he asks.

My temptation is to throw him a buck and get out as fast as possible, but an inner voice urges me to humor him. "Sure, Max. Why not?"

We go outside to the clear summer morning and Max starts right where he left off:

> "Once again
> Do I behold these steep and lofty cliffs,
> That on a wild secluded scene impress
> Thoughts of more deep seclusion; and connect
> The landscape with the quiet of the sky.
> The day is come when I again repose
> Here, under this dark sycamore, and view
> These plots of cottage ground, these orchard tufts,
> Which at this season, with their unripe fruits,
> Are clad in one green hue, and lose themselves
> 'Mid groves and copses."

Listening to Max's perfect dictation and resonating voice, I find myself wishing I were in a green, bucolic Welsh valley dotted with thatched-roof cottages instead of heading off to a stress-filled, windowless newsroom. How nice and peaceful that would be. How delightfully refreshing.

"Ahh, it's getting to you, isn't it?" Max says, his eyes twinkling. "That's what I'm going for, a life like that. A life of repose."

I give him a Tupperware container of the peach cobbler I'd intended for Arnie, along with a ten-dollar bill. "Take care, Max. You may be right."

At work, I hand Dolores the other slice of cobbler, to smooth her ruffled feathers.

"I'll put my name on it," she says, pulling out a black Sharpie, "and put it in the refrigerator for lunch. I already brought dessert, but so what."

"Yeah, so what." Arnie's gonna kill me. Luckily, his office is dark. "Where's our beloved leader this morning, anyway?"

Dolores points upward with the Sharpie, pantomime for Owen's lair. "Handling the daily crisis. Another day, another fire."

Glad to be off Arnie's radar, I head to my desk, ready to put in a decent morning's work going over the campaign finance reports from yesterday, separating new donors from old, tracing individuals to corporations and trying to determine who's switched their financial support. The fun just never ends when you're a glamorous TV journalist.

Valerie's computer monitor is off, which means she's hasn't come to work yet—not unusual for reporters who've put in late hours the night before. I expect she won't be in until noon, thank God. I can't imagine my young protégé's too pleased with me after last night. Not that I'm regretting anything.

First, however, a dose of procrastination as I flip through the *Boston Globe*. Two paragraphs into their story about Amy's murder and the phone rings. It's a woman screaming hysterically.

"Can you hear me?" *Tap. Tap. Bang.* "How's this? Is this better?"

It's Liza calling from the outskirts of Bucharest or some such former Communist hellhole. I repeatedly say yes, that I can hear her fine, but it's pointless. She keeps hitting the phone against something and cursing the local telephone company. My ears might never be the same.

Finally, she hangs up and calls again, so clear, she could be on the other side of the newsroom. "I've been dying to know," she says. "How did it go with my beloved Chef Rene?"

This is so Liza. "You're thousands of miles away in Romania and you're calling to ask about Chef Rene?"

"Of course! This isn't a passing fling, Julie. This is the real deal. Did you put in a good word for me, or what?"

Okay, now I feel really bad because I dropped the ball on the D'Ours front. To cover, I go on about how handsome he is and oh what personality.

"I know, right?" Liza sounds as if she's eating while on the phone. Then again, she's always eating. "At first he comes off as a little prick with his fussy French ways. But then, after a couple of conversations, he really loosens up a bit."

How many conversations, exactly, has she had with him? I ask.

"Two. One in the hallway and one on the sidewalk, but they were great! Best ever. We talked about food and wine and pairings. We have so much in common."

That's a surprise considering D'Ours is a snob about American cuisine, of which Liza is the shortcut queen. "And he knows that you're the famous writer of the Hot Haute series?"

"No way. I figured I'd let him fall for me first and then, when he's gotten to where he thinks I'm all out of intrigue, I'll totally impress him by revealing my vast oeuvre."

Usually, at that point in a relationship, Liza reveals other vast parts about her, so this is a switch. She must really like the guy.

"How's it going with Michael?"

When I relay Michael's line about me not following my heart, she lets out another screech. "I've been telling you that for years. Julie, quit this job because it's eating away at your soul. But do you listen to me, your best friend? *Nooo.* Then some man says the exact same thing and suddenly your life is changed."

I have to shift in my chair. "A peach cobbler does not a life change make."

"It's not the cobbler. See, that's what people don't get about food. It's never the food, it's the love that goes into making it. That's what's important."

When she finally gets off, it's eleven-thirty. I better get to work if I want to pitch this campaign finance report story to Arnie by our two p.m. meeting. Not exactly A-slot material, but that's okay. Can't be murders and five-alarm house fires every day.

And yet Valerie's still not in. Interesting.

At noon, I'm crunching the numbers, finance reports tossed all over the place, a calculator in my lap and a spreadsheet on my computer, when Raldo stops by looking for a lunch companion.

"Can't get a sandwich with you today," I say, trying to reconcile two conflicting donor reports. "These numbers don't make any sense at all."

"I give you credit for having enough guts to show your face," he says, towering over me. "I'd never expected you to sink so low. A little rivalry among colleagues can be healthy, but to intentionally cut her off at the knees and ridicule her in the press? She must be mortified."

I look up, baffled, to find Raldo wearing a rare sneer. "What are you talking about?"

"As if you don't know. You've got the paper right in front of you." And he thumbs through the *Globe* on my desk, turning to the jump of the Amy Michak murder. The jump I didn't get to because of Liza's phone call.

There, in a breakout sidebar, is a short article only three paragraphs long, headlined:

Amy's Mother Snubs Press
. . . But Not Cobbler.

With one eye open, I scan it quickly, like that will lessen the pain.

> *Rhonda Michak refused all comments. . . . Reporters waited for hours. . . . Only one was permitted entrance, Julie Mueller, of WBOS TV, who came carrying a peach cobbler. . . . According to Mueller's mother, Betty Mueller, of Watertown, her daughter was not there to cover the story, but to offer her sympathies.*

Whew. That's not *too* bad. And the article's almost over, except for this last line:

> *"Said Mrs. Mueller, 'Julie's appalled that some people at her station would invent out of whole cloth a rumor that Rhonda killed her own daughter. It's outrageous. Rhonda Michak called her and she went over with a peach cobbler D'Ours. So what?' "*

My mother!

Folding the newspaper and shoving it in the trash, I tell Raldo it was no big deal. "In fact, Valerie got off easy. I was the one who got the tongue-lashing from Ray."

"Don't tell it to me," Raldo says, pointing past my shoulder. "Tell it to him."

Which is when I spin around to find Arnie shaking his head and gleefully waving a pink slip.

"Peach cobbler," he says. "What the hell were you thinking?"

"You know, Julie," Owen begins, rolling up his French blue shirtsleeves, "I'm all for bribes. I've got no problem paying for a story as long as no one finds out. But . . . dessert? That, I don't get."

"Your ethics are very impressive, Owen. However, the peach cobbler was a condolence offering, not a bribe," I say, trying not to leave sweat marks on the fine English leather of his wing chair. We are in his sixth-floor wing, with its regulation billiard table and views overlooking the Cambridge skyline. "My visit to Rhonda's was purely personal and everything said was off the record."

"So that's why you didn't bring a cameraman or tape the interview."

"No need. It was a courtesy call."

"A courtesy call?" Arnie, who's been twirling one of Owen's pool cues, stops pacing. "You work for WBOS, Julie, not the goddamn ladies auxiliary."

"Really? I hadn't noticed, what with the way everyone is so demure and polite around here."

He wags his finger. "Watch it. You're on thin ice, Tinkerbell."

"Too late," Owen says, "Tinkerbell's fallen through. Our best reporter felled by a peach."

Best reporter. Goes to show Owen really loves me, as does Arnie. Otherwise they wouldn't half joke around. What I've got to do is get them to see my mother's innocent—albeit unfortunate—comments were harmless and then they'll lighten up again.

"Let's put this in perspective," I begin, oozing rationality. "It was a cobbler, not a nuclear bomb. If you ask me, you're being a couple of pansies."

"We didn't ask you, and people who bring cobblers are in no position to call other people pansies," says Arnie. "Besides, don't you realize the *Globe*'s moronic columnists are going to have a field day making fun of us for this? This does not add to the image we're trying to cultivate of being serious journalists. We'll be the laughingstock of Boston news."

Perhaps a different tack. "Have you considered that, instead, I *saved* the station's reputation?"

Owen leans forward. "How so?"

"It's kind of a bad cop–good cop routine. Valerie was the bad cop, I was the good cop. The *Globe* could have attacked us for floating the Rhonda rumor. Instead, they attacked me, bearer of delicious desserts."

"Except I didn't assign you to play cop, did I?" Arnie says. "Much less ask you to bring dessert."

"You should have posted a sign-up sheet like Dolores does for the company potluck barbecue."

"Do you *want* to be fired?" Owen demands of me, glancing at Arnie, who is back to pacing, head down, pool cue twirling. "Is that what these wisecracks are about? Maybe you've got another job lined up and you're looking for severance pay."

"Darn. Why didn't I think of that? Look, Owen, I've done nothing wrong and you know it. Now, why don't we let this ride and I'll go downstairs to finish my campaign finance story."

"I say fire her." Arnie sticks out his tongue at me. "She's getting wide in the caboose, anyway. She's no longer an *ass*et to the station."

"You fire me after that comment and you'll have a sexual harassment suit slapped on your own ass before you're out the elevator." I stick out my tongue in reply. "Anyway, you know the *Globe* will go crazy if you can me for this. Keep me on and they'll forget about it once their lazy columnists find another victim to hang. Fire me and it'll be front-page news."

Examining his green desk blotter, Owen says, "Okay. I'm not going to reach a decision on this until further investigation. I need to think."

"And I need to drink," chimes in Arnie. "Preferably something cold and malted in a small green stadium off Lansdowne Street during a Red Sox–Yankees doubleheader. In the meantime, what should we do with her? I could always stick her on night sports with Smelly Leo."

Owen strokes his chin, regarding me thoughtfully. "Obit update."

"Not that!" That's the worst. "In the basement?" A tedious job involving poring through archives and splicing films.

Arnie says, "Excellent idea. We haven't had our obit file updated in a year and Ted Kennedy's sure to kick it sooner than later and Barney Frank's not getting any younger, either."

"Also, you've got to apologize to Valerie." Owen scribbles something onto a sheet of paper and slides it across the desk to me. "She can be reached here."

"No way am I apologizing to Valerie, she was . . ." Wait. What's going on here? I have to read the address again. "This isn't her email address. This is the address for—"

"The Washington bureau." Owen keeps his gaze on the blotter, as if he can't face me. "Valerie left this morning for a two-week tryout."

Suddenly, the mood's not so light. *He picked her.* My initial instinct was right. That's why she was with Kirk all yesterday morning. Not to discuss Amy Michak, but because *he picked her* for the national election team.

"Sorry, Julie." A hand squeezes my shoulder. It's Arnie leaning on his pool cue. "If it's any comfort, Owen and I agree you were the better choice. And not just because you're learning how to cook."

"Unless I decide to fire you," Owen adds. "In which case, I will announce in a press release that you were the worst reporter we ever had and an embarrassment to the station."

"You're so supportive."

Owen nods. "You can always count on me to back you up when things are going well."

Chapter Eleven

We that are true lovers run into strange capers;
but as all is mortal in nature, so is all nature in love mortal in folly.

—AS YOU LIKE IT, ACT II, SCENE 4

Xanax.

That's what the DMV should hand out with every teenage driving permit. Who was the nimrod who decided seventeen was an ideal age to get behind the wheel, anyway? Like sex and marijuana and beer parties weren't enough to deal with, now these poor kids have got to learn how to handle a two-ton vehicle, too.

"How you doin', Mom?" Em's smiling bright eyes, those meticulously tweezed brows, appear in the rearview mirror. Does she have to be so pleased with herself?

"Just fine," I chirp, digging my fingers into the backseat. *Keep your eyes on the road and not on me, kiddo. Disaster is only a distraction away.*

Mom, riding shotgun because she insisted, points to the left. "Your exit's coming up. I don't know what bonehead designed this crazy road, but you're going to have to move across two lanes and pretty fast, too."

"Two lanes!" Em says.

Two lanes! I nearly scream.

"You can do it. Just check your mirrors and use your blinkers," Mom says.

Sure, like that will help. Doesn't Mom realize blinkers are a sign of weakness in this city? They'll run all over us. We'll be roadkill on the six-thirty news, my trusty green Subaru Outback a mangled burning heap, some loudmouth Southie opining as to how the ladies should stay off Storrow if they can't deal with "real" drivers.

"Maybe I should take over this part," I say, undoing my safety belt and crawling between the seats.

Mom pushes me down. "What the ho-hay are you trying to do, Julie? Cause an accident? Emmaline can handle this."

"Yeah, Mom." And, leaning out of her window, her blond ponytail flapping in the damp and dirty breeze, my seventeen-year-old daughter manages to do what I have never been able to in my decades of driving: sail across two lanes of Storrow Drive, one, two, exit—with merely a smile and a wave.

I have to admit, I am very impressed. Or is that relief to be alive?

"Good for you!" Mom pats a wrinkled hand on Em's bare shoulder. "I knew you could."

"Thanks, Grandma."

Gawd, I'm an awful parent. I mean, really, really lousy. Here all Em ever wants is a vote of confidence, a chance to drive and be independent, and where am I? Cowering in the rear seat, hiding my eyes. Thank heavens Mom's there to pick up the slack.

Though, come to think of it, since when did Mom get so cool? She wasn't this laid-back when I was learning how to drive, what with her gripping the dashboard and slamming her right foot against the invisible brake, letting out gasps whenever I moved the car an inch.

Watch out, Julie! Not so fast! What're you trying to do, kill us?

And that was just pulling out of the driveway.

The thing is, I'm simmering with a fair amount of inner resentment since I'm finding it hard to completely forgive her for what she did at the Michaks'. To violate the sacred boundary between kitchen gossip and work is unheard of. It's so . . . wrong (even if she was right). She had no business talking to that *Globe* reporter.

All week I've been paying the price in the basement of WBOS, updating obits. Listen, it's not easy paring Ted Kennedy's life to three precious minutes, two of which could go to Chappaquiddick alone. It's so unfair. Here Valerie's jetting off with the national election team to Denver and Sacramento while I'm trying to make sense of Boston native Bobby Brown's prison record. And why?

Mom.

This is what drives me up the wall about my mother. Her meddling. She can't simply listen to my troubles and leave them be. She has to *do* something. She has to make suggestions and "make calls," pull strings behind my back. She has to be Mrs. Buttinsky.

That might have been mildly acceptable in first grade when Mavis Buckhoe tripped me with her jump rope every day because she thought I liked her boyfriend, Michael Utard, and Mom had me switched to another class. But I am over forty! What's she thinking, blabbing to anyone and everyone about my troubles?

"Okay, so where is this famous cooking school?" Mom asks as traffic screeches to a halt.

From the backseat I answer, "On Newbury Street, but don't make Em drive me to the door. It's a zoo. Just drop me off at the Eliot Hotel and I'll walk up."

Unfortunately, Em takes a right too soon and ends up heading the wrong way on Beacon Street, a one-way corridor headed toward a mess of an intersection made more terrifying with the Red Sox in town.

"No problem," Mom says, her gripping fingers on the dash belying that statement. "We'll make it through."

Em is panicked, unsure what lane to be in as Boston drivers, sensing a weak one among them, cut her off and flip the bird. Her previous confidence has vaporized and she is no longer smiling at me in the rearview. Every muscle in her arms is tensed to snap.

"Get into the left," I tell her. "Check first, goddammit!"

I know, I know. You're not supposed to swear at your teenage daughter, but I can't help it. She was sliding into the next lane without looking at her mirrors. We could have been killed. Or . . . badly dinged.

Em checks, looks out the window, and gets over. "Good," I say, determined to be the one to walk Em through this and not my buttinsky mother. "Okay. This intersection's not too bad. Just packed with Red Sox fans. Better than if we'd been here an hour earlier. We never would have gotten through."

Mom, somewhere on Planet Plutron, muses whimsically, "Used to be a swamp, Kenmore Square. Literally, a swamp. Now, when was the last time we were down here to see the Sox? Was it with Nana?"

Holy Hank Aaron. "Now is not the time to be strolling la-di-da down memory lane, *Mother*." Not when Em nearly hit some guy in a wheelchair.

"The last game she ever saw," Mom adds. "Too bad you couldn't hold out longer to see them win the pennant. You might have tried, Mom."

In the rearview mirror, Em grimaces in alarm. I agree, weird. Mom talking to her own mother, who's been dead for ten years. Still, that's no reason to take one's eyes off the road.

"There's your left." I point to the craziness of Lansdowne Street blanketed by fans in the trademark navy and blue holding seat cushions and water bottles, signs, raincoats, and pink hats. "Do your best."

Em does her best, at one point actually closing her eyes. Perfectly okay. Lots of drivers around here drive with their eyes closed. It's the only way to stay sane.

The next challenge, getting from Lansdowne to Ipswich, to Boylston and back to Mass. Ave., she manages with very little swearing on my part. The back of Mom's seat, however, will be forever imprinted with the indentations of my right hand.

Pulling into a gas station, Em practically collapses. "That was the worst. I am never driving again."

"Of course you are," I say, opening the door to get out. "You did a fantastic job. Why, I couldn't have done that at your age. I didn't get the guts to drive through Boston until I was in my twenties."

"I dunno. I'm not ready for this. Grandma, can you drive back?"

Normally that would be fine. My mother's an old hand at taking on Southies. Shoot, she's been battling them long enough. But there was something about her talking to her mother just now. And the way she was tottering in the garden this morning. Like she might have been having another dizzy spell—an observation she refuted with an "I am not!" as though my loving inquiry was an outrageous insult.

The bottom line is, I don't want her driving Em. Awful, true, but there you have it. I don't trust her brain.

"If you want me to, Emmaline . . . ," Mom is saying.

"Actually, I'd like Em to have the experience of getting back on the horse." I give them both encouraging grins. "You understand, right, Mom?"

She understands all too well. "If this is about what happened in the garden, I told you, I just got up too fast, that's all." She folds her arms and frowns. "Honestly, Julie, you need to stop treating me like I'm an old lady. I'm only seventy-five, one year older than Gloria Steinem. Barbara Walters is seventy-eight and look at her!"

"Yes, but you haven't been living on a one-thousand-calorie-a-day diet," I say. "Nor have you been working out every morning with a personal trainer, sipping wheatgrass juice, and taking frequent trips to Canyon Ranch. And don't get me started on those Pepperidge Farm cookies you sneak every afternoon. I wouldn't be surprised if it's all the sugar you eat that's making you dizzy."

Em glances from me to her. "What are you two talking about?"

"Nothing," I say, keeping my gaze on Mom, who seems tinier somehow, more brittle. "Mom knows I want you to drive just for the experience. Anyway, that'll be a half hour of driving on your record that I won't have to stomach."

Then I give Mom a kiss on the cheek, Em a thumbs-up, and step onto the sidewalk right as a gentle summer rain begins to fall.

Michael is waiting for me.

Perhaps that's merely my imagination but . . . no. There he is lingering by the front door of the Boston Cooking School, his hands stuffed in the pockets of his navy North Face jacket as the rain that was gentle moments ago turns into a downpour. I am drenched.

"Here." Whipping off his jacket, he tosses it to me as I dash toward him to reach the safety of the green awning. I catch it before it can fall to the wet sidewalk, an amazing feat in itself considering my coordination quotient.

"Too late. I'm soaked through." Under the awning, I wiggle between the smoking students and return his coat. "Thanks for the gesture. You're very sweet."

Michael takes me in with the kind of approval women crave—if they are looking for that sort of affirmation. Having abandoned *The Little House on the Prairie* fashion statement of last week, I'm in a black-and-white sleeveless sundress with strappy black sandals and a matching patent leather belt cinched tight at the waist. It violates all of D'Ours's rules, but I don't care.

You might say I'm in a rule-breaking mood.

"I was waiting for you," he says.

I'm flattered, really, though I say, "Either that or you've taken up smoking."

We move away from the crowd to some fresher air. What is it with cooking school students and their love of cigarettes? I can't understand why they'd ingest something that kills taste buds.

"Read that bit about you in the *Globe* this week," he starts.

I pretend as if I can't quite remember that. "Oh! You meant that blurb about Mom. Yeah. That was odd, wasn't it?"

"I didn't think so. In fact, I was very glad to see you took our conversation to heart." He's grinning ear to ear, he's so pleased with himself. "It's a step in the right direction for you, Julie."

"You mean up the evolutionary ladder?" Brushing water off my skirt, I say, "It was nice to shed the scales and crawl out of the primordial ooze to join you warm-blooded types."

He laughs. "You were never that bad. I always suspected a softie inside your hardened shell."

"And like a softshell crab, I'm suddenly edible. Talk radio's been eating me alive and my station, too, for the cobbler. They're none too happy with me at WBOS."

"Oh, come on. They don't care about that at the station, do they? Isn't that free publicity or something?"

"Absolutely. Most serious news stations love to be mocked for employing journalists who wheedle their way into interviews with dessert."

Michael's not grinning anymore. He's starting to worry. "But you didn't do an interview, did you?"

"Which only goes to show how much of a girly-girl I really am. I bring my elderly mother. I bring a cobbler. *And* I forget to interview the mother of the murdered girl. I am a regular Nellie Bly."

"But . . ."

"That's not all. Add to that the rumor you and I had a relationship while I was covering the FitzWilliams campaign—by the way, thanks for telling Kirk to shove that question up his ass, did me a world of good—and I've lost the national election team post along with all credibility."

He's crestfallen, shock etched in his dropped jaw and furrowed brow. "That's outrageous. You shouldn't be penalized for a flip remark I made."

I shrug. "Well, I was. Turns out bureau chiefs don't like to be told to piss off when they're doing background checks. Who knew?"

"Michael?" It's Carol at the door in a thin red sheath that hangs over her collection of bones. "What are you doing out here? We've already started."

But he can't tear himself away. "I'm sorry, Julie. I had no idea."

"Forget it. You didn't do anything wrong and neither did I. It's them. They're the Neanderthals for being so thickheaded." Scraping my toe against a dropped butt, I turn my attention to the dirty sidewalk. "My bosses will cool down and I'll be sprung from my obit duty in the basement before long. Maybe by fall? It would be nice to see the colors this year."

"Shit," he says softly.

"Michael!" Carol says again as her owlish gaze drifts from him to me, her lips slowly turning upward into a knowing smirk. "Now, don't tell me your mother made *that* dress."

"No. This one I stole."

Which is kind of true since I took it from Liza's closet. Anyway, it sounds better than buying it on sale at Filene's.

Chapter Twelve

. . . he can speak French; and therefore he is a traitor.

—HENRY VI, PART TWO, ACT IV, SCENE 2

I am so ready for this class.

Last time, I was ill prepared in both dress and skill. But this week, with a reduced work schedule and lots of anxiety to whittle away, I cheated and looked ahead in D'Ours's cookbook. I know my tarte Tatin hands down. I even have a faint grasp of tiramisu.

D'Ours is going to be blown away, I think, gliding past Michael and Carol into the classroom, already perfumed by the wonderful smells of roasting nuts and spices for the spiced pear and Roquefort flan.

We know the drill: Wash hands, grab an apron plus a glass of champagne or sparkling cider, and gather around the long steel counter. Angela's back, her purple bangs now a kinky shade of midnight blue, along with D'Ours, who goes out of his way to sit me front and center. I swear he is giving me the eye.

And I'm not the only one who thinks so. As Michael takes the seat next to me, he whispers, "Seems as though your cobbler gained you another admirer."

Another admirer? Hmm. I'll have to think about that.

"I might have told you last class that in France we end our meals satisfied, but not full, with a wedge of Camembert on homemade crusty bread or a slice of apple to satisfy the palate," our fearless froggie French leader says, deftly slicing off a chunk of Granny Smith. "Or perhaps, in summer, one perfect strawberry and a sip of champagne."

"Is he crazy?" I murmur to Michael. "One strawberry does not a dessert make!"

"And *one* sip of champagne?" he scoffs. "It's hard enough to stop at a whole bottle."

"That is how I came to create my spiced pear and Roquefort flan." From the refrigerator, D'Ours pulls a pot in which five dark red peeled pears sit perfectly upright in their syrup of red wine, sugar, cinnamon, allspice, vanilla bean, star anise, and cloves that D'Ours informs us Angela stewed the night before.

Angela registers this with a quick wave, the tips of her fingers still stained. It can't be easy serving as D'Ours's sous-chef, especially when, in Angela's case, you'd much rather spend your nights roaming the streets sucking the blood of innocents than making sure the Bartletts don't turn mushy.

D'Ours slices the pears thinly. "My flan has all the essence of a perfect French dessert. Pears, cheese, nuts, and bread, along with sweet wine— except for the Moroccan spices. French cuisine eschews spices, aside from those grown fresh on our hillsides such as parsley, sage, rosemary, thyme . . ."

Michael begins softly humming the tune to "Scarborough Fair" and I have to stifle a giggle. I'd forgotten about his wonky Simon and Garfunkel period when he used to wile away the nights in my brother's room, strumming his guitar and torturing me with "I Am a Rock." Later, there was a point in my life when if one more egotistical man quoted me that song by explaining he was an island and "an island never cries," I was going to have to deck him.

"You're so sensitive," I whisper.

"Shhh." He frowns at D'Ours with feigned sincerity. "Pay attention."

Chris the redhead shoots up her hand to interrupt the flan instructions. "I have a recipe for doing pears in the Crock-Pot four hours on high."

I'm not quite sure, but I do believe D'Ours just staggered slightly upon hearing the word "Crock-Pot" uttered in his kitchen.

"Yes, well," he says, darting a glance at Angela. "I suppose if one were to own a 'Crock-Pot' and one weren't making Swedish meatballs at the moment or, say, potluck chicken wings, one could conceivably"—he gulps—"spice pears."

Chris says to me, "I'll never do pears any other way."

In a ready crust of crushed walnuts, flour, and butter, D'Ours lays the pear slices in a pinwheel design. Because they've soaked up the red wine, their edges are etched in burgundy while their centers are white, giving them a candy cane appearance. A perfect Christmas dessert.

Next, he crumbles the Roquefort over the pears, noting the irony of fruit desserts. Pairing fruit with sweet ingredients such as honey or sugar brings out the fruit's tartness while tangy cheese can make the fruit seem sweeter. Which might explain why my grandfather salted his grapefruit.

"Roquefort has an intriguing history," he says while whipping a traditional flan filling of cream, sugar, and eggs. "You might be surprised to learn . . ."

I stick up my hand and before D'Ours can object, I explain how Roquefort, like most blue cheeses, attributes its blue veins to penicillin mold and that in the past, Roquefort makers (there are only, like, nine in the world), used to put wrapped cheese next to humongous moldy rye bread in caves and let the spores from the rye bread seep into the cheese.

"Someone's been doing her homework," he says, smiling. "By the way, I'd like to see you after class."

There is a sharp pain in my rib cage and I look down to find Michael's elbow there. "Teacher's pet," he says under his breath.

The pear and Roquefort flan in the oven, D'Ours moves on to our next dish, a gingerbread that's so easy I'll tell Mom never to buy a mix again. The lemon sauce to drizzle over it is even more divine, a puckery combination of water, sugar, cornstarch, butter, lemon juice, and zest poured over the hot gingerbread so it seeps into the cake, perfectly crystallizing the outside.

We take a break to go to the bathroom and get some air while Angela and her lackey clean up the mess. When we come back, we taste test the tart and the gingerbread before regrouping for the tarte Tatin and the almond biscotti tiramisu.

Michael, the woman I've dubbed Lilly Pulitzer, and Carol are in a neat circle, talking and eating, so I float over to Chris, who's eagerly passing Crock-Pot tips to the nuns. Every once in a while I look over at Michael, trying to read his body language with Carol. They're side by side, but not close in a girlfriend-boyfriend kind of way. For the life of me, I can't figure out their relationship.

Champagne refilled, plates whisked away, we're back at the counter to learn about what I like to think of as upside-down apple pie. This time I'm wedged between Lilly Pulitzer and Chris, whose husband is next to Michael and Carol.

Odd. It's not nearly as much fun without Michael here.

"And now, the famous *tarte des demoiselles Tatin*," D'Ours declares, melting butter in a thick iron skillet, "created by the inventive Tatin sisters for their hotel in France around 1889. Quite by accident, by the way. It seems that during hunting season—"

"The sisters were preparing to make apple pie and left the apples cooking in the skillet too long and they were caramelized," I pipe up. "Though, honestly, who cooks apples before putting them in a pie?"

My fellow classmates laugh in agreement at such an absurd idea. These are my people, I'm thinking. We may be foodies; we are also savvy.

"Actually," D'Ours corrects, slightly peeved, "that's the flaw in the myth you just told. Stéphanie Tatin accidentally baked a tart upside down and this was the result."

"I see." Bull. That's even worse. Only an utter moron would bake a tart upside down.

Nevertheless, this is D'Ours's show, and I—who can barely make boxed macaroni and cheese—have no business taking him to the mat. Though it's killing me, the upside-down tart thing. Why can't he see that, clearly, she was making apple pie?

He gives me a warning look and goes on. "At any rate, the one rule is that tarte Tatin must be served hot straight from the oven with whipped cream or crème fraîche."

D'Ours cheats by using a prepared puff pastry sheet instead of making his own. Nice to know he's mortal. After melting sugar with butter and cramming apples into the skillet until it overflows, he bakes it at 425 degrees and then tops it with a chilled circle of the pastry. More baking, additional cooling, and then he inverts it precisely onto a platter.

We gasp at the delicious sight of baked apples and cinnamon in gooey golden caramel. D'Ours cuts it up right away and we pass around a bowl of fresh whipped cream to dollop on the side. If I am fired, I will make this every day until I'm too fat to care.

"The trick is firm apples," D'Ours says, after sipping his champagne. "In America you will have to make do with Golden Delicious." He sighs as if this is a great tragedy.

Since we are running out of time, he again separates the class. Half will make the warm cherry crisp with Vermont maple cream and the other half will make almond biscotti tiramisu.

Please oh please may I get almond biscotti tiramisu, I pray.

Yes. Everyone who did cobbler last week is on biscotti tiramisu duty.

Everyone who did ginger ice cream is on cherry crisp. Ipso facto, they get D'Ours and we get Angela.

Angela is all business. And if there's one thing I've learned from reading D'Ours's cookbook, it's that tiramisu is anything but business. So many flavors to play with—rum, coffee, chocolate, almond—and textures, too. From the rock-hard biscotti that turns chewy during the "setting" phase to the creamy mascarpone lightened by whipped cream.

"Translated, tiramisu means 'pick me up' in Italian," Sister Martha, one of the nuns, tells me, though I'm unsure whether she means "pick me up" as in a singles bar or "pick me up" like someone who wants to guess your weight, until she adds, "And it is a pick-me-up, isn't it? What with that strong coffee and chocolate."

Not with Angela at the controls, I think. Like an automaton, she shows us how to achieve the perfect pale yellow ribbons of the custard by whisking egg yolks and sugar that magically triples in volume when it's heated in a double boiler. When we ask her why it does that, she replies, "It just does."

Our job as underlings is to lay out half the almond biscotti while Angela uses a pastry brush to paint it with a syrup of amaretto liqueur combined with sugar and espresso powder. Next comes the filling and then more biscotti/amaretto-espresso syrup and finally the filling. Cocoa is sifted over everything and it's put in the refrigerator for at least four hours.

"That's impossible," I say. "Not in my house."

Angela cleans off a spoon and says, "Why?"

"Because it'd be eaten way before then, that's why."

Chris's husband says, "You got that right. My house, too."

"I don't understand." Angela blinks her large superblack eyelashes. "If you eat it before four hours, the biscotti won't have a chance to soften and the flavors won't have melded."

After she leaves, Chris, her husband, and I agree Angela is some sort of mutant alien who must have been hatched instead of raised in a family. How else to explain someone who doesn't sneak tiramisu?

I almost forgot about D'Ours's wish to see me after class, so I'm halfway out the door before I feel a hand on my arm and am hooked back in.

"I need to talk to you."

At first I wonder how much champagne he's had since he's slurring his words until I realize he's not slurring out of drunkenness but out of Frenchitude. His black tie is undone and his shirt collar is slightly open as he pins me against the doorjamb and leans toward me seductively. Suddenly, he's all mannerisms and suave, sexy French accent.

Liza would kill to be in my spot.

"I had no idea you were on television," he starts in, his eyes darting downward to check the state of my chest. "You should have told me."

"Why?"

"Because that's where I want to be. On TV."

I have to think about this. "You want to do the news?"

"No, silly." It comes out as *silleeee*. "I want to be on The Food Channel. We are closing in on a deal any day. Or so my people tell me."

Ah, yes. He has people. But of course!

"I was so pleased to read in the paper that you made sure to mention my name."

I stare back blankly. What's he talking about?

"Cobbler D'Ours? Not exactly right. It was Peach Cobbler D'Ours, but it will do. My agent tells me it might help with The Food Channel deal. Do you think so?"

"I have no idea. Food TV isn't exactly my bailiwick."

He repeats the word "bailiwick" and looks off as if an invisible English-French dictionary were behind me to define it.

Nearby, Michael pretends to be deep in conversation with Chris. A faint ruse since he keeps frowning at D'Ours as if he's hitting on me. I let him think so by giggling a bit and leaning close to catch each precious word.

"I think there is someone else who wants to talk to you, too." D'Ours cocks his dimpled chin at Michael. "You have to go, I understand. But let's get together after the next class. I would be very interested to talk more with you about this television business. I have the feeling there is much you could teach me, for a change."

"Absolutely," I say, fully aware Michael is overhearing everything. "I'd love to."

D'Ours leans down and brushes my cheek with a European kiss. "I am in your debt." I have to say, that kissing habit can be quite lovely.

"Didn't mean to interrupt," Michael says as soon as D'Ours is across the room, talking up Carol.

"Yes, you did."

"You're right. I did." Thumbing in the direction of D'Ours, he asks, "Is every woman in love with that pompous ass?"

"You mean, like Carol? Hmmm. I hadn't noticed."

Michael grins and shoves his hands in his pockets. "I just wanted to apologize for whatever part I might have had in screwing up your career. First I made that comment to Budso."

"Bledsoe," I correct. "Kirk Bledsoe."

"Totally unfair he took my sarcasm out on you. Anyway, and then that speech I had no business giving you about showing your bias. I . . . I guess I had no idea it would be such a big deal."

"All that Simon and Garfunkel. You've become too sensitive," I say, patting him on the shoulder. "Cheer up, old friend. Like I said, it's not your fault. It's theirs."

"Uh-huh." He doesn't believe me. "That aside, I'd like to make it up to you. I don't know if you're doing anything tomorrow, but I have to go up to the North Shore to visit my mother. I haven't seen her in a month."

Frankly, I'm surprised she's still around, considering she seemed to prefer being horizontal to vertical.

"She doesn't really recognize me, but the doctors and nurses claim the visits are worthwhile." He shoves his hands deeper into his pockets. "Alzheimer's."

Oh, God. That's the pits. I don't know how I'd cope if my mother came down with Alzheimer's and I became a stranger to her. Mom's so much a part of my daily life, gossiping, talking, lecturing. I couldn't go on without her advice and counsel—as nosy and unrequested as it can be.

"I'm so sorry, Michael. I had no idea."

" 'All the world's a stage,' " he says. " 'Last scene of all, / That ends this strange eventful history, / Is second childishness and mere oblivion.' "

"More Shakespeare?"

"A famous scene from *As You Like It*. Anyway, it'd be easier if you came with me. And afterward, I thought I might start making things up to you with a trip to the old Revere Beach and maybe dinner overlooking the ocean. Game?"

I must look shocked and I am. A week ago, Michael hated my guts and here he is asking me to visit his dying mother and go to the ocean. What gives? Unfortunately, he takes my shock for something else and, ripping his hands from his pockets, smacks his forehead.

"Oh, God. I didn't mean to put you in this position. Some people can't deal with Alzheimer's patients. Like Carol, for instance, she can't . . ."

That does it. "I can handle it," I tell him, straightening. "I'd love to, actually. It's been years since I saw your mom. Who knows? I might spark a memory."

He brightens. "That crossed my mind, too. You never know what will trigger something. It's often the people in her distant past she cherishes the most." Pausing, he adds softly, "I guess that's something she and I have in common."

"Me too." And I reach out and give his hand a reassuring squeeze. "Pick me up at noon. I'll bring a picnic lunch."

Chapter Thirteen

O, let me not be mad, not mad, sweet heaven,
Keep me in temper: I would not be mad!

—KING LEAR ACT I, SCENE 5

"Now who are you making dessert for? Another person your station's going to screw over?"

Ignoring Mom, I eye the tablespoon of ground espresso beans and carefully even off the top with a knife like Angela showed us. This is going to be tricky.

How do I possibly expect to pack this picnic—cold chicken bought ready roasted, green grapes, strawberries, French bread, some gooey cheese, and almond biscotti tiramisu—and sneak out of the house to meet Michael without my mother finding out?

I simply can't risk her knowing. The questions alone would take up most of my morning. And she'd make a much bigger deal out of it than necessary. *So? You're going to meet his mother? Sounds like things between you two have taken a turn. Could this be the beginning of a beau-*

tiful relationship? Two minutes out the door and she'd be on the phone to all her friends.

"Just making a tiramisu for fun," I tell her. "No big deal."

"Cooking in this heat?" She pinches her sleeveless yellow blouse and wafts it back and forth so that within seconds the floral scent of her Avon Smile perfume overtakes the more enticing smells of almond and coffee. "You know what you should make instead? That icebox log with the Nabisco cookies and whipped cream. Don't even have to turn on the stove. The recipe's in that barn box I gave you."

Keeping my tongue bitten, I carefully turn the tablespoon of espresso into the bowl of amaretto and sugar. . . .

Mom clutches my wrist in midair. "Holy Mary mother of God. I hope you're not thinking of putting that in."

"Please. I know what I'm doing. We made this at class last night."

"Impossible. You can't put in ground coffee beans. That's disgusting." She flicks my wrist and the espresso sprays all over the kitchen counter.

Great. Just great. This is going to be a mess to clean up and I'm running out of time. The tiramisu has to sit for at least four hours.

Already it's ten-thirty and I'm behind schedule thanks to the outrageously long line at the grocery store this morning. Everyone was trying to get their shopping out of the way so they could spend the rest of the day enjoying the glorious summer weather—a balmy eighty-three degrees with a slight breeze and clear blue sky. Summer Saturdays don't get much better than that in Boston.

Mom is frowning at D'Ours's recipe and muttering under her breath. Something about espresso *powder.*

Honestly, I have no idea what's wrong with her these days, I think, getting the broom and dustpan from the back hall. First she has these dizzy spells, then she's holding conversations with her dead mother. Now she's talking to herself. Could she be depressed? Maybe there are drugs she could take. I've seen ads for them on TV, women looking out rainy windows on the verge of tears.

"That's okay, Mom," I say, sweeping up the last of the coffee. "I've got more beans. It'll take no time to grind them into powder."

"Powder. *Powder*," she repeats, running to my pantry. "Like Sanka. Not grounds like what you throw under the azaleas. You do have Sanka, don't you. Or Postum?"

"World War II is over, Mother. No one drinks Postum." Or, for that matter, Sanka.

Yet another difference between my new professionally acquired culinary skills and my mother's, most of which she picked up from women's magazines and free shoppers.

Along with back-of-box recipes, Mom is a sucker for shortcuts. Instant coffee. Liquid Smoke. Minute pudding. No-bake pies made from Jell-O, and chicken stock from bullion cubes with enough sodium to incite a cranial hemorrhage. Artificial sweeteners in pink and blue packets. Fake butter that comes in plastic tubs. Even Ritz crackers in "mock" apple pie.

Whereas I am approaching *la art de la cuisine*, as D'Ours would say, from a more sophisticated background. The highest quality in the smallest doses. Granted, this background is only two weeks going while Mom has been cooking for fifty years and counting. Still, that's no reason to pooh-pooh the minimum I've learned, namely that Sanka cannot be substituted for fine Italian roast.

I head back to the coffee grinder.

"Look. Cut out the espresso powder. It's only a tablespoon or so." Mom gives the cream filling in the double boiler a stir and turns it off. "Or throw in some coffee left over from this morning."

While she goes back to the pantry to ferret for the Sanka she refuses to believe I don't have, I sneak behind her back, whisk the filling again, and test the temperature—a mere 130 degrees, far from the required 160. This is going to take forever unless I ratchet up the heat. Turning the flame to its highest, I cover the double boiler for good measure and go back to the grinder as if nothing happened.

"Coffee from this morning. That's what I'm grinding," I say, shaking some beans into my Krups, a wedding gift my ex-husband Donald and I received and, until now, have never used.

"Not grounds. I mean coffee as in the liquid. What the hell . . . ?" At which point Mom, so furious with me for disobeying her orders, leans against the kitchen wall and closes her eyes to gain composure.

And stays there.

I lift my finger off the grinder. "Are you okay?"

She doesn't say anything, though the deep crevices between her brows fold in, as if she can't bear the pain of me using real coffee.

Odd the way panic is delayed, how it seems so distant. Slipping over an overlooked patch of the ground espresso, I run to catch her before she falls. "All right, all right," I say, holding her by the shoulders. "I'll use the leftover coffee. Just sit down and take it easy."

"Chair." She slides into it and collapses. "Thank you."

"Are you okay?"

"Of course. It was nothing."

No, it's something. And this is not simply about her being upset over ground coffee. Or about her getting old, either.

"Do you want a glass of water?" Should I call Dad? Oh, forget him. He won't know what to do. Maybe Teenie across the street or Lois or—shoot—911!

Mom nods and I go to the sink. The kitchen thermometer says eighty degrees outside, eighty-five inside because of the stove and my lack of central air, which might be the problem right there. Yes, that's it, I decide, feeling only slightly better. I should break down and buy a couple of room air conditioners because the fans I have now are useless.

Mom takes a couple of sips of the ice-cold water and massages her forehead.

"Do you have a headache?"

"No. It's this dang blasted sauna you've created. How do you expect anyone to manage in this sweltering heat?"

Goodness sake. It's not *that* hot.

Her eyes open and not for the first time does it strike me how their color has watered down to a milky gray. Old eyes. Eyes that have seen Christmases come and go, along with hot summers and many cups of Sanka.

I take her warm hand in mine and, like when I was a child, fiddle with her antique diamond and platinum engagement ring. It's so loose and worn thin that the diamond falls to the side as if it, too, doesn't have the energy to stand.

I suppose these signs of aging—her eyes and dizziness, the liver spots on her translucent skin, her mumbling—are to be expected. After all, in most families she'd be considered old. Though by the standards of our clan—where women tend to live to their upper nineties and beyond (aside from my aunt Charlotte, who died from breast cancer, and Aunt Anne, who was rushing to a League of Women Voters meeting and got hit by a bus)—Mom is a good twenty-six years from kicking the bucket.

That's one whole Britney Spears away from eternity.

Color is returning to her face and I begin to relax, remembering that this morning Mom was out killing slugs and hammering the tomato posts into the ground before I was awake. (Actually, that's how I came to be awake.) The woman does not stop. She's always weeding or walking back and forth to Waverly Square or hanging out sheets. No wonder she's dizzy.

Listen to your instincts. It's more.

"I'm getting you to the doctor." Letting go of her hand, I reach for the phone, though I have no idea whom to call.

"Doctor?" Mom perks up immediately. "I can't. Not today."

"Why not? Doctors work on Saturday."

"I know and I'm going to see one, the optometrist. That's why you're taking me to the mall, remember?"

Boom! My heart nearly explodes as the top of the double boiler rockets up and lands on the floor while the frothy custard bubbles over the sides of the pot fueling sizzling flames of orange and blue.

"The filling!" I scream, turning off the burner. Immediately the froth subsides, releasing the nauseating odor of burned egg.

"Don't put it in the sink," Mom barks. "You'll ruin the pot. Let it cool on the stove, then soak it. It'll take you a couple of hours to get off that junk, but you don't want to toss it in the trash. That's a good pot. What were you doing covering it, anyway?"

Just back from the dead and already she's a critic. Slipping on my trusty red pot holders, I carry the double boiler to the sink and try very, very hard not to sound hysterical when I calmly ask what time she needs to be at the mall for her optometry appointment.

"I have to pick up my new glasses at twelve-thirty. Don't worry. It won't take long, only a half hour."

The most pivotal date I've had in eons and mom has to ruin it with a 12:30 eyeglass appointment. I mean, who makes an appointment smack in the middle of a summer Saturday? *Little old ladies with nothing better to do, that's who.*

Yet another example of my mother assuming I have no social life. Which, considering, is not that crazy of an assumption.

"Is it that you can't drive because of these dizzy spells?" I ask, scraping at the hardened filling.

"No." She takes another sip of water and squints at what I'm doing, clearly disapproving. "They're putting drops in my eyes. I'm not allowed to drive afterward. You'll gouge the coating on that pot if you're not careful."

"You mean, this is not just an eyeglass fitting. This is a whole *eye appointment.*"

"I suppose it is, if they're giving me a test, too. The girl on the phone did say my prescription had expired. Oh, well, I guess I'll be there longer than I thought."

Adding up the hours in my head—a half hour to get to the mall, a half hour to wait for her appointment, a half hour appointment, an hour plus to wait for the glasses, provided there's no line, which there will be, a half hour to get back. "Mom, that'll take all of three hours."

"What do you care? You got a date?"

Yes, I do. A date to visit Michael's mother and I've just realized I'm actually really excited about it. It's not his mother I'm interested in, really, though it would be nice if I could trigger some memory for her. It's *him*.

He's changed. Maybe it's the mellowing effect of middle age, but he doesn't seem nearly as egotistical as when he was at the height of his career running the FitzWilliams campaign.

Mom used to say Michael's self-absorption was a survival mechanism he developed in college to compensate for his slovenly family situation with their roaches and house that always smelled of rotted oranges. Kind of a fake-it-to-make-it thing, I suppose. To be among the best he had to pretend he wasn't from the worst.

Some women on the FitzWilliams campaign staff told me they found him irresistible when he was in his "master of the universe" mode. Not me. I liked him when he wasn't on guard, usually when he was telling me an interesting story or reminiscing about our childhoods. I liked how he'd lean close and look so deeply into my eyes, I'd forget where he ended and I began. It was intense. Too intense, perhaps, because he would inevitably catch himself, clam up, and go back to being Michael—smart, busy, and forever on his cell.

"How about Em?" I suggest to Mom. "She could drive you."

"I couldn't do that to Em. It's her one Saturday off. Besides, I don't trust her behind the wheel. She nearly killed us on the way back from your dessert class yesterday when she cut off a tractor trailer on Auburn Street."

"Okay. Then what about Dad?"

"Nope." Mom shakes her head as if that's not even up for discussion. "Can't do it."

"Why not? Why can't he do *something* for goddamn once."

"Julie! Don't swear at your father."

"I'm not . . ." Gripping the sink for composure, I lower my voice and say slowly, "I'm not swearing *at* him. He's not even here. I just want to know why he can't drive."

"Just can't. He's got plans."

As do we all. The selfish S.O.B. probably doesn't want to leave his TV and miss the Red Sox doubleheader. But I can't yell about it or at Dad because that'll upset Mom. And I can't yell at her because, my lord, she just collapsed. She's so fragile and annoying. Annoyingly fragile.

There's nothing I can do. I'm stuck.

Tossing the ruined pot in the sink, I say, "Gotta make a phone call. Maybe you should get ready."

Then I head for my bedroom to give Michael the bad news.

Chapter Fourteen

How poor are they that have not patience!
What wound did ever heal but by degrees?

—OTHELLO, ACT II, SCENE 3

When I called Michael, he was so understanding and sweet I wondered if his feelings for me really have changed.

"Don't worry. I know how mothers are. It's fine," he said. "Visiting hours are until five o'clock on Saturdays, so we have plenty of time. And if we get a late start, we'll skip the swimming among the flotsam and jetsam in Revere to go straight out to drinks and dinner." There was a moment of hesitation. "Unless you have other plans for tonight."

"Guess what? George Clooney just cancelled. You're in luck."

He laughed a bit and said, "Well, then. It's a date."

Is that what it was . . . a date?

What am I saying? Michael and I are old friends turned enemies with the possibility of turning back to friends again. Nothing more. Besides,

I'm not his type, being that I'm neither a) blond, b) a former debutante, or c) a waif.

As for *my* type, I'm not sure what that is anymore. Male. Responsible. Fairly good-looking. Able to take care of himself without being too needy. A kind personality and gentle sense of humor.

I think I've just described Aunt Charlotte's basset hound.

Anyway, my call to Michael has landed me in a relatively better mood when Mom, Em, and Nadia climb into my car. I'm thoroughly disgusted with my daughter for spending her one Saturday off from work at the mall when she could be outside soaking up the sun on this glorious day.

Hey, it's her life. I'm not going to tell her what to do—unlike some people present.

"Buckle up, everyone," Mom reminds us, as if this is a revolutionary idea.

"I don't even think about putting my safety belt on," Em says to Nadia. "Do you?"

"Nope." Nadia pulls her gum out of her mouth and wraps it around her finger.

"Well, you should," Mom scolds. "Seat belts save lives."

"They know that, Mother," I say. "They mean it's so automatic, they don't have to think about it."

Mom goes, "Oh." And pouts.

Too bad. I have resolved not to let her or anyone bring me down this afternoon. I am going to be upbeat and positive by doing a bit of shopping in preparation for my afternoon at the beach. I needed a new swimsuit, anyway.

A half an hour down the Mass Pike and we're at the humongous mall. I let Mom off at one of the one thousand entrances and then find a space way far away so I can get a little exercise. Nadia and Em complain, the couch potatoes, but they'll thank me when they're middle-aged and fitting into their daughters' jeans—a fantasy of which I've often dreamed.

Inside, Em and Nadia head to Abercrombie while I check on Mom, who's perusing through a copy of *20/20* magazine in the waiting area of C-Rite optometrists.

"They're backed up," Mom says. "Looks like I won't get in for another hour."

"An hour?" That's rubbish.

Obviously, Mom is being pushed around. They spot a little old lady, assume she has nothing better to do, and move her to the back of the line. Well, we'll have to see about that. One of the most helpful things I've learned as a reporter is not to accept the first answer to my question, the first seat assignment on a plane, or the first hotel room offered. There's always something better being held in reserve.

"It's been crazy today. Sorry," the receptionist says, tapping on the keyboard and (supposedly) checking the screen for sooner openings. "If your mom would like to come back on the twenty-fifth, we could do it then."

Perfect. Find Em and I'll be out of here in ten minutes. Revere Beach, here I come.

"How about Tuesday?" I ask Mom.

"Okay."

"The twenty-fifth isn't a Tuesday," the receptionist says. "It's a Friday. The twenty-fifth of August."

"That's two months away!"

Mom shakes her head. "Let's just get this over with now."

I'm getting a very, very bad feeling about this bad start to our mall adventure. But as I swing out of C-Rite and head for the food court to fetch Mom an iced tea, I remind myself there's no point in getting upset. The outcome will still be the same whether I'm anxious or not, so I might as well add a few days to my life by being not.

This is known as the Zen of middle age.

Having delivered an iced tea lemon, no sugar, to Mom, I head out to find a swimsuit that will cinch my waist, extend my legs, and uplift my apathetic breasts.

This is known as the pipe dream of middle age.

Like most "normal" women, I dread shopping for swimsuits. The deal is that for nine months out of the year, I maintain an image of my body as being fairly decent. Not great, but decent.

This illusion lasts until I get into the dressing room with five or six swimsuits for which I have extremely high hopes and discover much to my surprise I cannot pull any one over my thighs. Or that another makes my belly balloon out like a frog's.

Suddenly my body's not decent, it's hideous. I am so unsexy and fat it's unfathomable I could be attractive to any man besides lifers and hard-up hermits. The end result is me in tears, a pile of suits at my feet, and a saleswoman banging on the door asking if I'd like any help.

In my campaign to keep a positive attitude, however, I have resolved to approach today's swimsuit shopping with an open mind. The fashion industry's come a long way over the years, I remind myself. It's no longer ruled by sadistic misogynists who are out to mortify real women. New fabrics, new technology, a renewed appreciation for the Rubenesque frame—surely I'll be able to find something flattering.

Errr . . . no. Every "figure-flattering" suit I try is a tricky disaster, hidden panels or no hidden panels. Black, the color of choice, makes my skin as pale as the underbelly of a dead snake. The leopard prints on my middle-aged body scream Moira of Boca Raton, not Pam Anderson of Malibu, and anything in bright green, pink, or blue looks preteen. Who am I kidding? I'm no Barbie.

Plus, what the heck are all these bumps on my thighs? Cellulite, I know that. But this isn't cellu-*lite*, this is cellu-*palooza*. It's disgusting. I can't walk along a public beach looking like this.

Which leaves me with the one remaining option: the dreaded skirt suit. My mother wears those. Big one-piece numbers in navy or turquoise with crazy huge Hawaiian flowers stamped all over them. Yes, I am aware the skirted suit is making a comeback. It's not our grandmother's suit anymore. That said, a skirt is a skirt. It screams, I'M SELF-CONSCIOUS ABOUT MY CRAP BOD. Also, I'M OLD.

Thoroughly depressed, I leave a huge lump of suits in the dressing room of Macy's (serves them right for selling such cruel designs) and head back to the food court for the cold calorific comfort of an iced mocha latte. That's where I bump into Em and Nadia ordering carmellatos.

"We were looking for you," Em says. "Is it okay if we go to the one-thirty movie? We'll be out by three."

My tendency is to say no since Mom might get out earlier. Then I do the math and come to the conclusion that by the end of the matinee, Mom will just be picking out her new eyeglass case, floral or clear.

"Yeah, okay. But keep your cell phone on vibrate in case we need to go," I say. "We'll meet back here at the food court as soon as the movie's over. Be prompt. I don't want to have to sit around waiting."

"Sure." Their answer is in teenage singsong, a clear indication they haven't heard one little thing.

I check on Mom and find she's in with the doctor at last. Great. It can't be that much longer now. After all, C-Rite does promise to have glasses ready "in an hour," though I'm not clear if this is followed by an unspoken "or else." Like pizza. "Glasses ready in a hour, *or else* the pair is free." Or, on a more threatening note, "glasses ready in an hour *or else* every C-Rite employee is fired." When I'm freed from the basement of WBOS, that's something I'm going to look into, the whole eyeglasses-in-an-hour scam. It'll probably be the most popular story I ever do.

With plenty of time to kill, I'm leaning toward a manicure to boost my spirits but find the mall salons are booked solid, it being the wedding season.

"How about a spray tan?" Lanelle, the woman at Salon Goodbye, suggests. "I could do one right now for thirty-five dollars."

A spray tan. Why haven't I thought of that before? It'll completely take care of the fish-belly problem with the black swimsuits and it'll give me a healthy, golden, youthful glow that will peel years off. Plus, it's so much cheaper than a new suit. Pure genius.

Then I remember Raldo, who's a pumpkin-colored spray-tan addict and ask, "I'm not going to be orange, am I?"

What I expect her to say, I'm not quite sure. *Yes, you will be orange. Is that a problem?* Anyway, she assures me I'll love it and that the orange people are people who use poor product or slack off in maintenance. Yap, yap, yap.

Next thing I know, I'm on a table, naked, and Lanelle's rubbing sea salt scrub all over me to exfoliate. Very relaxing and yet invigorating at the same time. A conundrum. Even the tanning process itself isn't too bad except halfway through, the following announcement comes over the mall intercom:

"ATTENTION: JULIE MUELLER. WOULD A JULIE MUELLER PLEASE MEET DR. DANDY AT THE C-RITE OFFICE IMMEDIATELY."

Lanelle stops spraying. "Isn't that you?"

I picture Mom pestering them to page me so I can give her my opinion on UV coating. Practical prevention or scam? "It's only my mother. You can keep going."

Finished with my left side, Lanelle is about to start on the right when:

"ATTENTION: JULIE MUELLER. PLEASE COME TO C-RITE IMMEDIATELY. THIS IS A MEDICAL EMERGENCY."

A medical emergency? The dizzy spells. Suddenly, I have a vision of Mom flat out on Dr. Dandy's floor.

"Gotta go," I say, frantically trying to open the booth door.

"Wait!" Lanelle says. "You can't leave now."

"It's my mother. Something's happened. I'll come back and pay you later." I am heading down the hallway when Lanelle, in an athletic feat normally reserved for jaguars, sprints and hooks me from behind.

"Your clothes," she gasps, panting, brown streaks emerging on her smock. "They're back there. . . ."

Because mirrors are everywhere, every client in the salon—including one grinning preteen boy—is afforded a clear view of me in my pink bra and matching underwear with black lace. And let me say this: I do not always wear matching pink bras and underwear with black lace. It was seeing Liza changing the other day that inspired me to shape up. And now I'm a believer.

"Right," I say, rushing back, throwing on my clothes and tossing two twenties at Lanelle, who assures me I can return to finish the tan anytime.

"Hope your mom's okay!" she shouts as I dash out of Salon Goodbye and toward C-Rite, where I run into a crowd of people, onlookers gawking at—ohmigod—the Natick Emergency Squad rushing in with a gurney.

"Let me through!" I bark, jabbing my elbows here and there. "I'm Julie Mueller. Let me through."

Incredible. People are actually reluctant to let me pass. Did they not hear the announcement? Do they not know who Julie Mueller is?

"I'm her daughter!" I yell. "Let me through!"

Finally, a security officer parts the crowd and pushes me toward C-Rite, where my mother is being strapped to the gurney. She is out cold. An oxygen mask is being attached to her face, and they're wrapping her in blankets.

"She's fine," I hear someone tell me, though I don't believe it. "She just passed out." It's not until I clutch Mom's hand and feel her rapid pulse that I begin to calm myself. Asking the emergency crew questions proves futile. They completely ignore me since it appears my role is not to ask, but to answer.

How old is Mom? Does she take any medication? Is she suffering from any diseases? Does she have diabetes? Do I know the name of her doctor/

her health insurance provider? Is her husband alive? Can he meet them at MetroSouth Hospital?

I tell them seventy-five, tamoxifen and an aspirin a day, breast cancer survivor, no, Dr. Heller, Blue Cross Blue Shield, and yes, he's alive though you'd never know it. I'll call him and tell him to get off his &%#@ ass for once and be at his wife's side.

With that, they're gone, wheeling her past Banana Republic to the outside. It's surprising how silent it is now that the police radios are gone, too.

Dr. Dandy is off to the side looking nervous and yet defensive. He's young, in his late twenties, and my guess is Mom's collapse is one of those experiences they didn't prepare him for in C-Rite optometry school.

"We were giving her a cataract test. I blew in the air and the next thing I knew, she was out," he tells me. "I'm sure it must be a preexisting condition."

"Possibly." I'm curious as to whom he called first: 911 or his lawyer.

There's no answer at Mom and Dad's house, so on my way to the car, I call Teenie, who tells me Dad's truck is gone. Great. No doubt he's at a construction site "supervising"—his pretend job where he finds various road projects and stands around with other old men, their hands in back pockets, chewing the fat.

Teenie will call Lois, who will meet me at MetroSouth. I try calling Em but, per usual, my message goes straight to her dreamy voice mail.

Hi. This is me, Em, and if I could, I'd take your call. But I can't, so . . . uh, you know what to do.

She has turned off her phone instead of keeping it on like I'd asked.

Honestly, what is the point of paying sixty bucks a month for her to have a cell phone if she only uses it to call me and ask *me* for favors?

The next few hours are a mishmash of fighting traffic to get to MetroSouth, filling out paperwork, and staring at NASCAR on the waiting room TV until I'm allowed to see Mom. Throughout it all I feel sick with worry and anxiety. For all I know, she could be in serious, serious trouble, even—no, I can't think it—*the ultimate*, and they haven't yet told me.

You never know what you're going to run into in an emergency room. It's not like the regular part of the hospital where most of the drama happens behind closed doors. Here, all that separates you from bloody car crash victims, emergency tracheotomies, and sudden death are a few pale blue canvas curtains.

Finally, I'm allowed to see her. Mom is at the end of the hall, propped up with a black blood pressure gauge on her arm, sipping red fruit juice from a straw and surrounded by scary equipment. A cardiac monitor above her head reports regular triangles. An IV sticks out of her arm. And she's in a hospital gown. Despite that, she has never looked better.

"You're here, finally." She takes her mouth off the straw and curls a lip. "What's wrong with your arms?"

"Are you okay?" Instinctively, I stroke back her thinning gray hair and say a silent prayer, so glad, so very glad she's alive. "Have you seen a doctor yet? Do they know what happened?"

"Either my eyes are still not back to normal or . . . those arms of yours are two different colors." Mom seems not to know that she's in an emergency room. "Julie Ann Mueller, you fell asleep on your side suntanning this afternoon, didn't you? How many times have I told you not to do that? Skin cancer is no laughing matter. Remember Irma Fishbine? Beautiful girl, very pale . . ."

The curtain yanks back and in comes another young doctor. She's dark and beautiful, with a ponytail and glasses and a name tag that says DR. BAJAJ. Definitely the type to run marathons and abstain from sugar, alcohol, and fat. *She* wouldn't have a nervous breakdown in Macy's swimsuit department.

Moving past me and going straight to Mom, she shouts, "How are you doing, Mrs. Mueller?"

Mom murmurs she's fine, that it was the stupid cataract test that made her pass out. "You'd think if they could send men to the moon, they wouldn't have to blow air into a person's eyes."

"I don't like those, either. Yuck." Dr. Bajaj checks the papers on her clipboard. "Do you know where you are?"

"You're the fifteenth person to ask me that."

Dr. Bajaj is undaunted. "And the answer is?"

"The emergency room of MetroSouth Hospital. My sister, Charlotte, died here."

The doctor makes a tick mark and holds up her hand. "How many fingers?"

"Five."

"Who's the president of the United States?"

"Good question," Mom says, getting ornery. "I've got my personal opinion about that, if you have a half hour to spare."

I whisper into Dr. Bajaj's ear that this is a subject better not explored.

Nodding, Dr. Bajaj asks, "Have you been eating today?"

"Of course," I interject again. "This is Betty Mueller you're talking to."

Dr. Bajaj gives me a tolerant smile. "Are you a relative?"

"Her daughter." And then, to cement my status, I add, "I filled out all the forms."

"Okay, then, your mother's blood sugar is very low. Do you mind?"

Two terms I never thought I'd hear in the same sentence: "your mother" and "low blood sugar."

"Did you eat today?" Dr. Bajaj asks again.

"No," Mom says. "I forgot."

She forgot? That's like the earth forgetting to rotate around the sun. A physical impossibility. Mom never starts the day without half a grapefruit, black coffee, and a bowl of Grape-Nuts.

Dr. Bajaj says they'd like to keep her a little longer to run an EKG and maybe a CAT scan to make sure everything's hunky-dory before they release her. Meanwhile, Mom should continue to rest.

Beyond the curtain, Dr. Bajaj takes me aside. "It says here your mother's husband is still living with her."

"Yes, my father. He's, uh, out on a job."

"Look, she can walk out on her own, but my preference is not to release her until he's here to pick her up. I'll need to give him some instructions for her care over the next twenty-four hours. They could be crucial."

Good luck, I think. "She'll probably go home with me, then."

"Has your mother passed out before?"

"She's been dizzy lately. I don't know if she's completely passed out. But just this morning she had a spell and had to sit down. What's wrong with her?"

Dr. Bajaj shrugs. "Right now, I'm not sure. She seems fine, but she should come back next week for a follow-up. We need to rule out a few other possibilities."

"Like what?" I clench my fists, prepared for the worst.

"It could be anything. The fact that she didn't eat this morning. The heat. That she's dehydrated."

These, I know, are wimpy, made-up diagnoses, answers to keep me from flying off the handle. "Okay. I'll make sure she comes in."

"Good." Dr. Bajaj is about to go, when she turns and says, "Your dad . . . is he on his way, do you think?"

"Coming. It's her friend Lois you should talk to, though. She helped Mom through a bout of breast cancer a few years ago. She's almost like family. Better, really. If there's anything you need to know about Mom, Lois is your Shell Answer Girl."

"I see." She nods, getting it. "I see."

This Dr. Bajaj is no dummy.

A nurse is hooking up Mom to the EKG, pasting electrodes to her chest, when I return. I hate to see her like this in a hospital johnny with an IV in her arm. She looks so small and vulnerable, more like a child than my mother. I want her to be home in familiar surroundings, not in this clinical place that smells of urine and chicken soup.

"She'll be here for at least another hour," the nurse tells me. "So if you need to make any phone calls or something, now's the time. I wouldn't expect her to get out of here until well after five."

Five already? Shoot . . . it's past four! Em and Nadia's movie ended long ago and they're probably wandering the mall figuring I've dumped them.

Assuring Mom that I'll be right back and she's not to leave without me, I tell her I have to get the kids.

She nods and gives the nurse who's sticking on the electrodes a dirty look.

It's another traffic battle outside MetroSouth during which I call Michael and leave a message on his home answering machine telling him there's no point in him waiting, that he should see his mom without me. My own mother's in the hospital and I'll probably have to take care of her all night.

With a heavy heart, I say good-bye and hang up. Adulthood sucks.

This time I don't park far away in the mall lot for exercise, but flagrantly pull my car right up to the door and put on my flashers with the vain hope Em might be outside waiting. I have dialed this kid repeatedly and still no answer. After fifteen minutes pass I decide that, dammit, I'm going to have to get out, go in the mall, and hunt her down.

"Hey, Mom!" Em is sipping another carmellato outside the food court, right where I told her to be. "Where were you? The movie was over an hour ago."

Then, seeing my expression of unadulterated fury, she yells to Nadia, "She's on the warpath. Run!"

Nadia, though, is too preoccupied with the window display of Victoria's Secret to care. Or, rather, having enough brains to spot a mom on a rampage when she sees one, she effectively plays dumb. Not much of a stretch when you're Nadia.

"I've been calling you every two minutes," I say, grabbing Em's arm like she's six. "Why is your cell off?"

Em swallows hard. I never spanked her as a child and I rarely yell at her as a near adult, so my public display of anger is a new and unnerving experience. "It's not off," she scrambles. "I mean, it *is* off, but that's not my fault. The battery's dead."

"That *is* your fault, Em. Keeping your phone charged is part of the responsibility of ownership. Tomorrow, I'm calling up Verizon and canceling it."

I can't get over how much I sounded like Mom just then, right down to the responsibility line and the empty threat.

"No!" Em hisses, motioning for me to keep my voice down. "I promise. From now on I really will take care of it and keep it on and everything. I swear. Just don't cancel my phone."

"I needed to get hold of you this afternoon, Em. It was an emergency." Then, forcing myself to be more gentle, I say, "Grandma collapsed at her eyeglass appointment. She's at MetroSouth's emergency room."

"Oh, shit." Em slaps her hand across her mouth. "Is she going to be okay?"

"She seems fine. They're running tests, but I don't know. I should be with her. . . ." My anger's rising again. I need to cool it. "But I'm not in the emergency room because a certain someone did not leave her cell phone on."

"I told you I couldn't leave it on because the battery—"

"I know what you told me. You're missing the point."

"Hey!" Nadia gestures her carmellato toward the outside doors. "Isn't that your mom's car?"

My mother's car? I think stupidly, as I turn to see my trusty green

Subaru moving on its own, the front end up and attached to a blinking tow truck. A tow truck!

"Stop! Stop!" I scream, running to the revolving doors where a security officer—the same rent-a-cop who helped with crowd control outside of C-Rite—intercepts me.

"Is that your car?" he asks, taking out a pad.

"I was there five minutes. I had to get my daughter. You remember me, right?"

He cocks his head, puzzled.

"I'm Julie Mueller, the daughter of the woman who collapsed at C-Rite today. My mother's in the emergency room and . . . you've got to stop him. I need my car. I need to get back to the hospital."

"Can't." He shakes his head. "Once you're towed, you're towed."

Pointing to the walkie-talkie on his belt, I say, "Please, call him. You can call him. You called him to pick up my car. Surely, you can call him to drop it off."

"Mall policy," he says. "Liability issues. Code two, section 13C. Contracted hauler BTV Towing is not allowed to deposit vehicles on mall premises once said vehicles have been placed in possession of BTV Towing until BTV Towing arrives at a properly statuted repossession yard."

Bullshit. You don't even know the meaning of what you just said. *Properly statuted repossession yard.* What the heck is that?

You're not going to get anywhere yelling at this doofus, I remind myself. What you want is to get your car back and fast. Do what you have to do, Julie. Pull a girly.

"Officer?" I whimper. "Officer, I don't know what to do. You've got to help me. My mother's in the hospital . . ."

Em is hanging on my every word, every eyelash bat.

". . . dying. For all I know she might already be . . . gone."

Nadia says, "Get out. Your grandma's not dead, is she?"

Em tells Nadia to shut up.

A genuine tear rolls down my cheek. "I have no idea how I'll get to the properly statuted repossession yard, unless . . ." Doe eyes in his direction.

Like cake he crumbles. "Okay, okay. I know what you're trying to do. I'll give you a lift to the yard. Though my advice is to get out some cash now. They don't take credit cards or checks." He waves his arm to the ATM in the corner.

In all the days of my days, this has been the worst, ever. My afternoon with Michael has been ruined. I can't find a swimsuit to save my life, though I do find vast swaths of brand-new cellulite. I'm two colors, like the Riddler from Batman. My mother collapses and is taken to the hospital. I fight with my lovely, loving, and good daughter. My car is towed, and to top it off . . . ?

ATM fees. An outrageous three dollars to access my own money. Not the bank's—mine. Has our financial industry overlooked that little detail?

But I'm wrong. The ATM fees are not the worst part. Nor is my mother's collapse.

An hour later, after I've waited in line to pay one hundred dollars to retrieve my car, Nadia is riding shotgun and Em is in the backseat as we're a block from MetroSouth in Framingham when I feel a tap on my shoulder.

"Mom, I hate to bring this up," Em says in a little voice.

"If you have to go to the bathroom, you'll have to wait until the hospital. We're almost there."

"It's about Quinn McVeigh."

I have no idea who Quinn McVeigh is.

"My boss's daughter."

Oh, right. Chris McVeigh's daughter. Teeny girl. Strawberry blond with pigtails. Adorable. Sometimes Chris brings her down to Brigham's and we all take turns squeezing her.

"I was supposed to be at her house ten minutes ago to babysit."

My hands grip the wheel so hard the knuckles turn white. This cannot be happening. "Doesn't Chris McVeigh live in Natick?"

"Uh, yeah."

"Weren't we *just in* Natick?"

"Yes, but I thought we were going straight home and then I could drive myself."

How she came to the conclusion that we were going straight home, in the opposite direction of MetroSouth, is baffling. Did she think that I'd abandon my mother at the hospital and go home to check the mail, water the garden, get a soda? Pulling a U-turn and heading right back from whence I came, not for the first time do I ask myself, will this day end?

I hear a *sniff*, turn to find Em in the backseat crying, and my heart melts. "It's okay, Em. I'm sorry I got so mad," I say, patting her knee.

"It's not that it's, I wasn't thinking about what we were doing. I was too worried about Grandma. Is she going to . . . ?"

"NO!" Now I've done it. I screamed at a poor, rattled teenager who believes her beloved grandmother's on her deathbed. "She's fine. So fine that the doctor's releasing her right away. It was just a dizzy spell brought on by the fact Grandma was dehydrated in the heat and she hadn't eaten."

Em's eyes go wide. "Grandma not eating. Now I really know something's wrong."

After dropping off Em at the McVeighs', I stop by the hospital to check on Mom, who tells me she won't be leaving with me, she'll be leaving with Lois because Dad has gone on an overnight fishing trip to Maine with his old friend, Buster Rubick. Hence, his "reason" for not being able to drive Mom to the mall.

This seems like a fairly important fact, the kind you'd say right off if you were in your right mind. That Mom held off telling us until I was about to cruise Watertown's more popular public works projects looking for him tells me her mind is anything but right.

"Lois has central air," Mom tells me. "The doctor called that a medical necessity in my condition."

So I go home and pack a bag for Mom to take to Lois's. (Mom gave me a list.) Then I have to drop off Nadia, who seems perfectly happy to hang around like a witch's familiar sucking on lollypops and looking vacantly out the window as I tour her around the greater Boston area, from the mall to the hospital in Framingham, back to Natick, to the hospital again, and finally to her house in Watertown, where she gets out and says, "Thanks, Mrs. M. That was fun."

It's impossible not to love that girl.

Back at the hospital yet again, I find Mom has checked out without waiting for me.

Of course. *Of course* she's checked out. Because for her to have waited for me would have been . . . normal. And normal is something my family does not do.

Turns out Mom is at Lois's house all the way in Lexington, where I find her feet up, eating lime sherbet with raspberry sauce, and watching a rerun of *Keeping Up Appearances* on public television as if nothing out of the ordinary has happened, as if a day that was supposed to start as a half-hour glasses fitting hadn't ended up in the emergency room.

"By the way," Mom says, after I deposit her bag in Lois's doorway. "I left my glasses at the mall. You wouldn't mind picking them up, would you? They don't close until nine."

It's too much. It's too much!

Mom's shoulders begin to shake. And Lois, who's stepped out of the kitchen with a dishcloth over her shoulder, lets out a giggle. Soon they're both in hysterics over my reaction to Mom's "joke." Everyone's having a laugh riot but me. I want to cry.

"Lighten up, Julie," Mom says, dipping into her sherbet. "You take life way too seriously."

"I love you, Mom." I blow her a kiss and envision the sherbet bowl dumped upside down on her head, green and raspberry goo running over her cheeks. The imagination is a wonderful thing; it allows for all manner of undiscoverable sins.

Wearily and woozily, I teeter out to my car, start it up, check my mirrors, and get about ten miles down the road when a scruffy man in a rusted pickup truck pulls next to me at a light and begins gesturing obscenely at my rear bumper.

Being a veteran reporter, however, I am onto his tricks. I can't count how many stories I've done about sick men conning vulnerable women into pulling to the side of a deserted road or rolling down their windows all the way, only to find the man has a gun and evil deeds on his mind.

Surreptitiously, I lock my doors and stare straight ahead.

"Lady!" He's leaned over and rolled down his own window, even though the light's about to change. "Your left rear goddamn (and lots of other expletives) tire is fucking flat."

The light turns green and this being Boston, everyone behind us immediately leans on their horns.

I can't believe it. A flat tire. Of all the things to have happened on this, the lousiest of days. And in Lexington, too, where gas stations are few and far between. Yanking my car into a dirt parking lot at Minute Man Park, I get out and survey the damage. Oh, it's flat all right. It is dead and lifeless.

Well, no point feeling sorry for myself. Let's change this sucker and get home so I can take a shower, pour a nice cold glass of wine, and relax. Except . . . there's no spare tire in the trunk. What happened to the spare?

Then I remember. The tire that's flat IS the spare because the original was ripped to shreds last winter and I never replaced it.

I give up. Do you hear that, God! You win. I give up.

And I do. I don't even go back to the car. Instead, I walk into the woods, sit down against a big tree, and close my eyes. It's very peaceful here, site of the famous battle where the famous shot was heard around the world. Around me, stones mark the slow progression of the British and the minutemen as they shot their way from Concord to Lexington, the first bloody steps in the march toward American democracy.

Who am I to complain about a flat tire, then, when so many gave up their lives so future generations could be free?

My cell phone rings, jolting me back to the twenty-first century. It's Michael.

"Hi," he says. "I just got back from seeing Mom and picked up your message. I figured if you were tied up this afternoon we could do something else tonight. Is Betty okay?"

I relay a shortened version of her collapse and tell him she's fine. "I, however, am not. My car has a flat, I'm without a spare, so I'm sitting here in Minute Man Park waiting for the Rapture because I'm done. I want off this Earth."

He doesn't wait a beat. "Stay right there. I'll come to get you."

A lump rises in my throat. Yes, I know I'm not supposed to rely on men to save me and I'm proud to say I rarely do. But at a time like this, is anything more welcome than a capable man with a free ride?

"You don't have to do that," I lie. "I can call AAA."

"Shut up, Julie. Don't even pretend like you don't want me to get you out of this. Just sit still and try not to get mugged."

"It's Lexington. At worst, some prepper in multilayered Ralph Lauren will try to rush me."

"Now you've got me really worried. Whatever you do, don't let them talk you into a G&T. That's their gateway drug."

"Gotcha."

"Be right there." And he hangs up.

For the first time today, I find myself smiling.

Chapter Fifteen

The course of true love never did run smooth

—A MIDSUMMER NIGHT'S DREAM, ACT I, SCENE 1

"You're kidding me. You don't have even one air conditioner?"

"I can live with the heat, that's not the problem. It's my mother who can't deal," I tell him as we pull up to my house in his gorgeous silver BMW convertible, top down. "The doctor wouldn't even let her come home tonight because we didn't have A/C. So she had to stay at Lois's."

Michael says, "That's it," and starts up the car. "I'm going to get a couple of window units. She can't live like this."

"Don't be crazy. Mom will be fine as soon as the weather breaks."

He pays me no heed as we hook a left and head for the box stores. "Look, Julie. After all your mother did for me, the least I can do is install a couple of air conditioners—one for her, one for you. It's not like your father can lift those things anymore."

"But . . ."

"I'm sorry to disappoint you and I know going to Home Depot isn't the same as lobster on the dock, but have faith. I'm not entirely without charm. Let's just take care of your mother first, and then I'll take care of you."

An hour later the BMW is crammed with not one, but three Frigidaires. One for Em's bedroom, one for mine, and another for my parents, though I have my doubts. They're weird about A/C.

"The Legionnaires ruined it for them," I say, helping him haul the backbreaking unit up the steps of my parent's apartment. "Remember that? A bunch of guys at an American Legion convention in Philadelphia developed pneumonia from contaminated hotel air-conditioning and overnight they had their own disease."

"Lucky bastards." He winces, taking most of the weight as we back through the house from Mom's heavily upholstered living room done up in variations of dusty rose, through the colonial blue dining room with its matching dark mahogany furniture and polished silver tea sets, through the hallway with its fuzzy gold wallpaper and all our framed family photographs, and finally to her pristine white bedroom with its damask spread and maple headboard over which hangs a picture of a cherubic Jesus, hands clasped.

We drop the air conditioner by the window and immediately clutch our lower lumbars. Michael nods to the painting. "I could make a crack about that."

"He's either there to answer Dad's prayers to get laid or Mom's prayers not to." I can't believe I just said that. "Oh, my God. I made a crack about my parents' sex life. I'm sorry."

"Do yourself a favor, don't think about it. If I did, I'd go nuts."

He's referring, of course, to his mother, who turned her bedroom into the big top, come one, come all. Fortysomething years old and I still haven't learned to think before I speak. "Look . . . I didn't mean."

"Forget it." He waves me off and goes to the window to pop out the screen. "By the way, when I told my mom you'd planned on coming today, a miracle occurred."

I rip open the box with my mother's nail scissors. "Yeah?"

"She looked me straight in the eye and said, 'Julie Mueller. I remember her. The pudgy little fat girl.' "

"What?" I wasn't *that* fat, was I? Then I see a reflection of him grinning in my mother's vanity mirror. "She did not."

"Oh yes, she did." He bends down and tosses out two blocks of Styrofoam. "Pudgy little fat girl with her pretend playmate, Alice."

Now I definitely know he's teasing. "That's an Alzheimer's joke. Could you be any more politically incorrect?"

"I got plenty more where those came from," he says, lifting out the air conditioner and, grunting, shoving it into the window. "Six years' worth of digs to get back at you."

"I'm flattered."

"You should be. I spent many nights falling asleep planning my revenge." Steadying the heavy unit with one of his legs, carefully he lowers the sash. "Do you know how much I hate installing air conditioners? If I didn't love your mom more than my own, I'd be throwing a fit."

I tell him to quit whining and get to work. "So, six years, huh? How about before that?"

"Before that, it was other memories of you that kept me away. One memory of a certain August night in particular." He gives me a naughty smile and then revs up his power screwdriver.

Whoa, I think, standing back as he fastens the unit. He hasn't forgotten and here I hoped he might have. Not that I did anything out of the ordinary for my age, not really. Except he was twenty-one, an experienced man with an active sex life back in college, and I was a high school virgin with an overly developed imagination and a secret, passionate longing who'd read way too many romance novels.

I was so sure the reason he didn't pay any attention to me was because he still thought of me as a girl, not a woman. As Paul's little sister. But if I could show him I had breasts and legs and everything his gorgeous girlfriends had, then he would see me in a new light. He would fall in love.

Which was why I dragged him into the woods, where I foolishly . . . oh, I can't even think about it. Anyway, all I remember is him gently pulling my shirt closed and kissing me on the cheeks, softly. *Brotherly.* Then he said something about how he would always respect me and how I'd always have a special place in his heart but that I was kind of young.

Damn.

"What're you thinking about?" he asks, sealing the rest of the window.

"That shower," I say. "I really need one." Preferably, cold. Like ice.

It's pitch-black by the time we've finished installing, screwing in, and sealing all the units and the house is buzzing and clicking with the delicious sound of our rooms cooling. I insist on going down to Corner Beverage to buy him a six-pack in gratitude, but Michael will have nothing of it.

"How about a glass of wine, then?"

"No thanks." He's washing his hands at the sink and drying them on the towel, getting ready to go.

"Look, I have to repay you some way. You spent a Saturday night putting in three air conditioners, for heaven sakes, not to mention driving all the way out to Lexington to pick me up."

"Tell you what." He drops the towel, leaving it in a lump. Bachelor brain. "Why don't you take that shower and afterward we can discuss dinner."

We're still on for dinner? At this late hour? "It's nine-thirty. Nothing around here's open." *And, after the day I've had, I really don't want to drive someplace.*

"You know, that's another one of your problems. You always insist on micromanaging everything. How about kicking back and trusting a guy for a change?"

"Last time I trusted a guy a pink plus sign showed up on the little white stick."

"Ah, right. Well, that wasn't my fault, was it?"

"No. That was Donald's. Too bad he got to me before you could."

Michael shakes his head. "It's only dinner, Julie. I'm not trying to get you into bed."

"I didn't think you were." *Snort.* Spinning around, I practically run down the hall. I cannot get into that shower fast enough. *Too bad he got to me before you could.* It must be the heat or the stress of the day because my mouth is going off on its own.

There's a lot of banging and clanging going on outside my cooling bedroom as I towel off and change into a white cotton sundress. Pots, it sounds like, and I bet he's cooking dinner. That is so sweet. First he picks me up in Lexington, then he installs the air conditioners, and now this. He must really feel guilty for screwing up with Kirk. Brushing my hair back into a ponytail, I add a shimmer of pink gloss simply because my lips are dry. No other reason, I swear.

The banging stops and I wait a minute to make sure I'm not going to ruin his surprise. Then I tiptoe out, excited to see what he's been up to, only to find him staring at a white bag in the middle of the kitchen floor.

"I can't do it," he says, throwing up his arms. "I got the water ready. Salted it. Even found some butter and . . . I just can't do it."

The bag moves. On its own.

My goodness. Men are such weenies. "Lobsters?"

"Two five-pounders."

Holy mackerel! "Where did they come from?"

"My car." Seeing my alarm, he adds, "Don't worry. I had them on ice. This nurse who takes care of my mother gave them to me this morning as thanks for the help I gave her in a dispute with city hall. Her husband's a lobsterman in Hingham."

Ahh. "Nice friend to have."

"I'll say. And I love lobster. It's my favorite food in the world. But no matter what"—he puts his hands on his hips, as if in defeat—"I can't bring myself to kill the damn things."

I pretend that for me, she who is experienced in the ways of murdering crustaceans, executing a lobster hit is no big deal.

"How about you go in the next room, turn on some loud music, and I'll call you when the worst is over. Okay, big boy?"

"Better yet, on the way up the stairs, I noticed the front railing's loose. I'll go see if I can fix it so your mother won't lean on that one day and fall right over."

"That sounds good. And very macho."

"It's a safety issue, Julie. Nothing more."

"And all the way out there, you'll never hear the lobsters scream."

"They scr—?" He stops and grins. "Got me back for the fat girl remark, didn't you?"

"No. They really do scream. So high-pitched only dogs can hear them."

"Right." And with one last look of regret, he goes.

Regarding the lobsters in their bag, I psych myself up by reminding myself they are huge mutant arthropods descended from the same ancestor that brought us such enjoyable creatures as the poisonous scorpion. And that, contrary to erroneous reports, they do not mate for life. The male, in fact, mates as many females as he can.

On second thought, boiling's too good for them.

But first, a trick taught to me by my beloved grandmother. Rub the carapace between their eyes, thereby confusing and stunning them into unconsciousness. Then dunk them headfirst into rapidly boiling water. No pain, guaranteed.

That's what I'm doing, scratching the lobsters between the eyes, when the swinging door to the kitchen opens a crack.

"You're petting them?" Michael exclaims, wielding a hammer as if to remind me of his masculinity.

"Not petting. Stunning. You better go."

"I can take it," he says.

"Okay." With a pot holder in one hand, I scoop up the lobster with my left and perform a synchronized lid lifting/lobster dunking/lid returning maneuver that's so quick I don't even know what's happened—and I'm the one doing it.

"There," I say, my hand firmly on the lid in case he tries to escape. "It's done."

"What about him?" He gestures at the remaining lobster still in its foggy state. " 'If it were done when 'tis done, then 'twere well / It were done quickly:' "

"*Hamlet*?"

"*Macbeth*."

"Too bad, Macduff, I have to wait for the water to reach boiling again."

It's a gruesome act, killing lobsters. But the reward is so worth it. Moments later, Michael and I are swatting at mosquitoes (despite the citronella candle on the middle of the picnic table—do those things ever work?) and cracking lobster over newspapers under a full moon. Sweet, delicate white meat in melted butter, tomatoes from Mom's garden with a splash of vinaigrette, and a glass of chilled chardonnay.

Life does not get any better.

"As I recall, the last time you made us dinner was when you stole food from the Star," I say, picking at a claw. "Actually, it was more stole from the Star's Dumpster."

Michael puts down his beer with indignation. "I did not. That's another one of your lies."

"Yes, you did. This was during your Americans-waste-so-much phase. You came over with a huge spread of lettuce and a whole assortment of salad vegetables, even a package of ground beef, and rolls, and you grilled burgers for us on the backyard barbecue. It wasn't until we were done that you announced you'd picked everything from a Dumpster outside a grocery store."

He nods, remembering. "That's right. I did. And, unless I'm mistaken, no one got sick, did they?"

"As long as I didn't think about what you'd done, I was fine."

"But at least I made you think, right?"

"You always made me think. That's your most attractive body part, Michael. Your brain," I say, grinning to myself. *Take that, Frank Zappa.* Tossing the claw into the bowl, I settle down to debate what to attack next. The tail? That's kind of like the big bang of fireworks in lobster cuisine. When that's gone, what's left?

"Why didn't we ever get together?"

The question uppercuts me, right when I'm struggling with the tail. "What do you mean?"

"I mean, even when you were a bratty kid you were kind of cute."

"With my joyful singing and dancing?" Or when I was throwing myself at you in the woods?

"There was that. But then one day when I was home from college, you walked into the room and I was stunned. I thought, what happened to Paul's sister? Who replaced the dorky, giggly schoolgirl with this beautiful woman?"

"That's a total crock." Though I'm sucking it up, praying he'll keep laying it on. "You're just angling for the rest of my lobster."

"I'm telling you, it's true." He leans over and breaks off the tail I've been wrestling, pushing the meat through like a pro.

"Thanks."

"De nada."

"If so, then why did you slam me when I made a pass at you?"

"Oh, that." He fiddles with a claw shell, twirling it on his plate. "That was a very dicey situation. I'm not sure I can adequately explain it."

"Please. If this is going to be some philosophical lecture, I don't want to hear it. It's late enough as it is and I'd hate to fall asleep out here," I say, licking butter off my fingers.

"Okay, smarty-pants, I'll tell you why." He holds up his thumb. "First, you were seventeen and I was twenty-one. Though not a huge age difference, kind of an important one from a legal perspective."

Lame. "You were such a nerd. What other healthy, red-blooded American, twenty-one-year-old male would push off a seventeen-year-old girl in short-shorts who was willing to do anything?"

"Anything?"

"Anything."

"See, I didn't know about the anything." He wags his claw. "Had I known, I might have reevaluated my position."

"Too late now, buster. You missed out. What's the second reason?"

"Your brother and my relationship with him. Namely, the one time he caught me checking you out, he threatened—in far more colorful language than I'm about to use—that should I ever feel inclined to make a move on you, he would have to knock my lights out."

Note to self: Murder brother.

The portable phone rings. It's Em to say the McVeighs are back and she'll be sleeping over there since Chris doesn't want to drive all the way to Watertown. Like a slutty high school cheerleader who's just learned her parents are going away for the weekend, I think, *Yes!*

Mom and Dad are out. Em's gone. I have the place to myself.

"That was Em," I say, clicking off and daintily wiping my lips. "She's not coming home tonight."

"Hmm." Michael takes another swig and gives me an interesting look. "So you're all alone, little girl."

"I am. And I'm not so little."

"I've noticed."

"Watch it."

He leans forward suggestively. "And I'm not twenty-one anymore."

"And I'm not seventeen."

"You're better than when you were seventeen. You've gotten better with age."

Pushing away my plate, I say, "That's not what you said six years ago. What were your exact words? That's right. You called me a ratings-grubbing ice queen with no heart or soul or principles. A picture-perfect sellout."

"Did I say that? I'm sure I must have been referring to someone else."

"No. I was standing right there."

"The good news," he says, crumpling his napkin, "is that we're even. You screwed me over, I screwed you over. We can start anew."

"I'm not so sure."

"Come on, Julie. Don't play this game. You always had a crush on me, admit it."

I will admit nothing. "Perhaps I did have a crush on you once upon a time."

"And I always had a soft spot for you, too."

"Soft spot? That's all I get? Rotten apples have soft spots."

"Babies, too, and they're adorable just like you."

With a gentle grab of his forearm I enlighten him that no woman over the age of six wants to be referred to as adorable. "Try intriguing,"

He runs his large hand over mine. "Okay, intriguing. Now, what's the caveat?"

"The caveat," I say, summoning strength, "is why are you flirting with me when you're going out with a beautiful woman who thinks you walk on water?"

"Ah." He pulls away and studies the label on his beer. "You're referring to Carol."

That stuff I mentioned about him not being so egotistical? Scratch that. "There's more than one beautiful woman who adores you?"

Michael thinks about this, stripping off the beer label and then stripping that into strips. "You may have a misimpression about our relationship."

"She doe-eyes you all through dessert class. What's to misimpress?"

"Carol's a complicated situation. What she needs, I can't give. Unfortunately."

That old line. I could write the script blindfolded—marriage, commitment, a lifelong partnership. "You mean an engagement ring."

"No." He strips off another part of the label. "Nothing like that."

"Then what? Monogamy?"

"Well, for starters," he says slowly, as if selecting each word. "Love. I don't love her."

"But you don't mind sleeping with her."

"Who said I was sleeping with her?"

I give him a look. "Be real."

"Okay, let's say I were. Just for the sake of argument, for figuring out how Julie Mueller operates, tell me—do you have to be in love to sleep with someone? I mean, we're adults, right? We're not innocents. We've both been married. You to a guy who left you with a nine-month-old baby, me to a woman who found my disdain for parties and country clubs got in the way of her personal and social fulfillment."

So that's why he and Cassie split, over such a trivial matter. And from what Mom tells me it was a huge wedding with all the bells and whistles. I would have gone except I was out to there with Em. Or, at least, that's what I told myself.

"What are you saying, Michael? Are you saying because we failed at marriage we are doomed to a future of loveless sex? Because I don't buy that."

"What I'm saying is that there's love and then there's sex and that sex without love, though not as ideal, does have its merits."

This is what he wants. That's why he's flirting with me. He's just looking to get me into bed, nothing more. Curse him.

Unable to sit across from him one more minute, I jump up and promptly tip over the bowl of lobster shells. Super. Lobster water's all over my hands, turning them sticky and the table now smells like low tide.

"What's wrong?" he says, mopping up the water with the newspapers. "You act like I've insulted you."

"Because you have." I crumble the newspapers into a big ball. *You don't give good, noble, loving women like me a chance.* "It all goes back to how you're such an idealist. You're waiting for a perfect woman out there who might look like Cassie and act like Cassie without the flaws. When there is no such thing. Don't you get that, even at your age? There are no perfect women!"

He takes the newspaper out of my hands and comes around to my side of the table. He's so close, I can smell the faint trace of sweat and a mild, vinegary scent of beer. It's been a long time since I was so close to a man I liked. Ages since I was so close to one I once loved.

"You underestimate me, Julie."

"Do I?" Heart beating hard. Must will it to behave.

"It's not perfection I'm after. It's something else, something stupidly romantic." Bowing his head, he says, "I'm more, as you would say, old-fashioned. I actually do believe in true love."

"Oh, please," I scoff and turn to get the rest of the dishes, though deep down I'm incredibly touched by his sentiment. Provided he's sincere, of course.

Something happens and his hand's on mine and he's pulling me toward him, making me understand. "That's where I went wrong with Cassie. Cassie was beautiful and fun and, yes, sexy. Most important, she liked me. Back then, I figured if a girl really liked me, then I should like her. It's hard to describe, really."

"But marriage? That's more than just agreeing to take her to the movies, Michael."

"At the time, I'd reached what I thought was a mature conclusion by deciding there was no point in waiting for this idealistic construct of true love. Cassie loved me. I loved her, in a way. She wanted to get married and so I proposed. She was persistent, but she was not my true love. That hasn't happened. Yet."

An ominous silence punctuated by the occasional cricket chirp and passing car comes over us. What I should do is drop the issue and finish cleaning the table. But this feels like a one-in-a-million moment. Maybe it's the full moon or the sultry night air or the lobster and wine on top of body-aching exhaustion. Whatever the reason, I can't stop myself.

"You didn't need to wait, Michael." I can barely get out the words. "You met your true love when you were about ten. You just never realized it."

A phone rings in his pocket, though he doesn't answer it right away because he seems to be frozen. Finally, he frees my hand and takes the call, strolling to the end of the yard for privacy. Meanwhile, I gather up the plates and bowl and find as I climb the back stairs that my knees are wobbling in the strangest way.

What have I done? I have basically admitted that I've loved him all along. Still. Hurriedly, I set to washing the dishes and dreading his footsteps up the back stairs.

"That was Carol," he says, coming inside with the rest of the newspaper and stuffing it into my garbage can. "She's alone this weekend and doesn't have the kids. Thinks she may have seen a burglar or Peeping Tom or someone lurking on her lawn."

That woman must be a witch to have picked up on our vibes all the way from Newton.

"I told her I'd stop by and make sure she's okay."

"Uh-huh. Well, thanks for the lobster and the air conditioners and picking me up." Squeezing out the Palmolive, I invest myself in washing these plates right away.

"Julie." His arm is around my waist and it is all I can do to keep scrubbing and rinsing as Betty Mueller taught me. Clean, clean and your troubles will disappear. "You've given me a lot to think about tonight. Thank you."

I stop scrubbing. The water's still flowing, but I don't dare turn it off. I'm too afraid to move.

With barely a brush of a kiss on my cheek, his arm slips away and the front door slams.

Gone at last. Flicking off the water, I have to lean against the sink, I'm shaking so hard. *Why did I say that?* No wonder he flew out of here. I scared him off, is what I did, sent him running for the hills. Well, at least I won't have to ever see him again.

And then I remember: my last dessert class. Damn.

At the thought of having to face him next Friday, my heart revs up again, beating so hard with anxiety that I have to sit down and place my hand over it as if I could keep it from flying out of my chest. Only, when I do, I feel the strangest thing.

Hard and too large for comfort. In the upper-left-hand quadrant of my left breast. The same quadrant in which my mother and my aunt and their mother and her mother found theirs, too.

A lump.

Chapter Sixteen

Friendship is constant in all things
Save in the office and affairs of love

—MUCH ADO ABOUT NOTHING, ACT II, SCENE 1

"It's nothing. You know it's nothing. Ninety percent of lumps turn out to be benign," Liza says when I call her, almost in a panic, the next morning.

"Easy for you to say, Liza. You're thousands of miles away in Romania dining on crap."

"Crap is the Romanian word for carp and I'm back in civilization. I'm in Venice eating *pesci del traitor,* thank you very much."

"Fish of the traitor?"

"I don't know. I don't speak Italian."

But as a cookbook author she should at least know . . . oh, forget it.

"Clearly everything's gone to hell in a handbasket in my absence," she says, "what with you losing the national election team spot and finding a lump and saying good night to your lifelong crush with a peck on the cheek."

I haven't told her or anyone about my soul-baring comment because I'm trying very hard to put it out of my mind. "He's not my lifelong crush," I state, "and if he were, he's already involved with someone else. Besides, Liza, my days as a wanton sexual woman are over. I was too busy raising Em and slaving at WBOS to notice when they were here and now that I've come up for air, it's too late."

Liza has no truck with this. "Listen to you. You sound like some bad country-western song crooning about your baby and the bills. When did you turn frigid all of a sudden? And to think I left you in charge of seducing D'Ours for me. I'd have been better off calling Mother Teresa."

"She's dead."

"Exactly."

Carefully, I apply a translucent strip of Pink Buff to my newly manicured thumbnail and weigh the pros and cons of suggesting she give up on D'Ours. It was fairly freaky the way he cornered me after class, oozing Frenchness and acting terribly interested in my career as a lowly local TV reporter. Thank goodness Michael was there to keep him in check.

I've been relatively frosty with D'Ours compared to the woman I refer to as Lilly Pulitzer, who managed to undo one more button at the top of her hot-pink Lacoste shirt somewhere between the pear flan and almond biscotti tiramisu. Then she breathlessly begged him to instruct her in the right mixing technique. Who knew it required the exact same gyrations as your average pole dancer?

The thing is, Liza's very unpredictable. And kinky. In her twisted mind a chef who bumps and grinds his way through a cherry crumble could be a total turn-on.

No. There's no easy solution here. The best course of action is to change the subject.

"I just want to know why stuff like this has to happen smack in the middle of a weekend," I say, moving on to another nail. "You always come across a lump or weird bleeding or a suspicious spot when you're on vacation overseas or during a Christmas holiday. Why don't these things pop up at ten a.m. on Wednesdays when the doctor's in?"

"Why do you switch lines at the grocery store only to find the one you left is faster? How come the one time you download tickets to a movie, you get held up and miss the show? Why does the call you've been waiting for happen when you're in the shower or out to get the mail? That's the way the cookie crumbles."

"There's an expression I haven't heard since my fifth-grade teacher, 'cookie crumbles.' "

"When you're in the culinary lines, every metaphor is food related. What I want to know is whether you're going to tell Michael."

This question is so odd that I miss my nail and drop a tiny blob of pink buff acrylic on my desk. "Why should I?"

"*Exactly.* Because you know how men are. . . ."

"I'm beginning to think I don't."

"Men can't deal with disease." Liza pauses and then says cautiously, "Like your dad, remember? To him, your mom's breast cancer was his fault for not protecting her better, as if he'd let the team down."

"That's my mother's theory." I finish my fingers and blow on them, wondering just how many carcinogens are in a bottle of polish, anyway. "I've never been convinced."

"Still," she says, "I wouldn't go blabbing to him."

This is advice I don't need. Not only am I not going to tell Michael, I'm not going to tell anyone at work. This could be the kiss of death to any remaining hope of Kirk Bledsoe changing his mind. I can't even let myself think of it being the kiss of death in any other way.

Not to mention the effect of this on Mom and Em, both of whom will worry way too much about me. Mom has her own health issues and Em should be enjoying her last year of school, applying to colleges and skipping classes with her friends, not checking my temperature and making tea.

"You're not saying anything," Liza says. "Does this mean I over-stepped my bounds again?"

"Forget it." Capping the bottle, I say, "You probably have to go, any-way. This call must be costing you a fortune."

"Quick. Ask me the ingredients of a *riso e bisi con pancietta* I sampled on Saturday."

"What are the ingredients of the *riso e bisi con pancietta* you sampled on Saturday?"

"Arborio rice, pancetta, peas, the best Parmesan possible, and other junk. There. This call is now a business expense."

"I'm so glad I could do you the favor."

"In return, I want you to do yourself a favor. At one-thirty today go to the Renew Day Spa and check in for a massage, facial, and pedicure. If you can't make it, call them and reschedule, but do it soon. It's imperative for your mental health."

I'm having trouble comprehending what she's suggesting. "You mean you, in Italy, made an appointment for me at a spa down the street?"

"It's a gift, not an appointment. I'm not that crass. Now will you do it?"

This is vintage Liza. Always with a trick up her sleeve, an unexpected delivery of flowers, a kitten in a box, and a Candygram at work.

"Are you kidding? I'm not going to blow off a spa trip you paid for. It's been too long since you showered me with an expensive gift."

"That's what I love about you, Julie. You're cheap and greedy."

"And you're generous and extravagant. We have the perfect friendship."

But when I hang up, I resolve to pay back Liza in spades. The question is, should I set her up with D'Ours? Or should I do what she does for me: surprise her with a gift she doesn't realize she desperately needs?

The next morning, I wake up in my cool air-conditioned room, shower, make coffee, and sit by the phone, my doctor's number programmed into redial so I am the first in line when the office opens at eight.

Which is right . . . now.

"The earliest I can get you in," the receptionist informs me, "is Thursday at one."

"Thursday at one? I can't wait until Thursday at one. I'll be clinically insane with worry by then."

"You better take it," she says. "I've got three other people on hold who will if you don't."

I take it.

Man. I am so tired of being yanked around, I groan, hanging up the phone with a slam. I get yanked around at work, by Arnie, by Kirk Bledsoe, even at C-Rite.

How come whatever *I* want gets a low priority? Even Em, though the greatest teenager ever, still leaves her stuff around like I'm the maid and she just expects me to do her bidding. Does scolding her about her discarded yogurt tops and piles of dirty clothes do any good? No.

Look. There are her gum wrappers on the couch. Five of them. Does she expect them to walk themselves to the trash? Guess so, because here I am once again cleaning up after her. Tossing them into the wastepaper basket under the sink, I give the door a good hard kick when I'm done. And is this her strawberry shortcake bowl left over from last night still on the dining room table sticky hard with dried whipped cream?

I throw the bowl into the sink so hard it almost breaks. Then I dump her socks—still holding the shape of Em's foot—into the hamper and slam the hamper lid. For good measure I give the bathroom door a hard slam, too, on my way out. It feels terrific. I might slam every door in the house.

Nothing. I'm (slam!) nothing to anyone. Only a doormat. (Slam and slam!) I can't even get a doctor's appointment (slam!) when I want to. I have to wait (slam!) and wait (slam!) and wait (slam!).

There is a knock on the front door. "Julie!" Mom calls. "Are you okay?"

My father picked up Mom from Lois's house on his way home from

Maine last night. I had to bite my tongue when I discovered he let her make dinner—despite her condition. The good news is he let Em and me borrow his car so we could drive out to Lexington with a new spare and fetch mine.

But the bad news? I can't tell her about the lump. That's the last thing she needs to worry about on top of everything else.

"I'm okay," I tell her. "Just pissed."

"Well, keep it down. You're so loud your father can't hear the *Today* show."

That's it. That's the final straw. "The *Today* show!" I yell, throwing open the door to find her still in that hideous pink quilted housecoat. "He shouldn't be watching that junk. Anyway, why doesn't he tell me himself? Why does he always get you to do his dirty work? He lets you make dinner, lets you stay at Lois's house while you recover from a collapse, and he has enough nerve to ask me to keep it down?"

Mom's wrinkled lips press into a hard line, a sure sign that she's hurt, and immediately I wish I could take it back. But I don't want to.

"Listen," she starts in, jabbing me with her bony finger. "I don't know what's gotten into you lately. Ever since yesterday you've been a pill to put up with. As if I don't have enough problems."

"I'm sorry, Mom. I didn't mean to upset you. It's just that—"

"You meant it. I know what you think of me and lemme tell you something, kiddo, you don't know squat." Her eyes are watering and her cheeks are getting red and I'm afraid she's going to keel over again. "What goes on between your father and me is our business. It works for us and we've got fifty years of marriage to back us up. So why don't you keep your bossy trap shut."

She doesn't say it, but I know what she's thinking. For someone whose marriage lasted all of two years, I'm not one to be sitting in judgment. That's rich coming from a woman who never had a career but who never hesitates to give me career advice.

"Look, Mom," I say, trying to keep it cool and not doing a very good job. "You have no idea what I'm going through. *No* idea. You've never had to be a single mother *and* worry about how to pay the bills. You've always been taken care of by a man."

I'm really on a roll now. I'm feeling self-destructive like a thresher out of control cutting down everything in its path. "So pardon me if I slam a few doors. A few slammed doors seem like a small price to pay for what I'm going through. And if you don't like that, you can butt out."

"Fine," she says, stepping away, disgust written all over her face. "If that's what you want, it can be arranged. I'll butt out of your life, you butt out of mine. Though you might want to consider that daughter of yours. She doesn't have a choice. She's stuck with you and your foul moods."

There is a momentary exchange of glares and then she goes and I slam the door feeling guilty as well as angry now. "Too bad," I murmur, though loud enough for Em, who's standing in the doorway, to hear.

"What?" I snap.

"What?" She throws up her hands. "You're in a shouting match with Grandma and you want to know *what*? How am I supposed to sleep with all this racket?"

"Well, maybe you ought to try waking up before noon."

"It's not anywhere close to noon. Grandma's right. What *is* wrong with you?"

I hadn't intended to tell Em. Honest. My plan was to get this checked out and then, if everything came back fine, to never speak of it again. But here she is, a half-grown woman, and here I am, acting like a baby, and it hits me that this is not the kind of cloud I can live under without her taking stock.

"I found a lump."

There. I said it.

"In my breast."

"Oh." Em stares straight at my chest. "Which one?"

Putting my hand on "the spot," I say, "Left. Upper-left-hand quadrant."

"Most common place."

"Yes." I'm impressed. She must have been reading up.

"That's a bummer," she says, leaning against the door. "What are you going to do about it?"

It's a relief Em's taking this so well. I'd have expected she'd be wailing and worrying about the "what-ifs" by now. "I called the doctor this morning and they said they can't see me until Thursday. Which means I probably won't get a mammogram until next week. Hence my slamming doors."

"And that's that—you slam a few doors? Isn't there another doctor? Isn't there someplace else you can go?"

"I don't think so. I'm on an HMO. I need her approval before I can take the next step. It's complicated. Adult stuff."

"Let me get this straight." Em folds her arms, a simple gesture that turns her normally whimsical figure womanly. "You're always telling me to stand up for myself and fight for what's really important. But then you find a lump and you know that Grandma had breast cancer and her mother before her and her mother before her and you're just going to wait? How fucked up is that?"

The swear catches me off guard, but she's right. Moreover, so is Mom. I've got to be the role model here. Even if I can't get in to see my doctor before Thursday, I've at least got to show Em I tried.

Without saying a word, I go over to the phone and press redial. The receptionist answers on the third ring and asks if she can put me on hold.

"No, thank you," I answer as politely as possible. "I need to speak to Dr. Foulk now."

"Dr. Foulk's with a patient. She won't be returning phone calls until three. Is this an emergency?"

Okay, I want to cave. I'll wait until three. But there's Em on the couch, studying me, watching every move, thinking no doubt about how she'll react when she finds a lump. If she will slam doors and vent her frustration on her family instead of the medical establishment. If she will belittle and berate me, her mother.

"Yes," I say, "it's an emergency."

Em gives me the thumbs-up.

The receptionist sighs. I know she wants to ask me the nature of my emergency and all sorts of nosy questions. I don't let her, though. I ask her to get Dr. Foulk now.

When Dr. Foulk gets on, she is slightly clipped and professional. Two sentences into my description of what I've found, however, and she's scolding the receptionist for making me wait until Thursday.

Turns out, all I need from her is a prescription to get a mammogram and she can fax one over to the breast-imaging center within the next few minutes. She even goes so far as to say she'll call them right away and make sure I get in tomorrow.

"With your family history," she says, "you don't mess around, Julie, though I'm sure it's fine. Ninety percent of all lumps are benign."

"So everyone keeps telling me."

I thank her and hang up, choked with fresh emotion at the sight of my daughter—my beautiful, strong and oh-so-smart daughter—looking up at me victoriously.

"Emmaline," I say, trying not to cry. "You might have just saved my life."

"And for that you're going to hug me, right? No cash? No car? No all-expense-paid trip to Europe?"

"A car, you can buy anytime," I say, throwing myself on the couch and wrapping my arms around her. "But a mother's love . . ."

"Free."

Chapter Seventeen

. . . those that are betray'd
Do feel the treason sharply, yet the traitor
Stands in worse case of woe.

—CYMBELINE, ACT III, SCENE 4

Later that night, while lying in bed trying not to let my mind drift to Michael or my hand drift to the upper-left quadrant of my breast, I have an epiphany: Max the homeless man. Of course! Why didn't I ask him before?

I've seen a lot of Max lately, partly because I've been eager for any excuse not to go to work, where I'll only be relegated to the basement. We've finished "Tintern Abbey" and moved on to other brief, occasionally rambling discussions about Shakespeare (Michael's influence). But mostly we've been dishing dessert.

It started with the peach cobbler and, ever since, Max has asked me if I have a "taste treat" to go with the dollar or two I hand him each morning for opening the Davis Square T station door. A muffin, a chocolate croissant, once some almond biscotti tiramisu—that's what I usually bring. He's a recovering alcoholic, he's told me, and like a lot of recovering alcoholics he craves the sugar that used to come with his wine and rum.

He also didn't just quit his investment banker job, as Michael had said. He was fired. As for the Back Bay town house, that, too, is a myth. It was more like he had a tiny Cape in Westwood from which he was booted by a wife fed up with his addiction. Now he's on the streets, sober—or so he says—for three years, immersing himself in library books to escape the demons that poke and prod him to go back to the bottle.

And yet for all our exchanges, it never occurred to me that, being a virtual resident of the Somerville Public Library, Max might have been a witness to the abduction of Amy Michak.

This is why, on the morning of my mammogram, I bound out of the T and make a beeline for Max's old haunts. He's not by the subway door or at the coffee shop or Woolworth's. He's not huddled with his friends in one of the other T entrances. When I do find him, he's relieving himself against the wall of an abandoned garage.

"Oh, sorry." Slinking back in embarrassment, I avert my eyes.

"Got to do it somewhere. Try to be as out of the way as possible," he says, zipping up his fly and gesturing to a newspaper lying at his feet. "Just read about you in the *Phoenix*. They won't give you a break for that Michak bullshit, will they?"

Exactly what I came here to ask him about. "Do you know about the Michak case?"

"Naturally." He bristles, insulted. "I don't just read books. I read the papers. That's one thing there's no shortage of at a T station."

If he knows, then . . . well, I'd better ask him. "And what's your take on that murder?"

Max reaches down to wipe his hands on a discarded McDonald's napkin. "What's my take? My take is that the police aren't looking very hard."

"And why's that?"

"Why are you asking me?"

"Because you practically live at the Somerville Library, where Amy Michak was last seen alive."

He gives me a dirty look and starts walking, picking up cans and throwing them into a plastic Shaw's bag, toeing foil gum wrappers smashed on the sidewalk with the faint hope they might be change. "I was there that night," he says at last.

I knew it. "You see anything?"

"Yup." Pausing in front of a community garbage can, he reaches in and fishes around, his eyes closed as he lets his mind wander.

This is frustrating. My instinct is to shake him and make him talk, but he's getting too much attention from me to answer quickly. "Can you describe what you saw?"

"Yup." From the garbage can he removes an almost spent legal pad, one white page barely clinging on. "Got a writing implement?"

I fish a pen from my purse and he immediately begins to draw. As he proceeds to brag about his innate aptitude as an artist, a figure emerges beneath his hand. Its familiar stoop and potbelly, the bald dome, and goatee send chills down my spine.

My first thought is, another tragedy for Rhonda. I think that makes three.

"That was who she walked out with." Max thumps the pad with his forefinger. "I'd bet my life."

"Are you sure?"

"Never more so."

This is so not the outcome I wanted.

"Did you tell this to the police?" I ask.

A corner of his lip curls. "No, dear. They never asked me if I saw someone. They asked me if I did it. Don't you see? I'm nobody. I am the scum o' the earth."

Again I examine the drawing, mesmerized by how accurately Max captured the personality as well as the physical form. That's the mark of a true artist, isn't it? To be able to convey a person's *je ne sais quoi*.

"Do you know who this is?" I say.

"Yes, dear," Max says. " 'A little more than kin, and less than kind.' "

Hamlet speaking of his uncle Claudius.

Max is definitely no ordinary bum.

It's while I'm closing out my third conversation of the morning with Detective Sinesky from the Somerville Police Department that Arnie barges into my basement prison all aflutter.

"Owen's office in ten minutes. We've reached a decision about you and your cobbler nuisance."

Covering the mouthpiece, I try to explain that I'm working on a hot story, but Arnie puts up his hands. "Don't give me that. You knew this was coming. Ten minutes."

When I get back on, Detective Sinesky says, "Who was that?"

"My boss. The general manager wants to see me about the cobbler brouhaha. I'm in a heap of trouble."

Sinesky chuckles to himself. "They haven't a clue that you brought us one step closer to solving the most heinous murder of last year, do they?"

Peaches are serious business, I tell him. They are not to be entered into a cobbler lightly.

When I get to Owen's office, Arnie and Owen are there along with a gray-suited man with dark circles under his eyes and the morbid pallor of the chronic insomniac. Of all the days to have a mammogram, I couldn't have chosen worse. No deodorant or antiperspirant allowed, and my armpits are getting soaked in nervous sweat.

"Julie, this is Tom Wrye," Owen says. "Our counsel."

Whose counsel? Certainly not mine as well.

I shake Tom's hand and he slips me a business card with CHAIM AND WRYE in raised gold lettering.

"You're kidding, right?"

He gives me a *wry* smile. "Most people say hold the mayo. I get it all the time."

"Okay, knock off the monkey business." Owen smoothes back his hair and hitches up his pants. "You and I like to joke around, but now we got Tom here and he charges $350 an hour. That's no laughing matter."

Arnie says, "Then you won't mind if I cut to the chase. Julie, we're putting you on unpaid leave for a week, commonly referred to as a 'temporary suspension.' I've laid this out in a press release Dolores is faxing to the morning zoo radio stations so they'll stop calling us wusses. Now, let's go back to work."

A week of leave? Yippeee. Could not have come at a better time, aside from the money. That sucks. But, forgetting about that for the moment, this means I have a week off smack in the middle of summer. For once, kismet's on my side.

Tom asks him to hold on. "Julie, I'm just curious. What was your intention, bringing over that cobbler?"

"She wanted to—" Arnie cuts in, but Owen stops him. "Tell him, Julie. It's okay."

I frown and go on. "I brought that cobbler over because Ray Schmuler, Rhonda Michak's boyfriend, called me at home to complain about Valerie badgering Rhonda and airing unfounded rumors that she murdered her own daughter. Speaking of which—"

"Did you at any moment extend any promises to Mr. Schmuler?" Tom asks.

Folding my arms tightly to hide potential underarm stains, I try to remember if I said something out of line. "I don't think so. Which brings me to—"

"And were you on your shift at that moment?"

Arnie, who's been swinging an imaginary golf club, stops midair. "Does that matter?"

"I'm playing devil's advocate," Tom explains patiently. "Now that I've had a chance to depose her informally and having recently reviewed the station bylaws, I'm not sure she deserves a suspension. If Julie was off her shift, then she was on her own time. To suspend her for acting out her own goodwill would, for example, require us to suspend all the reporters who go to church."

Arnie says, "We have reporters who go to church?"

"No, I wasn't working," I say. "I was on my own time."

Tom goes, "Hmph. I don't know, gentlemen. This is a gray area."

"Well, that's lousy," Owen says, hitching up his pants. "I'd hoped to put an end to this today by sticking her in the public stocks."

"Yeah," says Arnie. "Public stocks. Now, how are we ever gonna get our credibility back?"

"I know," I say. "I just got off the phone with Detective Sinesky, who said—"

Tom interrupts. "You could broadcast a roundtable discussion, a thoughtful examination of the fine lines journalists must be careful not to cross."

"Interesting," Owen says. "Dull as dishwater, but interesting. Would it lower our insurance rates?"

"Possibly," Tom says.

I can't take it anymore. "Listen to me," I practically yell. "You're paying Tom $350 an hour to come up with roundtable discussions, but I've got big, big news."

"Well, stop beating around the bush," Arnie says. "Spit it out."

"Am I still suspended?"

The three men exchange questioning glances, mentally passing off the question like a hot potato. Finally, Arnie asks, "This news of yours. How big is it?"

"Big enough to shut up the fat traps on morning radio."

Owen waves his hand. "Then this suspension is hereby foreshortened."

"And erased from my personnel file," I remind him.

Owen agrees.

"Next she's going to ask for a pay raise," Arnie says.

"Not a bad idea." I look to Owen. "How about it?"

"How about you tell us what this big news is first?"

From my tablet, I remove the drawing Max made earlier that morning. "This is a sketch of the man who abducted Amy from the Somerville Library. It was drawn by a homeless man named Max who saw the whole thing and I've faxed it over to Detective Sinesky. They've interviewed him and will be bringing in the suspect for questioning. My guess is there'll be an arrest just in time for the six-thirty news and Sinesky has promised to give us first dibs in gratitude for my contribution."

Peering at the drawing, Arnie says, "Why does he look familiar?"

"Because he's been all over the Amy Michak case, handing out flyers and serving as spokesman for the family. We've had him on our broadcasts every time we do an Amy update."

Shocked, Owen says, "This is the mother's boyfriend."

Arnie lets out a bunch of swears.

"You mean the boyfriend who called you at home?" Tom asks.

"That's the guy." And saying this reminds me of how many sessions I sat with Rhonda and Ray, Ray always with a comforting hand on Rhonda's thigh, the loyal escort guiding her through the mass of reporters and putting himself on the public pedestal. "The cops brought him in for questioning on numerous occasions. But he had an airtight alibi."

"Which was?" Arnie asks.

"Rhonda. She claimed Ray was outside in the parking lot of the Brown Derby waiting to pick her up from work during the window of time police figure Amy was supposedly abducted."

"Which means Valerie wasn't so off the mark," Arnie rushes to note.

"Wasn't so on the mark, either. Sinesky firmly believes Rhonda's an innocent party who had no idea what her boyfriend was up to. The library is a block from the Brown Derby. It's possible Ray . . ." This part I'm not prepared for, and I find it hard to continue.

Of all the men, it's Tom the lawyer who gives me a reassuring pat on the back. "We get the picture. Ray did what he did, strangled Amy out of panic, and stashed the body. Came back later that night and took her remains to Walden Pond."

"Right." That unfortunate, terrified girl.

"So what the hell are you doing here flapping your gums at us?" Arnie yells. "You should be out there getting this story."

"You were the one who relegated Julie to the basement," Owen reminds him. "And then you made me suspend her. You're an awful, cruel man with no regard for my employees."

"Forget it. Forget it." Arnie's waving madly and hopping about like a chimpanzee in a briar patch. "This is big. We've got to get a crew down to the cop station. You, too, Mueller."

"Don't want to tip off the competition," I warn him. "And I'm sorry, but my exclusive will have to wait. I found a lump in my left breast two days ago and I've got to get a mammogram in an hour."

Arnie stops gesticulating and Owen's jaw drops.

"But as soon as I'm done, I'll be right on top of it, no matter the test results." I cross my heart. "Promise."

On that note, I walk out of Owen's office, glad to be away from the morbid subject of Amy's murder and the prospect of confronting Rhonda with the truth.

You know it's time to rethink your career when a mammogram comes as a welcome relief.

Chapter Eighteen

[Thou art] a disease that must be cut away.

—CORIOLANUS, ACT III, SCENE 1

Suddenly, I'm a comedienne. A bad comedienne at that. Think Joan Rivers at the Berkshires dinner theater.

"When was the date of your most recent mammogram?" the nurse asks me when I check in to the Mt. Olive Breast Care Center.

"April twenty-second of this year."

"That's impressive," she says, writing it down. "Most women can't recall."

"How could I not? It was the last time I took off my shirt for a man." I can't help it. It's a nervous reaction.

"Okay," she says, handing me a clipboard. "Go down the hall to the right. The waiting room is the third door. Take off your top and bra and put them in an empty locker. Slip into the johnny so it ties in the front. A technician will be right with you. Did you wear antiperspirant today?"

I'm about to make another tasteless crack when I catch myself. "No. I didn't."

My nerves don't truly give out, though, until I'm waiting in the changing room with the other women. It's very bizarre how nervous I am. Why? Here I've had so many mammograms over the years it's a wonder my boobs don't glow in the dark, and yet I can't concentrate on this *Time* magazine. Why are my palms sweating and my heart racing? Why am I being such a baby?

Mt. Olive has done everything possible to provide a soothing atmosphere, but not even the peach walls or framed prints of flowers and waterfalls can ease my fears. The odds are (though I've read disputes on this statistic) that one in eight women will get breast cancer. Here we are, exactly eight in this room.

Which one of us will be the odd one out?

I'm sure I'm not alone in playing this morbid roulette. Maybe the woman calmly knitting next to me is also mentally running through the odds, though you'd never know it the way yarn flies over her needles, even and measured, her lips set in a bucolic smile.

Then again we women are trained to fake serenity, aren't we? Nine months of pregnancy and hours of backbreaking labor, annual Pap smears and blood tests, not to mention impatient husbands, angry bosses, and vomiting children have conditioned us to keep going, to keep smiling no matter what.

We stare at the *Prevention* magazine and the wrinkled *Newsweek* like we're at Jiffy Lube waiting for our twenty-point oil change, instead of in a hospital waiting to find out if our breasts have turned on us like buxom secret agents conspiring with the enemy. The telltale difference is that rarely does Jiffy Lube require a pink-flowered johnny that opens in the front.

After what seems like forever, the door flies open and a young woman with a sharp chin and even sharper eyes gazes around the room. "Julie Mueller?"

I'm never called right away. I think—not good.

Her name is Sondra and she tells me that she does fifty-three mammo-grams a day at Mt. Olive's Breast Care Center. It's all digital now, though the machines themselves aren't any softer. I try to ask her a bunch of questions about her job and training and whether she dreams boobs, but she cuts me off. I know I'm number forty-six and she's got seven more be-fore she can call it quits.

Mammograms never hurt as much as people claim. Pinch, maybe, but not hurt. Honestly, there were guys I dated in high school—this one quar-terback in particular—who really knew how to mash a breast. I tell her that and she steps behind a Plexiglas wall and reminds me to hold my breath.

"So he really mashed your breast, huh?" she asks, remolding my left boob and pushing me into a new contortion. "This is the breast with the lump, right?"

I swallow. "Right."

"I'll pay extra attention to this one."

"Oh, joy."

"Don't worry. Eighty-five percent of lumps are benign."

Down from ninety so soon?

She lowers the plate so that I can't possibly breathe and retreats to the booth. We repeat this with the other breast until both are sore and throb-bing. It takes forever. Much longer than I remember. At last I'm asked to change and wait in a different room where the radiologist will meet me if necessary.

It's a small place at the end of the hall with the door open so I can see everyone coming and going. I have one plastic chair and a chart about breasts and various forms of irregularities with which to entertain myself. There's a box of bright purple Latex gloves and a white curtain.

There's also a ready box of tissues.

I've been here before, I think, swinging my legs, trying to be grateful that the days of waiting for a phone call from the radiologist are over. We've really come far thanks to those pink ribbons and road races. This is the result: an entire hospital wing devoted to breast issues and a more sensitive medical community that realizes women need to know, fast.

Has it always taken this long? In the past, the radiologist—often a balding man with a bow tie—comes down the hall immediately, asks a few perfunctory questions about family history, and advises me to keep up the annual screening. It's such a relief. As if MasterCard called up and told me to forget about my $5,000 balance.

But this . . . this is too long.

I debate calling Liza, a ridiculous idea since she's in Italy. I even think of calling my ex-husband, Donald, since he's a doctor. The truth is, there's only one person I need right now. And she and I aren't exactly on speaking terms.

"Mrs. Mueller?"

That's right. How did he guess?

I look up. A short, somewhat handsome man with wavy brown hair is smiling at me, maintaining perfect eye contact.

"*Ms.* Mueller," I say. "Are you . . . ?"

He sticks out his hand. "Dr. Horton. I'm with the center."

It's then that I notice Sondra is standing next to him and that the door is closed. This is not what we did in April. The door has never been closed. I lean over to open it, but Sondra steps forward and I realize Dr. Horton didn't identify himself. He's not just any radiologist.

He specializes in breast cancer.

"If you don't mind, I'd like to examine the left breast," he says, still smiling. "May I have permission to touch your breast?"

I fight the urge to burst out laughing, to act giddy over this carefully crafted request, the product of lawsuits and sexual harassment claims. I will do anything to keep stalling.

A joke about copping a feel crosses my mind, but for once, thank God,

I'm too frightened to say it. I simply nod and take my shirt off, then my bra. It was wishful thinking putting those on. They don't ask you to take them off when the mammogram comes back negative.

Dr. Horton palpates this and that. He looks away and mutters something to Sondra, who jots down notes. What is she jotting down?

"What's going on? You found something, didn't you?" The hysteria in my voice is embarrassing. I want to apologize for it.

He offers to let me put on my shirt and meet him in his office, but I grab his arm, forgetting that I'm completely naked from the waist up. "How about we get this over with now."

What he says next, I don't know. My brain seems unable to absorb it. Something about a mass on the mammogram and a lesion. Though lesion doesn't sound right. Isn't a lesion a wound? And then more reassuring stuff about most lesions being benign.

I don't know what I'm saying. Mostly I'm asking over and over again if this is cancer. Just a yes or a no. How hard is that?

"We don't know. The odds are in your favor that the answer is no," he says. "The question now is how to proceed. We can do an ultrasound, though all that will do is confirm we've found a lesion, and clearly we have. The next choice is an ultra-fine or core needle biopsy. . . ."

"What about a regular biopsy?" A fog has lifted and I'm remembering my mother's experience. *Ask, push, and research. Don't delay. Don't dither. Fight. Go all the way.*

"If the lesion is penetrable, then a core needle biopsy should tell us what we need to know. If it's calcified, then we'll have to remove the lesion surgically."

I think about this. "I'd like it done by the end of this week."

Sondra and he exchange glances. "If possible, that would be ideal. However, these are the summer months and with so many people on vacation. . . ."

"Please, by the end of this week. It may not matter to you, but I'm the single mother of a teenage daughter who needs me right now and, frankly, I can't risk another day."

He hesitates, probably considering his other patients. "I'm sorry. We're so booked right now that even next week is a stretch. The best I can do is next Friday at the earliest."

"Okay," I say, resigned. Take it or leave it.

There is more stuff. Paperwork and blood work and questionnaires about my family history and more questionnaires about whether I'd like to participate in a clinical study. Part of me can't believe it's happening, that the shoe has finally dropped and now I'm going through the screening process for breast cancer. And yet the other part of me is not surprised. It's as if I've been waiting for this moment my entire life. Like I'm prepared.

By the end of the biopsy prep, I consider calling Arnie to have him assign Ray's arrest to someone else. It's a fleeting whim, however, and I scold myself for giving in after a measly old mammogram. Shoot, there are cancer patients who go to work the day after chemotherapy. What kind of wimp am I?

Searching for my car in the vast expanses of hoods and roofs in the searing Parking Lot C for Mt. Olive, I think how nice it would be to have someone to lean on—specifically someone with broad, strong shoulders. I don't mind being divorced, but this is one of those special moments when a loving, caring husband would really come in handy.

Instead, as I get closer, I see someone better sitting on the hood of my car reading a book, her familiar straw hat shading her from the sun. And my heart breaks. My mother.

How did she know? How does she always know?

Chapter Nineteen

Kindness in women, not their beauteous looks,
Shall win my love

—THE TAMING OF THE SHREW, ACT IV, SCENE 2

As far as ex-husbands go, I suppose mine, Donald Bishop . . . Excuse me—*Dr*. Donald Bishop—is not the worst. I mean, he doesn't show up drunk and smash the windshield of my car and it's not as if he badmouths me to our mutual acquaintances.

If anything, Donald errs on the opposite end of the emotional spectrum. His feelings of anger and resentment, especially toward his mother, are stuffed in a heavy mental box, sealed for eternity, along with what little abundant love and sympathy once lodged in his cold black heart.

That he spends his days helping strangers open their own mental boxes is, at the very least, sadly ironic.

Sometimes I wonder what would happen to Donald's practice if his patients learned he abandoned his young wife and infant daughter and hid in his mother's Back Bay town house because he couldn't handle the responsibility of parenthood. That he did not stop by once for six months until I went over there myself with Em in tow and thrust her into his arms.

It's the threat of exposure, I suspect, that keeps him sending those $500 child support checks the first of each month, that dutifully brings him to our house every Sunday afternoon for an "outing" with Em— usually shopping. Now I hope he will go one step further. That's why I'm meeting him for coffee this afternoon.

It is the day after my mammogram and I'm waiting at a sunny table outside 1369 Coffee, in Central Square, right down the street from Cambridge Hospital, where Donald practices. Summer students in shorts and backpacks are giving me the eye since, without coffee or a partner, I cannot justify hogging the whole table. And just when it seems things might turn sketchy with a waitress ready to give me the heave-ho, Donald pops up looking nauseatingly preppy in a rumpled tweed blazer.

"Two soy decaf lattes, no sugar, Pippa," he says to the waitress. "And I love what you've done to your hair."

Pippa pats her asymmetrical cut and reminds him that with one more punch on his card, he could get a free coffee. Then she wipes off our table, sneers at the student who tattled on me, and rushes off.

This is Donald's forte, his charm. Though not classically handsome— especially now that he's bearing in on fifty and losing his hair—his manners and style are so winning that most women's first impressions are that he's dashing. He's definitely one of those men you love before you get to know.

"This is unexpected," he says, linking his neatly manicured fingers in front of him—body language for self-protection. "Is everything okay with Emmaline?"

I inform him she couldn't be better and watch with naughty glee as the question he really wants to ask plays on his lips.

"Then . . . it's not something with your parents, is it? Frank's heart is on track and Betty's cancer hasn't returned, right?"

"My parents are fine."

He sighs. "Then it's money, exactly as I thought. Look, I've tried to explain that I don't have as much as you think. Yes, we have the house in Newton and the vacation home in Maine. But Jillian is a stay-at-home mom and Angus is going to a private preschool. Those things don't come free, Julie, and it's not as though we have a choice. Angus is a highly intelligent child with a 190 IQ and his daily requirements are not like most children. He needs constant stimulation. . . ."

I let him go on, though internally my resentment inches toward the red zone. Em is a highly intelligent child, too, but he never bothered to consider her educational needs. And Jillian is, well, a whore. A lazy, self-centered whore who latched on to a man twenty years her senior and pulled every trick imaginable to land him as a husband so she wouldn't have to break another nail in the secretarial pool.

Again I ask myself, what did I see in this bozo when I married at the tender age of twenty-three? He has no chin. No *backbone*. Oh, right. Now I remember. That pink plus sign. That's what I saw.

"As for—"

"Donald." I lean over and cover his mouth right as Pippa arrives with our coffees. "Stop."

He turns bright red and as soon as Pippa leaves he scolds me for deploying embarrassing physical contact. "These are people I see every day," he says. "Have some dignity."

Ugh. "Look, Donald, I didn't ask you to meet me for money. Though do I think you could afford to spend more than $6,000 a year in child support when your wife spends that much in shoes? Yes."

He purses his lips and takes a stingy sip.

"That said, I do need a favor." Okay, Julie, here goes. "I wonder if you could 'surprise' "—I make my fingers into quotation marks for the surprise part—"Em with a trip to Maine next week."

A knowing smirk eases across Donald's pudgy lips. "It's finally happened, hasn't it? After all that waiting and worrying."

Horrified, it occurs to me Dr. Horton and Donald are friends and that the sacred doctor-patient relationship has been violated over fat-free yogurts in the hospital cafeteria. "How did you find out?"

"Please, Julie. I'm a psychiatrist. If I can't tell when a person is having an affair, then I should lose my license."

"You should lose your license then," I say, choking back a laugh. "Because I'm not having an affair."

"So you want Emmaline out of the way for your"—he lifts his shoulders—"knitting club, is it?"

"I want Em out of the way," I say evenly, "because they've found what appears to be a four-centimeter lesion in my left breast and they need to do a biopsy a week from Friday."

To Donald's credit he is truly dismayed. "Who's doing the biopsy?"

"Dr. Horton. I met with him yesterday and—"

"No, no, no." He shakes his head as only pompous WASPs can. "Absolutely not. You cannot have a Dr. Horton, a character out of a Dr. Seuss book, handle this. And at four centimeters you cannot wait until a week from Friday, for heaven sakes." Whipping out his cell, he says, "Who's your insurance carrier? Are you still in the Harvard HMO?"

"Hold on." I try to snatch the phone from his hand, but Donald, apparently having forgotten his own admonitions to maintain public dignity, keeps it out of my reach like a child. "I've got an appointment, Donald. It's summer and there are staffing shortages. Don't screw this up."

"Staffing shortages. Is that what they told you?" He sniffs. "That might be fine for the masses out there, but you're the mother of my child. I cannot risk you becoming permanently incapacitated during Emmaline's crucial teenage years. She needs monitoring and stability more than ever."

I sit back, flabbergasted by what's really at issue here. I am not a person in Donald's universe, a woman with a life to lead. I am the nanny of his loved but neglected spawn. When this breast cancer scare is through, he is definitely going to spend more time with Em, and not shopping sprees, either. Real family time. Whole weekends living, eating, talking, and driving together. Laundry. Homework.

"Okay. I give up." Pretending to be defeated, I give him the go-ahead sign. "Do your will."

Donald punches in a few numbers and, polite as always, walks to the end of the block to make the call. When he returns, everything has been arranged. "How's Friday?" he asks.

"I have my last dessert class. Can't go."

"Dessert class can take a backseat to your health. I've managed to get you in with a preeminent radiologist, a man who practically invented this form of biopsy, Dr. Martin Spitzer. Friday at 1:30."

Friday at 1:30. That's it, then, I think. That's when I'll find out if my life's changed or simply inconvenienced. In a mere two days.

"Thank you, Donald." And I say this sincerely. "The long wait was bothering me, I have to admit. It'll be good to know what we've got here. And you'll surprise Em this Friday, then?"

"Yes, well, I was meaning to ask her, anyway," he says with a pout. "You just beat me to it."

When I return home that night, the last person I expect to be sitting on the front steps chatting with my mother is Michael.

"Oh!" I say, clutching my brown bag of groceries. "Oh!"

Michael gives me such a knowing grin, I have to look away before Mom sees me blushing. "Hi, Julie. Long time no see."

"I meant to return your calls," I gush, putting down the bag of tuna fish, instant salad, toilet paper, and a large bar of extra-dark chocolate. "It's just . . . I've been busy."

In fact, Michael has called me every day since our lobster date and I've been too chicken to talk. I blame Liza for spooking me into worrying that

I'll let something slip about my mammogram if I connect with him in a weak moment—which has raised problems because, lately, my moments have been nothing but weak.

"Michael stopped by to fix the front railing. Isn't that nice?" Mom says, shading her eyes to look at a flock of robins. "Guess he was by here the other night and noticed it was loose. Too bad Frank and I weren't around when you stopped by. Or Em." Then she clears her throat.

Okay, what's that with the clearing of the throat?

"Your mother and I have been sitting here catching up on old times, haven't we, Betty?" he says with a wink. "She's been telling me everything I should do with my life. Must be a Mueller woman trait."

I'll ignore that.

"Lord, how he's grown. I'm so proud of you." Like a mother, she rubs his back in wide circles. "Seems like you're getting a bit of a curvature there, Michael. Is your chair at work okay?"

"It's fine," he says, laughing. "Next, you're probably going to tell me to sit up straight and eat my vegetables."

Mom says, "Did cross my mind."

Picking up the bag, I announce that, "I'd love to stick around, but I've got ice cream. Better get going."

"Here, let me get that," he says, coming down the stairs for my groceries. "I'll carry them up for you."

And before I can object, the bag's in his arms and Michael's taking the stairs to my apartment two at a time, leaving me to face Mom.

"He's a good man, Julie," she says evenly. "I don't blame you for having a crush on him."

Crush? "I'm not seventeen, Mother. It's not like that anymore."

"It'll always be like that for you. You've never loved any man as much as you love him. I only wish I'd realized it years ago instead of being a stubborn Yankee prude." Without another word, she pulls herself up on the repaired railing and goes inside—leaving me flat.

"You lied!" Michael says when I get upstairs. "There's no ice cream here. You just wanted to get away from me."

Kicking off my shoes and going into the kitchen for a glass of water, I tell him that's not true. "It's been a lousy week and . . . I'm not at my best." I wish he would leave until this phase of my life was over.

I want him to see the fun me, the pretty me, not the pathetic, anxious, frazzled me. "I'm sorry I'm not in a very good mood," I say, trying to be nice. "Right now, I feel as far from the perfect woman as you can get." *And what I really want is for you to hold me and tell me you'll love me no matter what.*

"You look pretty good to me." He smiles, leaning against the fridge. "But how lousy a week could it have been? Max tells me you made him a star."

I down half a glass of water and position myself so the kitchen table separates us. "He was a star on his own, and thanks for introducing me to him. Otherwise, we might never have found Amy's killer and I wouldn't be out of the basement of WBOS. I owe you. Again."

"Should we shake on that? Or will you send me a memo?" he asks, scowling.

"What have I done wrong now?"

"Look at you standing all the way over there, shooting darts. You've done everything but wrap yourself in barbed wire to keep me away."

"I didn't know you wanted to get closer."

"You didn't, huh?" Reaching in his back pocket, he pulls out a couple of nails. "These are yours, by the way. I needed some more for the railing and your mother told me to look in your toolbox in the back. I hope you don't mind."

"No, uh, great." Sitting at the table, I play with the nails, positioning them so they make a house. "Is that it?"

"How are the air conditioners working out?"

"Great. Thanks again."

He squints. "I love it when you go all monosyllabic."

"How's Carol? Did you find her Peeping Tom?"

"Ahh, there's the rub. Beware of jealousy, that green-eyed monster, Julie. It doesn't become you."

"I've got a much scarier monster I'm dealing with now, thank you very much," I say, not taking my eyes off the nails.

He's silent for a minute, waiting for me to spill. "I don't know what's bothering you and clearly you're not about to tell me. But whatever it is, you can call me any time of day or night to talk. And if you don't want to?"

I look up to find his face as blank of a mask as it was during our first dessert class. "Yes?

"Then get over it."

Before I can catch him and apologize, he's gone.

Chapter Twenty

Out, damned spot! Out, I say!

—MACBETH ACT V, SCENE 1

Two days later I am waiting to leave for the hospital and sitting in my living room watching Raldo mangle the story of Ray's arraignment on the noon news. It's surreal to see Ray, his head hanging sheepishly, enter a plea of not guilty when, clearly, he's as guilty as sin. I can't even think about Rhonda or the guilt she must be feeling knowing she allowed into her house a man who would later rape and murder her cherished daughter.

No peach cobbler's going to ease that kind of pain.

Punching off the television, I get my stuff together and am about to walk out the door when there's a knock. The familiar *tappity tap tap* of my mother, who probably wants to know why I haven't left already for the hospital.

"I'm leaving right now," I say, opening the door. "And I promise to call you as soon as it's over."

"You're going like that." She shakes her head at my jeans and white tee.

Neat. Clean. Nary a spot. "Sure. Why not?"

"Because you're not dressed enough for the limousine parked outside for you. That's why."

A limo? Really? How exciting. Rushing to the window, I climb onto the couch and look. There's a limo all right. A long black stretch limousine complete with chauffeur on the sidewalk waiting. Could Donald have sent that? No, that's impossible. Perhaps this is a service Dr. Spitzer provides to all his patients.

"Gotta go," I say, flying past Mom. "I'll call later."

"Hold on, Julie," she says.

I stop and look up at my mother, who is perched at the top of the stairs with her hands on her hips, wearing one of her crazy BIRDS OF NEW ENGLAND shirts. From this angle, she's as tall and authoritative as when I was a little girl.

"I just want you to keep in mind," she says, "that whatever happens—*whatever* happens—you will survive this just fine."

There's an ominous quality to this statement—as if she might be referring to more than the biopsy.

"I know, Mom," I tell her. "I love you."

"Ditto," she says. "Who sent the limo?"

"No one," I cry as the chauffeur opens the door and ushers me inside.

"No one my ass," a woman inside says. "This is pretty fancy shmancy car to be hired by a *no one*."

Liza!

Tumbling into the car, I throw myself at her, hugging her so tight I risk spilling the champagne she's trying to pour. Fortunately, Liza's an old pro when it comes to champagne and she manages not to lose a drop.

"Please," she says, extricating herself. "Not so close. I don't want to pick up cancer cooties." Her eyes twinkle mischievously. "I figured if you had to go to a stinky biopsy, you might as well go in style."

"You're the best." I'm still stunned. It's like I'm having visitor jet lag. It doesn't make sense that Liza's right in front of me when just yesterday she was in Florence trying to Americanize *Sogliola Cestello* into haddock and Cheez Whiz.

"What are you doing here? You're supposed to be in Italy."

"Right. I'm going hang around Italy while my best friend gets hole-punched." She hands me a glass of Veuve Clicquot. "Besides, do you have any idea what that country's like in the middle of summer? Dreadful. No wonder the Gauls sacked Rome in July. The Romans were too hot to fight back."

Having Liza here chattering away makes me realize how desperately I've needed a friend during this minor ordeal. Mom and Em are fine, but there is no substitute for a tried-and-true girlfriend.

"No waterworks, puh-leeze." Liza tosses me a tissue. "The way I see it, champagne can dull the pain of most troubles, right? So drink up."

"Right!" And we toast to friendship and hot Rome.

The champagne is cold and dry and deliciously soothing. I could really get used to this. How will I ever go back to Diet Coke and driving my own Subaru?

There are more Liza touches I'm just noticing: the bud vases filled with cheerful yellow daisies, the banner that reads 90 PERCENT! "I can't tell you how much this helps. You spent too much, Liza. Way too much just for a biopsy. Now if this turns into something more . . ."

"Quick," she says, "ask me how to make authentic Hungarian chicken paprikash with potato dumplings."

"How do you make authentic Hungarian chicken paprikash with potato dumplings?"

"Sautée onions in oil and butter, remove them, and brown chicken pieces on both sides. Remove the chicken, add back the onions, and mix with Hungarian paprika. Add the chicken, water, cover and simmer. When done, stir in sour cream. Meanwhile make potato dumplings using instant potato mix. . . ."

"That would be your Liza shortcut."

"Right. Just mush them with water like we used to do with Ivory Soap Flakes as kids and roll into balls and add to boiling water."

I tell her that's disgusting and she tells me that paid for the limo. All I know is Liza must have one heck of an accountant.

It actually wasn't too bad.

Not that lying still for a half hour while a nurse held my breast against a paddle while Dr. Spitzer went around punching holes out of my flesh is how I'd like to spend every Friday. No, I'd definitely have to say shoe shopping is a bit more fun.

And it would have been nice if, once they hooked me up to the machine, Dr. Spitzer could have slapped his forehead and declared it all a huge mistake. *Why, there was no lesion at all, just a smudge on the mammogram. Get dressed and go home, you silly girl.*

Instead, Spitzer parroted the 90 percent line and said not to move an inch. Depositing the tissue samples in bottles, he told me they would be sent to the lab, which should send back a pathology report on Monday, thereby ruining my whole weekend.

I told him this was the first time I'd ever paid a man to go to second base, and asked him if this was the beginning of my slide into moral depravity.

"Wait till you get my bill," he said as the nurse slapped Butterfly bandages over the biopsy sites. "You'll want to send me a Dear John letter."

I'm tempted to reply that I wouldn't mind sending him one now.

Liza's waiting with offers to go shopping or out for anything when I leave the hospital. Very wonderful and all that, but having watched Raldo butcher the basic facts of Ray's arraignment by, for example, asserting

Ray could face the death penalty when there is no death penalty in Massachusetts, has me more nervous than the results of my path report.

Right now, work would be the best therapy, I tell her.

"You and work," Liza says as we bid good-bye. "What's it going to take for you to get over that?"

You never know. All it might take is a bad biopsy.

Work is wonderful, though I don't get much done. I waste an hour moving back into my desk and returning phone calls, trying to ignore the pain emerging now that the Lidocaine is wearing off.

Arnie passing by does a double take. "I thought I gave you the day off."

"I couldn't stay away from you or your charming personality."

He gestures for me to follow him to his office. Probably he wants to analyze the chances of the Sox beating the Mariners tonight, that's how serious he looks.

But I'm wrong. Once inside, Arnie pulls the shades to his glass walls and throws his tablet on the desk. "I'm going to come right out and say it."

"You love me." I bat my eyes. "I love you, too. Let's elope."

"That mammogram wasn't good, was it?"

Shit. That's the last thing I wanted him to find out. There is absolutely no privacy in this office. Collapsing into his comfy chair, I say, "How'd you guess?"

"We went through this two years ago with my wife, June," he says. "It was hell for a week or so, but she was fine. The waiting's the bitch."

"Yes, it is."

"Luckily she had me to keep her spirits up." He gives me a weak smile. "You may not know this about me, but I'm a prince of a husband. That weekend we were waiting for the results, June didn't have to touch a dish and made dinner only once and that was because she insisted."

Meaning she was tired of eating hot dogs and beans. "How generous."

"That's me." Coming around the desk, he adds, "There's another reason I brought you in here. Valerie's not working out so well down in D.C., and Kirk's restrategizing. He wants to know if you're still interested."

Holy . . . I don't know what to say. Here I'd pretty much put that dream aside and now it's back. I feel like a kid who's ridden the roller coaster one too many rides and is now getting slightly sick.

"What about all the concern over my behavior with Michael Slayton? I thought that was the deal breaker."

Folding his arms, Arnie says, "Apparently Slayton called him this week and apologized. . . ."

"Apologized?" But he had no regrets about what he said. Why would he call Kirk Bledsoe and demean himself like that?

"Kirk said he was very gracious. They had a nice long chat and Slayton said you were nothing but professional in your coverage of the Fitz-Williams campaign. He also said that he'd asked you as a friend to tell him the details two days before the story ran so he could check out the allegations himself and that you had refused because you didn't want us to be scooped. Is that true?"

"Of course it's true. That peach cobbler incident must have gone to your head, Arnie. I'm not that much of a softie."

"Hmph." Arnie narrows his eyes and keeps going. "Kirk was pretty impressed with you—and with Slayton for eating humble pie. With that issue resolved and with the cobbler thing over . . . and now that you redeemed yourself with Ray's arrest, your star's fairly high in the WBOS universe."

Isn't that always the way. When work is high, my love life is down. And vice versa.

"So what say you? You still interested in being on the national election team?"

A shooting pain brings me back to reality. "How about we wait for the results on Monday and then I'll decide?"

Arnie nods. "Sounds good. I'll tell Kirk you need the weekend to consider, but I'll leave out all the gory details. By the way, got any plans? I could take you out for a beer at Duggy's and we could catch the end of the Mariners–Red Sox afternoon game."

"Sounds great, but I've got my last dessert class and I can't miss it. It's unending chocolate orgasm."

Arnie blinks. "You food types are kinda hard up in the sex department, aren't you?"

Chapter Twenty-one

. . . in the end the truth will out.

—THE MERCHANT OF VENICE, ACT II, SCENE 2

Michael's not there when I arrive at our last dessert class. Neither is Carol.

Actually, the class is pared down to the nuns and Chris the orange-haired foodie and her bald husband. Lilly Pulitzer, Michael, and Carol are off doing something much more exciting, I'm sure. That makes sense seeing as how they were in the cool ginger ice cream group to begin with.

Since the prospect of having to face Michael filled me with dread since our last tense meeting, I'm surprised by how disappointed I am he's not here. Or is it that I'm disappointed he *and Carol* aren't here?

That's not it, I think, washing my hands and quickly tying on the apron. Our lobster dinner was a perfect demonstration of why there can't be anything between us. He's looking for the "one true love" like a romantic teenager and I'm willing to settle for a house-trained dog like a practical, middle-aged woman. In the end, it all comes down to maturity.

D'Ours pulls out a stool and graciously hands me a glass of champagne. "I need to talk to you after class," he whispers in my ear. "Big TV stuff."

I get this sometimes. I suppose it's like being a doctor at a party when strangers start showing you their moles and asking if a pain below the shoulder blade is lung cancer or gas. TV is such an omnipresent, yet mysterious, industry to most people outside the West Coast that I'm often approached by the starstruck who are eager for inside knowledge.

"Okay," I say, and wink.

If the plate of discarded stems is any indication, I've missed chocolate-dipped strawberries and have arrived in the middle of the Grand Marnier chocolate mousse. Good timing!

"The mousse and the soufflé are much like cousins," D'Our says as the long-suffering Angela, bangs still midnight blue, chops dark chocolate into fine pieces. "One is baked, one is not. So for summer, I recommend the mousse. It never fails to entertain the unworldly."

"However," he adds, stealing Angela's chopped chocolate and whisking it into a bowl of heated milk, "when the temperature drops, there is no better way to welcome dinner guests than by greeting them into your house fragrant with the warm scent of baking chocolate. Can you smell it? Inhale. Drink in the perfume."

D'Ours takes a deep breath and we imitate, lifting our noses and closing our eyes. He's right. Deep, rich, comforting chocolate. Always reminds me of Monday nights when Mom would bake brownies straight out of the Duncan Hines box.

Emptying the chocolate mixture of eggs, sugar, and flour into a bowl, he slips it into the refrigerator, where it is to chill for two hours.

"In the meantime, let's turn our attention to the mousse. It is simplicity itself. Cream, egg yolks, sugar, chocolate, and Grand Marnier. With the added advantage that you impress your guests who know no better, having never taken my class. Though soon I will be in everyone's house!"

We laugh and Chris says to me, "He told us at the beginning of class he just got his own show on The Food Channel."

Ahh, no wonder he's in such an indulgent mood.

Whisking the yolks and sugar in a bowl, he slowly adds heated cream and then cooks the custard over low heat. Then he strains it through a fine-mesh sieve and adds a heavy splash of Grand Marnier before whisking in melted chocolate. Spooned into red wineglasses and refrigerated for at least six hours. Done.

The door slams and I whip my head around. A confused student scratches his head and backs out. Wrong class.

Too bad, no Michael. Not that I'm waiting for him or obsessing or anything. I'm only interested because I need to apologize for being so rude the other day. And to thank him for fixing Mom's railing. Nothing more.

One of my bandages itches and I try to sneak a scratch. D'Ours catches me and raises an eyebrow.

"The difference with the soufflé is we take it out of the refrigerator after two hours." He removes a pre-prepared bowl of soufflé. "Fold in the egg whites Angela is whipping."

Angela minding the KitchenAid gives us a wave.

"And then bake." From the oven he removes the soufflé boasting a perfect cracked top. I have to hold back Chris, who's about ready to leap over the counter and attack it with her spoon. We all applaud as the soufflé remains erect. Another miracle.

"How about we take a quick break, wash our hands, and come back for a taste test after this cools, eh?"

I am barely halfway off my stool when D'Ours pounces. "Have you heard my big news?"

"I did and congratulations! How exciting to have your own show."

"Still in the pilot stages. I am going to New York next week to do a couple of test runs and then we'll see. I am thinking maybe some local publicity might help, no?"

That's what he's after. A segment on WBOS. "Why not? If you can build a fan base here, then they'll be inclined to buy up more segments."

"*Exactement!*" He claps his hands and we exchange numbers and emails. Arnie's going to kill me for this. His two most loathsome activities—cooking and the French—on his show. He'll *plotz*.

We sample the mousse and soufflés before tackling the more heady *Torta Caprese* and profiteroles with dark chocolate Kahlúa sauce. These are the highlights of the cooking class, according to Chris.

"You want a chocolate orgasm," she says. "You eat D'Ours's *Torta Caprese*."

It's a little after 8:30 and still Michael's not here. I'd been hanging on to the possibility, however faint, that he might have been held up with clients or at a dinner. But no. Clearly he's avoiding me.

Well, too bad for him. He's going to totally miss out on how to make *Torta Caprese* and should he ever want to make profiteroles, he'll be out of luck. Not to mention his ineptitude should he attempt the dark chocolate sauce with Kahlúa.

Because we've been such excellent students and this is the last class, he's going to let Chris and the nuns make the *Torta Caprese*.

First Chris pulses blanched almonds in a Cuisinart, adds sugar, and empties the paste into a bowl for later. In the same food processor, she adds chopped Valrhona chocolate and sugar until it, too, is ground fine, later mixing that with the almonds. Meanwhile one of the nuns, Sister Martha, beats egg yolks and sugar until the old yellow ribbons emerge. That's added to the almonds and chocolate along with some almond extract and lemon peel.

As with the mousse and soufflés, beaten egg whites (courtesy of Angela) are folded in (by the nuns) and then poured into a springform pan. It takes all of ten minutes.

Chocolate + egg yolks + sugar + egg whites. I'm beginning to see a pattern here.

Despite the teamwork on the *Torta Caprese* we're almost out of time, which means D'Ours has to rush through the profiteroles. "I need someone to help me with the chocolate Kahlúa sauce." Ignoring all hands raised but mine, he says, "Julie, you're the only one who hasn't had a chance up here yet."

Actually, it's not that I don't want to help. It's that I've been daydreaming, picturing Carol and Michael hand in hand on a beach. Maybe my little lecture the other night pricked his conscience and he decided that sleeping with a woman he doesn't love was both sleazy and wrong. Which means he could have a) broken up with her, or b) done the opposite: tried to find out if there was some love there, after all.

"Julie?" D'Ours says again.

"Oh, right." I've totally missed what he wants. "Absolutely. Uh . . . what?"

Sister Martha rolls her eyes.

"Come, come," he says, leading me to the stove. My one job, it seems, is to keep stirring what's in the pot—a simple recipe of cream, chocolate, and Kahlúa—while D'Ours demonstrates how to make something called the *pâte au choux*, a fancy name for dough that's heated, and Angela is whipping up *crème pâtissière*.

What the heck am I supposed to do here? I think, staring at the pot dumbly.

"Just whisk until melted. Surely you can do this by now," Angela says as if I'm a child. "Here. I'll turn on the flame."

She turns on a teeny tiny flame and shoves a whisk into my hand with a strict order: "Stir."

Stir, stir, stir. I'm getting nowhere with this sauce business. The chocolate's not melting and the cream is still ice cold. Plus my wrist is getting sore, as is my elbow. Meanwhile, my classmates are over by D'Ours, laughing and refilling on champagne. This is so boring.

Checking the flame, I find it's almost out. Well, no wonder this is taking forever. How in the hell am I supposed to melt chocolate over the equivalent of a lit match? When Angela's not looking I bend down and turn up the flame full blast. See, here's the problem with fancy cooks. They're always taking forever, *simmering* instead of speeding things up with a boil.

"That's too high," Angela says.

"No, it's not." I block her so she can't get to the controls. "Trust me."

"Right, as if I would." Nudging her boss, she says, "Problem in sector seven, Chef."

"Please. Not while I'm putting out the *pâte au choux*," he barks.

Not to worry. Things are cooking just fine on my end. Tiny white bubbles are rising up the sides, the ugly lumps of chocolate have disappeared and it smells wonderful—cream and chocolate and that intoxicating overlay of liquor. This whole culinary industry needs an efficiency makeover, I think as I stir happily. If I get fired for real, I might look into that as a new career.

"Sacre bleu!" All of a sudden D'Ours is next to me, throwing a fit. "That's sugar and chocolate in there. It'll burn. I'd have thought you'd know better."

Behind him, Angela has her arms folded, victorious.

"It won't burn," I say. "It'll just cook faster."

The class laughs and D'Ours pauses, a funny expression coming over his face. "What did you just say?"

"I said it would cook faster."

"Julie, you are a product of the microwave generation," he says, removing the pot from my supervision. "Class, as amusing as our Julie is, I cannot stress enough the virtue of patience in coaxing flavor from the chocolate. You must treat it with care, with love, with respect. Much like how you treat a woman."

Chris is swooning, but I'm stuck on that microwave idea. Why didn't I think of that? Zip. One minute and you're done.

Which is when I look up and see not only that it's past nine and class is over, but that Michael has arrived, soaked by the rain outside, breathless, panting, and focusing straight at me and no one else.

All he says is, "Sorry I'm late."

"Why didn't you tell me?"

Michael takes me aside as everyone else lingers talking to D'Ours.

"Tell you what?" I say, snagging a filled profiterole for Mom.

"That you had a biopsy today."

"Oh." My cheeks grow hot and suddenly I'm self-conscious. "That."

"No wonder you were in such a bad mood when I was at your house. I feel like such an ass for not being more aware."

"Who told you?" I ask in a low voice, studying my pastry.

"Who do you think? Your mother. I stopped by on my way to the Cape to drop off a couple of books I promised her and she was at her wit's end because she hadn't heard from you and she thought I might have."

Brain slap. I should have called and left a message. "She wasn't home when I got home. And, anyway, there's nothing to tell. I won't know until Monday." My throat is tight all of a sudden, as is my chest. "Can we go outside? I'm feeling a bit claustrophobic."

Outside it's raining hard and I can tell my profiterole is a goner. There's no choice, I'll just have to eat it. Sigh. The sacrifices I have to make.

"You have to wait until Monday, eh?" The rain has ruined his expensive haircut, bringing out dark curls where usually there are restrained waves. "Then come with me to the Cape."

Half a profiterole is hanging out of my mouth and I have to—I know, gross—stuff in the rest of it and swallow it whole.

"Mum mid vou?" I mumble. "Mow?"

"Why not? It's just a weekend. Betty says Em's in Maine, so why not? Unless you have to work."

Oh, no. I made sure I had this weekend free. "I can't go with you. What about . . . Carol?"

His expression turns inward. "Don't worry about Carol. Carol's not in the picture, and I would really love it if you and I spent some time together. It's a great house in Truro and it would be just the two of us. No FitzWilliams campaign. No dessert class. No Betty. No Paul. For once, you and me . . . as adults."

It's the adult part that cinches it. That and the biopsy. Nothing like a four-centimeter lesion to remind you life is short, and offers to spend a weekend in Truro with the childhood love you've never quite gotten over don't land at your feet every day.

I tell him to pick me up in an hour.

Chapter Twenty-two

So we grow old together, Like to a double cherry. . . .

—A MIDSUMMER NIGHT'S DREAM, ACT III, SCENE 2

I wake the next morning with that disconcerting feeling of not knowing where I am. What is this airy room with its pale blue walls and bleached floorboards, the shells on the dresser opposite under a mirror that is too warped to reflect anything but light? And why does it smell like the sea?

Then I hear a chair scraping against the floor and I remember. I'm in Truro with Michael.

For a woman who never listed "wildly impulsive" on her résumé of attributes, going off with Michael—even if we spent the night in separate bedrooms—is a big step. And as I pull myself up on the cool white sheets, my left side registers a protest. Far sorer today than yesterday. I must have been insane to do this.

Oh, well. *C'est la vie*, I think, tugging up a pair of jeans and gingerly slipping into a sweatshirt. Face washed, teeth brushed, hair pulled into a ponytail, I pad downstairs to begin the rest of my life.

"Hey, you're up." Michael's in a ragged red T-shirt and navy running shorts. I never noticed his legs before. A shame since they're very nice, still muscular and taut. "I was going to wake you up and ask you if you want to go running, but I wasn't sure if in your, uh, condition . . ."

Now, now. We'll have none of that "in your condition" stuff. "Gee, that's a shame. I would have loved to go for a run," I gush, surveying the coffee situation.

"Really?" He brightens. "Because I wouldn't mind doing another one this evening. Running on the beach is the best in my mind."

"My mind, too." I give the coffee a stir. "In fact, that's the only way I run."

"On the beach?"

"In my mind. Many a morning I lie in bed and imagine what it would be like to be running. And then I roll over and go back to sleep."

He gapes for a second and then laughs. "So that whole running thing . . ."

"Let's just say I'll be with you in spirit."

We take our coffee out to the back deck that overlooks a green salt marsh stretching out to a blue bay. I drink in the healing salt air. No rain here and the sun is out along with an early sailor who's guiding a yellow Sunfish to sea.

"I once saw a real sunfish at the ocean beach in Eastham," I tell him as we grab two worn blue Adirondack chairs. "The fin was huge on the horizon and the lifeguard, to whom I ran hysterically pointing to what I thought was a man-eating shark, told me underneath the surface, the fish was probably the size of a Volkswagen Beetle."

Michael says, "We should do that."

"What?"

"Take a Sunfish out. They've got one here in the garage."

After taking a long sip of coffee, I say, "This is going to be one of those athletic weekends, isn't it? Not one of those 'let's putter around the antique shops and lunch' kind."

He acts horrified and I pat him on his bare leg and reassure him I'm game for anything.

"Anything?" he asks, cocking an eyebrow.

Which is when I remember our conversation over lobster during which I confessed I was willing to do anything when I was seventeen. "*Almost* anything."

"Damn."

It's strange being alone with Michael in that it's so easy. I'd have expected there to be some awkwardness like the other night when I was so snappy with him. But now that we've cleared the air, so to speak, I'm much more relaxed, and Liza's warning hasn't come true. He hasn't abandoned me like my father did my mother.

We spend the next hour or so drinking coffee and discussing this small, old, shingled cabin. (It's owned by a friend of his whom, I suspect, loaned it to Michael so he could take Carol.) We also gripe about how the Cape has changed since we were kids. Much more crowded and the beaches are disappearing.

Finding one of the deck boards is dangerously rotted through, Michael kneels down to pry it off. I can't help noticing how his shirt hangs off his shoulder blades and the muscles of his arms.

"This has got to be replaced," he says, lifting his head suddenly, catching me staring. With a slight grin, he adds, "Unless you have something else in mind."

"No. Hardware store." I leap up. "Top on my list for a weekend at the Cape."

On the way back from Aubuchon's on Route 6, we're distracted by a book fair in Wellfleet and a detour to the ocean. The freezing ocean, I might add. Our decking all but forgotten, we leave it in the car and walk as far as we can, our ability to talk seemingly as inexhaustible as our feet.

"There's something I need to clear up," he says after chatting about nothing. "When I was talking to Kirk Bledsoe, it seemed like he was under the impression FitzWilliams had fired me."

"Didn't he?"

"Hell, no. After your . . ."

"Incredibly insightful exposé."

He chucks a shell into the water. "After your hastily cobbled together slapdash muckraking . . ."

"Says you."

"I did my own investigation."

"Oh? And was I right? Is an apology in order?"

"Not so fast. I couldn't find any proof that FitzWilliams coerced those women into having sex with him, like you claimed. To me they were the kind of women who find politics to be an aphrodisiac, which is why they were on the campaign in the first place."

"I'm sure you know all about that."

"You know," he says, stopping me. "I do have some principles. It's not like I sleep with any woman I want and then dump her. In fact, that's why I quit the FitzWilliams campaign."

"You quit because women were throwing themselves at you and you were, what, scared?" I say as we start walking again.

He laughs. "In my dreams. No, I quit because when I confronted Carlos with my facts, my carefully researched facts—unlike some people's—he was alarmingly cavalier. His attitude was that sleeping with campaign workers was one of the perks of running for office. It was so slimy, I had to ask myself, do I really want to be working for a guy like that?"

"Even though he had all the right ideas and could have saved the public school system and ended world hunger?"

"I know. A killer, right? How come these visionaries can't keep it in their pants?"

"There must be a Shakespeare quote for that."

"Nothing except maybe the famous line from Julius Caesar: 'The fault, dear Brutus, is not in our stars, / But in ourselves, that we are underlings.' "

"The fault, dear Carlos, is not in our stars, but in our underwear, that we cannot keep it on."

Michael grins. "If you ever get sick of TV news, you could always look into a career bastardizing the Bard."

By the time we've circled back to the car, we've resolved to get out the Sunfish even though this violates my number one rule about going to the Cape: no exercise aside from swimming, walking, and biking for ice cream. Michael completely disregards me on this matter, hauling up the sails and pushing the boat out to the bay.

I've done my part with sandwiches and water and sunscreen, though my swimsuited body is covered up, anyway, in a sarong and button-down shirt.

"The sun's murder on my skin," I lie. It's not the sun, it's my skin I fear. All that cellulite.

As we push out to water, he gives me a look like he knows what's really up. "You don't have to be shy in front of me, Julie. We've known each other for decades."

And you've known women without an ounce of fat, I think. "I'm not seventeen anymore, Michael. A lot of water's gone under that bridge." And a lot of cannoli have gone in this mouth.

"You don't get me, do you?" We're out in the bay and he's doing what he can to pick up the wind that's died down. "Why do you think I invited you out here?"

For sex, is my first thought. "It's pretty obvious, isn't it?"

"What?"

"To cook lobsters. Not like you're going to do it."

A gust of wind comes out of nowhere and Michael has to hook the sail or whatever it is to catch it. Leaning way back, I miss the boom so I don't get conked in the head and, quick as a wink, fall right overboard.

Crap. *My bandages*! I think as my cuts sting in the salt water. Ripping off my shirt so it doesn't cling to the wounds and irritate them, I manage to loosen my sarong now drifting to the bottom of the bay. No way. I love that sarong. Liza bought it in Jamaica. Diving deep, I snag it at the last minute, hauling the water-logged cloth to the surface, where I hand it to Michael.

Now comes the fun part.

"It's better if I go to the opposite side to counterweight you when you haul yourself up," he says, smiling. "Guess I should go way, way, *way* over, huh?"

"I'm going to murder you if I live through this," I threaten.

In what I predict will be a tale to be retold at many a dinner party, I haul myself up onto the rocking Sunfish and beach the rest of me onto it like a walrus, panting. All I can think is how Carol would have looked in my predicament, like Venus on the half shell. Not Daughter of Flubber.

There's nothing to dry me with, so Michael starts to take off his shirt. "Keep it on. You'll get burned."

"Don't be silly," he says, handing me his shirt, anyway.

It is an incredibly nice chest, tanned and muscled, though not too. A good A side to the B side of his back. Until he starts laughing.

"I don't know which was funnier," he says. "You going over or coming back. For a second there, I thought the Sunfish was going to spin around like a kayak when you threw yourself onboard."

"That joke's getting stale, don't you think? Besides, I can't help it if you have a puny boat."

But I resolve to get him back, my chance coming sooner than expected when the wind completely stops and we are stranded a few feet from shore.

"Low tide," I say. "You forgot about that, didn't you?"

"Dead low." He shakes his head. "That's why everyone was out earlier. I'm going to have to go into the water and pull us in."

"Like the *African Queen*," I say. "How fun. Now, don't be slow, Mr. Allnut. It's hot out here."

With one last dirty look, he dives overboard perfectly and comes up to inform me that the bottom's not so far down, that he can probably drag it in.

"Mind where you put your feet," I say, pulling back the boom. The boat would be lighter and we'd get to shore faster if we both jumped out, but no way am I dipping my toe into the pinching crabs and icky jelly creatures slithering below.

"It's fine. What are you talking about?" he says, the water chest high. "Nothing but sand down here."

Uh-huh. "Don't look too closely."

Eventually we get to the point where I have to get out as well. Yanking down my trusty black suit, I jump overboard and promptly land in a patch of brown, hairy seaweed. Yuck.

The water's only up to my thighs, so I can see what's below, circumnavigating this and that until I feel the familiar lump under my arch. I stop. Move my foot to the left and to the right. "I found a clam."

Michael turns around, his hair drying into black curls. "What kind of clam?"

"A quahog. Gotta shell?"

He finds a huge scallop shell and tosses it to me and I begin to dig. Sometimes these can be razor clams that zip away before you can catch them. Or else—a crab. But, no, this is a huge quahog.

"Aha!" I say, holding it up.

"You need a license for that."

"I'm not going to cook it." And I toss it into the water with a splash, much to the consternation of seagulls hovering overheard. We dig around some more, finding mostly the telltale exit paths of razor clams and once a snapping angry crab. Then we sit on the beach and watch the sun dip into the horizon, leaving clouds of red and gold over Cape Cod Bay.

As soon as it disappears, a breeze blows down the beach and Michael puts his arm around me. "How are you feeling?" he asks.

"Cold. Sticky."

"I mean . . ."

"Oh, those." Peering down my suit, I check the bandages and find they're coming off, but otherwise everything's okay. "I think I'll live."

"That's what I'm counting on."

We watch a seagull angling sideways at us, checking for food. "If this turns out to be . . . cancer," I ask tentatively, "would you freak out?"

"If you're asking would I be like your father and split until the worst was over, absolutely not. That's not the way I operate, Julie. You know that. I love nothing more than rallying for a good cause and I can't think of a better one than you."

He lies down in the sand and pulls me to him so my head's on his chest and I can feel his heart beating. It's steady and soothing and I find my hand is idly stroking his thighs, raising all sorts of long-buried feelings within me.

"I wouldn't do that, if I were you," he says.

"No? Why, what will happen?"

"I might not be able to restrain myself and, trust me, right now I'm using all my last will."

Leaning on one elbow, I bend down and kiss him gently on his salty lips. He hesitates and then brings me to him, rolling me in the sand until our legs are intertwined and his whole body is wrapped around me. He's hard and strong, exactly as I imagined he would be, and I know that, after this, there's no turning back our relationship.

"Finally," I exhale. "After all these years you returned that pass."

He grins. "You have no idea how long I've wanted to."

"Really?"

"We've got a lot of missed time to make up for, Julie. So be prepared. From now until we leave, I'm never letting you out of my arms."

Night falls, morning breaks, it is sunny and beautiful and still we don't get out of bed except to drink wine, take showers, nibble food, and hop back in again.

I'd forgotten—or forced myself to forget—how great sex could be. Not just the *Torta Caprese* at the end but all the *crème pâtissiere* in the middle, bare skin on bare skin, the giddiness, the mindlessness, and hammering pulses. Even that male musky smell. Sounds odd, but I missed that.

But mostly I missed the sex.

Also, the heady, magical hope he might love me, too, and we had just embarked on a trip that would intertwine and change our lives forever.

The female temptation, of course, is to start posing this question by disguising it in casual conversation. Turning a basic question like "Where do you want to eat tonight?" into "Where do you want to eat in five years?"

We can't help it. That's what women do. We need to know where we stand. If, for example, when Monday's over and we're back home, will he stop by Carol's place and do to her that move with his thighs that he just did to me?

I can't bear to think about that.

Which is why, when Monday rolls around and we're cleaning up the cabin to go home, I pick a fight.

It starts when I call Arnie to tell him I'll be in late to work partly because I don't want to be in the office when I get the results. He tells me to take the day off, that he completely understands and, oh, by the way, have I given any more consideration to Kirk's offer if the results are okay?

At which point I step outside where Michael's fixing the deck, shirt off, his hair still nice and curly with flecks of gray. He looks up, winks, and I say to Arnie, "I think I'll pass on Kirk's offer. I've got too much going on here at the moment."

"You mean with Emmaline and such. I gotcha. It'd be a tough call if I were in your situation, too. My gut tells me you're making the right choice and, anyway, I'd hate to lose a reporter like you."

I don't say anything about this to Michael on the ride home until we've crossed the Sagamore Bridge in his BMW convertible and he checks his messages at home. Pretending to be thoroughly fascinated with a map I've picked up in Plymouth describing the various Pilgrim house sites, I can't help but overhear Carol's purring tones asking him to stop by on his way home from the Cape.

He clicks off and smiles. Nothing else. No "That was my old girl-friend, Carol. Boy, is she annoying." No "I'm so glad we had this week-end together because I realize, now, you are my true love and I'll never look at anyone else."

Just a smile. And a hum. He's humming!

"I got the job," I tell him.

He stops humming. "The one in Washington doing the national election team?"

"Your apology to Kirk Bledsoe worked, I guess. Only . . ."

"That's fantastic!" He puts up his hand to high-five me and I'm crestfallen.

"I thought Washington was a big mistake, that no one's your friend and they only invite you to parties to get you to return favors," I say. "That's what you told me."

"Yeah, I thought about what you said, about being a big girl, and I realized my lecture there was fairly insulting. You definitely should go. It's a presidential election, Julie. Who knows . . . it might get you on the network."

It might get me on the network?

"But that would mean I'd have to work in New York."

He shrugs. "So?"

"What about . . . Em?"

"Well, I don't know about kids, never having had one. But having been a kid, I can tell you that at seventeen your first priority is not your mother's address. Can't she stay up here and stay with Donald to finish her senior year?"

"Uh, yes. I'm sure I could talk him into that."

"Then problem solved. You're going to D.C. to join the national election team and at night I'll turn on the television and there you'll be, right in Katie Couric's spot. Congratulations."

I've been seduced! And hoodwinked and . . . used! This rat bastard just wanted to get me into bed. That was his goal when we were having lobsters and that was his goal when he invited me to the Cape on the spur of the moment so I couldn't back down.

You know, I wouldn't put it past him to have planned this . . . as revenge for the FitzWilliams debacle. Forget what I ever said about him being an idealist. He's a disillusioned idealist, in other words—a cynic.

Were I twenty years younger, I might have brought this up, verbalized the incendiary accusations darting around my mind. But I'm older and wiser now. I've learned the hard way that those types of confrontations only diminish the accuser and provide an upper hand to the scum.

No, if he wants to play that game, fine. I can be as cool and sophisticated as his other girlfriends, though inside I'm positively seething.

I'm so angry even when we turn up the road to my house that when the cell phone rings, I snap it open and bark, "Hello."

"Sorry," says an older man's voice. "I was looking for Julie Mueller."

Who is this? Turning the phone I see it's Mt. Olive Hospital. Oh, crap. The results!

"This is she," I say, my heart fluttering faster than a bird's. "Is this Dr. Spitzer?"

Michael parks the car and puts his hand on my knee, squeezing it slightly in comfort. I'm tempted to bat it off, but having it there helps me focus on anger instead of fear.

What Dr. Spitzer says next, I'm not quite sure. Something about "calcifications" and "checking back in six months." All I hear is the magical, wonderful word: "benign." No cancer.

"I told you," he says. "Ninety percent."

Yes! As soon as I hang up the phone, I shout it from the top of my lungs. "Yes! Yes!"

Michael's smiling and he might want to give me a hug and a kiss, but I don't let him. Instead I open the car, get my bag, and thank him for a terrific time.

"We should celebrate," he says. "You up for it?"

When, I think, *after you stop by Carol's?*

"How about I call you?" I make the universal sign of the telephone, slam the door, say thanks again, and tell him I'll be in touch.

Clearly a bit confused, he shifts into reverse, waves good-bye, and drives off, looking so magnificent in that car with those shades and that hair I scold myself for being so naïve as to think a man like him could want to keep a tired old horse like me.

"Is it good news?" Teenie asks, tottering across the street in lime-green capris and sneakers. "If you're here, it must be good."

Mom must have told her about my lump and subsequent tests. Oh, well. Can't stuff that genie back in the bottle.

"Good news, absolutely. Everything's clear."

"That's such a relief." Teenie clasps her hand across her tiny, sunken chest. "I've been worrying all day. I told Lois I wanted to go to the hospital, too, but she said I should stay here in case you got home."

There have been times when I've known or felt awful events before actually hearing the words. Like when the Watertown Preschool called to say that Em had had an accident and I knew, instinctively, that it wasn't any old accident like a scraped knee or a black eye and I was right. She'd broken her collarbone.

Or then, when she was older, with a stomachache that the doctor on the other end of the line assured me was the flu and a nagging voice inside disagreed. So I rushed her to the hospital feeling foolish and determined to get her to Mt. Olive, where Em's appendix was removed an hour from bursting.

This is one of those times.

Dad has had a heart attack.

"Teenie," I say, dropping my suitcase. "Where's Dad?"

"At the hospital, of course," she says, "with Lois."

With Lois? But why would he be with Lois when. . . . All of a sudden, my whole body begins to shake. I can barely say the word. Surely, they would have found a way to get in touch with me. "Em?"

"Frank told Emmaline to stay in Maine. What's wrong with you, Julie? You said it was good news." Teenie is coming toward me, her bright orange hair with its gray roots silly, clown silly. "It's the shock of it, isn't it? I remember when my own mother passed on . . ."

My hands have somehow landed on Teenie's tiny shoulders and Teenie's mouth is open in horror. Mom couldn't have died. She couldn't have. I just saw her Friday when I breezed past her to go to the limo . . . and I never got to tell her about the test results.

"My mother . . . she's not . . ."

"Oh, no!" Teenie lets out a gasp. "Your mother collapsed in the garden this morning. The paramedics came. I talked to your father an hour ago and he says it probably was a stroke."

"A stroke!" I know nothing about strokes. People survive them, don't they? "Is it bad?"

"They don't know. It's still early." Then Teenie reaches up and with her withered little hands removes mine from her shoulders. "This is not where you should be, Julie. Go to Mt. Olive. Go take care of your mother."

Chapter Twenty-three

I wasted time, and now doth time waste me

—RICHARD II, ACT V, SCENE 5

She's alive. She's alive. She's alive.

That's my mantra as I (finally!) get to Mt. Olive and (finally!) find a parking space. Something in the universe has shifted. I sense it, that the blissful era I took for granted in which my mother was resilient and healthy is forever gone.

More than ever I need to be in control and calm. I need to show everyone—including Dad and especially Mom—that this is no big deal. People recover from strokes all the time and go on to lead productive lives.

"Betty Mueller. I'm not seeing her on my sheet." An ancient volunteer at the patient inquiry desk runs a finger down a list of names. Don't they have computers for this? "Are you sure she's been admitted?"

A dart of panic surges through me. Nonsense. There'll be none of that mom-is-dying thinking, I tell myself, asking the snow white–haired man if perhaps my mother is under Elizabeth Mueller, only to find that he thought I'd said Nooler. (A first. Never have I or anyone in my family been confused for "Noolers.")

"Intensive care," he says, patting the sheets on his clipboard. "Third floor."

Intensive care? Somehow, I'd have expected her to be in recovery. Blindly, I follow the signs to intensive care, through the artificial normalcy of the lower lobby to the more intimate upper lobby where patients wearing light blue cotton robes hobble with the aid of loved ones and new mothers practice walking again at the insistence of taskmaster nurses.

"You're Mrs. Mueller's daughter?" a nurse asks, flipping through her checklists.

"Yes. Julie Mueller."

The nurse's name tag says A. ARONSON, RN, MS, ICU. I want to know her first name. I want her to tell me Mom's going to be just fine as she leads me down the circular hallway, past the other rooms with high metal beds and blinking machines, past other sagas and family tragedies in the making.

"Your mother came to us only an hour ago and she's scheduled for another MRI, so I'm not fully up to speed on her condition. She's asleep right now. Your father's with her."

"Is she going to be okay?" What a child I sound like. What an idiotic baby.

"It's a bleeding stroke, what we call a hemorrhagic—"

"Excuse me." I stop her outside the door. "It *is* or it *was* a bleeding stroke?"

A. Aronson looks up at me. She is tiny, but wise. Like every other nurse I've met, she's learned how to deliver bad news with the minimum necessary information and emotion, yet with steely compassion. "Is. Your mother's brain is still bleeding. That's why the doctor ordered another MRI, to see where the leak is, if you will."

"Ah."

Her brain is bleeding. This is incomprehensible, that my mother could be here, right around the corner, with a bleeding brain.

We turn into the room and I ready myself for whatever may come—which happens to be quite a lot.

There are so many machines beeping and blinking, so many tubes around the high metal bed that it's hard to see my mother in the middle of it, lost in the maze of technology. She looks smaller, shrunken, gray, and fragile, though the smile on her sleeping face is that of a child's.

This is what she must have looked like as a little girl.

The window to her right opens onto the green trees that line the Charles and, beyond them, the Boston skyline. A room with a view.

"Now, that's odd," A. Aronson is saying. "Your father was here a minute ago. He must have stepped out."

Not so odd. Though I'd have thought he'd have the decency to be here in the beginning.

"He knew you were on the way," A. Aronson is saying. "He told me."

Of course. That's why he left. I was on the way. He figured there'd be someone to relieve him.

This is when I'll have to set the groundwork, as A. Aronson checks Mom's vitals and waits a few minutes for Dad, who will never come.

I ask, "Do you know if the doctor's going to stop by?"

"Evening rounds start at seven, but if you want I can see if he can stop here first." She pauses and adds awkwardly, "We don't have you authorized as a primary caregiver, so the doctor won't be able to tell you anything without your father signing a waiver. Now, if your father were to sign off . . ."

"Nurse Aronson?" I begin, the rhythmic in, out of Mom's respirator suddenly noticeable.

She doesn't correct me or say "Amy" or "Alice" or "Arlene."

"My father won't be around until tomorrow. In fact, I'll be completely upfront and tell you that he won't be around much at all. He can't stand sickness."

Tucking in Mom's sheet, Aronson says, "I see. Well, I'm afraid those are the hospital rules and if your father won't be in any shape to care for your mother, then we should know now because we like to start physical therapy as soon as possible. Her primary caregiver is going to have a huge responsibility. It's not an easy job."

"I can do it!" Suddenly, I have a revelation: This is why the D.C. job won't work out. Not because of Michael, but because I need to take care of Mom. "I can cook for her and do her wash. Help her up and down stairs."

"I'm not sure your mother will ever go up and down stairs again."

Another icy shot of panic. "What do you mean? People recover from strokes all the time."

"Some do and some don't. It depends on the brain damage."

The hideous words "brain damage" hang in the air as A. Aronson goes to the door and closes it so we have privacy. "Look. I shouldn't be telling you this, but I think I have the picture of the family dynamic here. Your mother is very, very ill. The intracerebral hemorrhage she suffered was massive and probably not the first. Likely, she's been suffering minor strokes all along."

Didn't she see the doctor for a follow-up after her dizzy spell on the day I took her to the mall? I don't know. I was so wrapped up in my breast cancer *nothingness* that I didn't stop to make sure. If I had, she might not be here now. How could I have let her down like that?

"Her CAT scan and MRI show a significant portion of the right side of her brain has been, in laymen's terms, drowned by blood."

"What? I'm not sure I caught that."

She takes a breath. "The blood is cutting off oxygen to your mother's brain."

Nurse Aronson's nuggets of crucial information for which I hunger feel like bullets being fired at me from all sides. *Right side drowned. Intracerebral hemorrhage. Very, very ill.*

There is no hopeful "however." No "on the bright side," or even a mention of recovery. I feel not quite steady, though an inner voice—my mother's, I know it—urges me to stand still and act unfazed if I want Aronson to keep talking.

"This is a lot of information coming at you at once," Aronson says. "And I realize you might not be able to comprehend it. I admire you for not getting hysterical. Believe me, many people in your situation have before."

"I comprehend it. The right side of my mother's brain has died in part, which means the left side of her body will be affected." I am as clinical as she, forthright.

"By affected you mean paralyzed."

A beat goes by before I say, "You're joking, right?"

"Do you have a sibling or another family member who can help you sort through this? There are going to be a lot of decisions to make. Around forty-eight hours from admission the hospital's going to start asking you about long-term arrangements for your mother after discharge and I'm afraid that means a nursing home, unless you can afford around-the-clock nursing care. Which also raises the question of disability insurance. Do you know if your mother has any? The social worker will want to see a copy of her policy."

Paralyzed.

It can't be. They're wrong. *Temporarily* paralyzed maybe, but not forever. Doesn't the brain have the ability to rewire itself around bruised spots? I know it does. Otherwise, how to explain Bobby Newsome, who got hit on the head with a baseball and lay unconscious for three days when he was six and went on to become state representative?

Paralyzed.

My mother's left hand lies weakly above the sheet, her platinum and diamond engagement band ridiculous on those old veiny fingers. I want to wake her up and tell her this awful story that I heard about a daughter whose beloved mother fell in the garden one day and woke up paralyzed. I want her to click her tongue and tell me that reminds her of something that happened to Teenie's niece or Lois's best friend.

"Do you have a brother or a sister, Julie?" Aronson is next to me, her arm around my shoulder comfortingly.

"I have a brother, Paul, in Manhattan. He's a stockbroker and very busy. He can never get away. They work him to death." My mother's words. They come as easy to me as if she'd said them with my own mouth.

"If he were my brother, I'd call him right now and get him on a flight to Boston. If he has anything he needs to say to your mother, he should say it soon."

Chapter Twenty-four

There are more things in heaven and earth, Horatio,
Than are dreamt of in your philosophy.

—HAMLET, ACT I, SCENE 5

It is around midnight, when I'm waiting for my brother's delayed American Airlines shuttle from New York, that I realize I have completely forgotten about Michael and the Cape. Did we make love years ago or just this morning? It's all a blur.

I am going through the motions, recording each minor action so I can process them later when I am alert and sane. That is—if I'm ever sane again.

Here is the moment I've dreaded, waiting at Logan for my brother because something horrible has happened to Mom. These are my companions as the airport shuts down for the night: a couple of college students, an Indian man in a short-sleeved plaid shirt, a woman holding a brightly wrapped gift looking worried. This is what I'm wearing: a white scooped-neck T-shirt, and jeans that, unbelievable as it is, I put on this morning in

Truro. When I got out of the car in the Logan lot, sand fell from the cuffs.

I should have apologized wholly and fully to Mom. I should have taken back every bratty thing I said about Dad. Instead, I acted like an adolescent. (Em would have behaved better.) She needed me to take charge and instead I wrapped myself in my own petty personal problems—my idiotic obsession with landing on the national election team, my love/hate relationship with Michael, the brouhaha over bringing the cobbler to Rhonda's house. Even the mammogram that turned out to be no big deal.

If I could take back those weeks and redo them, I would. But I can't and now it's too late.

A fresh stream of stragglers drags themselves through the exit gate. I'm annoyed with every single one of them because I'm tired and haggard and haven't eaten since a bag of chips from the hospital vending machine.

When at last I see Paul in his gorgeous black double-breasted suit, his gray sideburns that are ridiculous with his boyish grin, I burst into tears. He is the only one who's in my place, who can share my pain.

"I know I'm a hunk, but you don't have to lose control," he says, slapping an arm around my neck. He smells like stale airline air and New York City metal. "Where's the nearest drink?"

"My apartment."

"And why am I not there?"

I tell him everything on the drive back from the airport, an ideal arrangement since I can pretend to keep my eyes on the road while pretending not to notice him quickly wiping away tears. In the Callahan Tunnel I drop the bomb that Mom has suffered brain damage and, on Storrow Drive, I gently inform him that this is more than a garden-variety stroke, that her left side is paralyzed with little hope of recovery

After that we talk about Em and his on-again, off-again fiancée, Scooter (thirty-five and she still goes by Scooter, I ask you). We are filling space and time with words as Paul tries to comprehend what I don't understand, either: that our mother might be dying.

At home, having changed into jeans and a loose Amherst T-shirt left over from when he went there (he's never gained a pound, the fink), he pours me a vodka tonic and pushes me onto the couch.

"At a time like this, drinking is a small, good thing." A spin on Raymond Carver's "eating is a small, good thing." "I forgot Boston could be so fucking sweltering in the summer. You're telling me Michael installed these air conditioners?"

"He did," I say, demurely giving my drink a stir.

"A man brings you flowers and chocolate, he's trying to get laid. He brings you air conditioners, he's trying to move in."

"Let's not talk about it."

Paul cocks his head. "Trouble in paradise so soon?"

"Please. Do me a favor and for the rest of your visit don't mention his name. If you see him, if you talk to him, which I'm sure you will, leave me out of it." My mind is reeling from his heavy hand of the vodka he'd brought from New York. "What is this?"

"Grey Goose. Expensive, but it's worth it. I can't deal with the swill you've got. So, is Dad handling this stroke thing okay or is he . . ."

"Not around."

"Not around? What do you mean, not around?" There's an edge to his voice and I see his right hand flex. "Don't tell me he's pulling that same shit as when Mom had cancer."

"We'll talk about it in the morning." Paul and Dad have a rocky relationship at best and there's no point in getting him riled up when he needs to get his rest and focus on Mom. "I'll make us a couple of sandwiches and then you can sleep in Em's room. She's in Maine with Donald."

"Donald." Paul snorts and flips through a copy of *Boston* magazine on my end table. "How is the pompous git? Has his buggering finally caught up with him?"

"He's consoling Em, that's how he is," I snap, and then, feeling bad about that, I apologize and make him the most incredible ham and Swiss cheese sandwich ever, followed by brownies Mom left for me in my refrigerator.

Like magic, Paul and I are back on friendly terms.

The next morning I wake to the sound of Paul stealing my car.

It's late, after nine, and my whole body aches either from the Grey Goose or stress or both. I suspect Paul's gone to see Mom alone, which is fine by me. Not that I'm the Mom gatekeeper or anything. Just that I know what it's like to want to have Mom all to yourself. He deserves that. She does, too.

I do the usual morning routine of checking my email while the coffee perks. When was the last time I checked email? Friday morning, before I went in for my test. A century in cyberspace time, I think, clicking through 123 messages, including a few from Arnie signing off on my emergency request for a leave of absence to take care of Mom and one from someone named "kittyluvr" about a "Dessert Class After Party."

> FROM: kittyluvr@bcs.org
>
> TO: Julie.Mueller@wbostvnews.com
>
> RE: Dessert Class After Party
>
> Dear Students of Chef Rene's Recreational Dessert Class:
>
> The Boston Cooking School wishes to invite you to a Dessert Class "After" Party at the Boston Cooking School this Friday at 7 p.m. to celebrate his latest creation: *D'Ours, D'Jour* to debut on The Food Channel later this fall.
>
> As a twist, we're asking guests to bring a dessert of their choice, either one made in class or a favorite family recipe. Also, please

feel free to invite friends and/or family since we are very eager to spread the news about this exciting TV show to be hosted by one of our most deserved chefs.

Until then, bon appétit!

Angela

That Angela? She of the severe bangs and midnight-blue hair—she's the kitty lover?

The front door slams and Paul walks in carrying a bag of bagels. He's wearing khakis and a yellow and white Ralph Lauren Polo shirt Mom bought him for his birthday last year. Nice touch.

"She's awake and wants to talk to you," he says, tossing the keys on the table. "You are such an alarmist. She's going to be perfectly fine."

"How did the biopsy go?"

This is my half-conscious mother's first question after I tiptoe into her quiet, darkened room. Her brain is still bleeding, her doctors aren't quite sure of her prognosis, and yet she remembers to inquire about the biopsy.

"I'm fine," I say, pained that I've been on her mind, so grateful for a chance to tell her myself. Sitting by her side, I take her good right hand and gently stroke it. "How are *you?*"

"Been better," she mumbles.

"You're going to make a full recovery, I hear. You're going to walk out."

Half awake, she barely stirs. "So no cancer?"

"No cancer."

She nods slightly and slurs, "I told you so," before falling back to sleep. Then I spend the rest of the day sitting by her side.

Waiting and thinking, about Mom and Dad and Em. About work and Michael.

Michael calls me every night to ask how things are going and if it's okay for him to visit. He's already sent Mom flowers and offered to help in any way, even pulling strings to get her into the best local nursing home—an inevitability I dread. The truth is, I'm not sure I'm up to facing him right now, not after overhearing Carol's sexy breathless message asking him to stop by on his way home from the Cape.

What's the story with those two? I have no clue. I'd ask him if I didn't think he'd spit back an obnoxious line about me being a green-eyed monster. So, for protection, I've shut myself down, tucking in my vulnerable heart like a turtle hides his body until danger has passed.

"I'm worried about you," he said the other night. "Why don't you let me come over or take you out? You can cry on my shoulder, or any other part of me you want."

It was a tempting image and I would have said yes if I hadn't been in turtle mode. "Are you going to the dessert class after party?" I asked, changing the subject.

"Are you?" The answer of a true noncommitter.

"I don't know. It depends on how my mother is."

"I can understand that" was all he said.

By the end of the week, Mom is sitting up and talking. It's a miraculous recovery, even the nurses agree, though I still haven't gotten used to how her body drops on one side like a puppet with broken strings.

"I'm hideous, aren't I?" she asks when I breeze in with exaggerated cheeriness.

"Of course not. You're gorgeous."

"I bet you say that to all the stroke victims."

That's the weird thing, how she hasn't lost her sense of humor. All week she's been making cracks about being a "lamebrain" and having a "stroke of genius."

"It was a stroke of genius," she slurs when her friends visit. "I always was a lamebrain."

Mom gets lots of visitors: Teenie, Lois, women from her Meals-On-Wheels program, even Liza, and once, when I was out picking up Em from Donald's, Michael. The only one missing, really, is my father.

Dad's line is that he has a new job supervising a construction site somewhere. What site? We have no idea. All we know is that he stops by to see Mom between seven and eight in the morning, before he "goes to work," and returns at five at night filled with stories about what bonehead employee accidentally lit his truck on fire or who dropped what.

During these evening meetings, Mom nods and smiles as if she's in the kitchen serving up dinner and Dad's relaying his report of the day. As if everything is normal.

But nothing's normal anymore.

"What happened with the biopsy?" she asks on Friday, four days after I told her the first time.

A lunch tray of inedible puréed food sits between us practically untouched. The nurses fret she's not eating, but who would want to eat that? Baby food. Mushed-up carrots, applesauce, and puréed white gunk.

"The biopsy went fine. No cancer," I say, dipping a spoon into the applesauce.

Mom says, "How many times have I asked you that?"

"I've lost count."

"Oh, brother. That's a doozy."

This is her new post-stroke phrase. "That's a doozy." Also, "Oh, brother," and, "Would ya get a load of that." As in, "They say if my next MRI is okay, I can go home. Would ya get a load of that."

I have no idea where these phrases come from. Liza says they sound like they're from her childhood, 1940s lingo. Next she'll be saying things like, "Hey, sister" and "Say, what's the big idea, big boy?"

"You going to dessert class tonight?" she asks, picking at a yellow blouse I brought her from home. My father told her she looked pretty in it and now she refuses to wear anything else.

"No dessert class tonight. Though there is a party for D'Ours. He's getting his own cooking show and the class is having a celebration." I hold up a spoon of applesauce. "How about you eat a little something so the nurses will call off their dogs."

She feebly opens her mouth and I spoon it in, feeling a strange sense of victory, like when I finally got Em to eat her first solid food of rice cereal. It's all I can do to stop myself from saying, "Good girl."

"You've got to go to that party," she says as I dab her lips. "Life goes on, you know."

"Well . . . I was thinking of taking Liza. She's got the hots for D'Ours."

"No, she won't get together with him. Liza's meant to be with Paul." Mom takes another spoon of the applesauce. I'm really doing well. "Aunt Charlotte says so."

"Aunt Charlotte?" I pause, empty spoon in midair.

"We talked about it when she came to visit yesterday. You know, what with Liza's wildness and Paul's reserve, they could be quite a match. Hey, that applesauce isn't half bad."

Perhaps I misunderstood. "Did you say Aunt Charlotte came to visit yesterday?"

"As bossy as ever. She wants me to go to Green Forest, where Nana went. Charlotte says the care there is top-notch. There are lectures and movies and cake every night. Can you call them for me?"

Okay. Stroke brain. Mom's other nurse, Nurse Kennedy, warned me about this and how important it is to reel Mom back to reality. "Look, Mom. Aunt Charlotte has been dead for seven years."

Mom wipes applesauce from her chin with her good hand, her droopy blind eye seemingly fixated on the floor. "No, she's not. She spends a lot of time at Green Forest reading in the library. Check it out."

"She's dead. She died in her sleep on May seventh, after ten years of battling breast cancer. I wouldn't lie to you about that."

"That's funny." Mom scratches her head as if trying to remember where she'd placed her glasses. "Well, she was sitting right where you were sitting last night. Even pooh-poohed the broken blind behind me. Said it was a disgrace. They'd never allow that at Green Forest. I can't even see over there. Is there a broken blind?"

I look up and, sure enough, there's a broken blind.

"Say, when you go to that dessert party, bring me back a goody, would ya?" she asks, as if nothing is out the ordinary, as if she hadn't been holding a discussion with her long-dead sister. "I'm jonesing for something really sweet."

Chapter Twenty-five

Sigh no more, ladies, sigh no more,
Men were deceivers ever

—MUCH ADO ABOUT NOTHING, ACT II, SCENE 3

For the dessert party, I cop out and bring one of my mother's quick refrigerator specialties: limeade pie made with cream cheese, limeade, lime zest, and a purchased graham cracker crust. About ten minutes to make and an hour in the fridge. So easy and quick, it's one step up from bringing Carvel.

Fortunately, I'm not to be outdone by Liza.

"It's a test," she says, drawing out a pan of cinnamon baked apples stuffed with chopped pecans, brown sugar, butter, cinnamon, and raisins. "It's from *The Hot Cook's Guide to Haute Cuisine, Volume IV*. Our entire future as a couple depends on his reaction to my pommes de Librecz."

"Pommes deLibrecz. You just made that up, didn't you?"

She scoops the apples into a serving tray. "He has a peach cobbler D'Ours. It's only fair."

Liza is smashing in a dramatic purple and silver silk sheath with a plunging neckline she picked up in Florence to go with a pair of Emilio Pucci crisscross sandals. Me? I'm much more reserved in a white skirt and green top to match my pie.

"We need code words," Liza says as we search for the "tasting room" where the party's being held. "If I plan on leaving with Chef Rene, I'll talk about the wallpaper I'm buying for the guestroom. If he's a total washout, I'll claim food poisoning and run to the bathroom."

"That won't be too obvious." The party's right ahead. Lots of laughter and music. "And what if Michael shows?"

"Without Carol, then you're leaving with him, no question. With Carol, then we'll have to round him up and force-feed him that pie of yours in retribution."

In fact, neither Michael nor Carol are here, though everyone else is, even the nuns who are surveying the dessert table piled high with the new old familiars.

There are two *Torta Capreses* and one almond biscotti tiramisu. Someone's brought a cherry crisp and a cold English summer pudding. Next to them, my limeade pie stands out like a hooker at a Park Avenue cotillion. All tarted up and frothy.

Snatching a glass of champagne off a silver tray, Liza sizes up D'Ours, who's talking to the woman known as Lilly Pulitzer. "What's her deal?"

"I don't know. I think she's a friend of Carol's. Not much of a threat. Want me to introduce you?"

Liza says, "I didn't come here for the tiramisu, that's for sure."

"Ah, Julie," D'Ours purrs, kissing my hand as we approach. "Just the woman I wished to speak with."

Liza shoots me a curious look.

"Actually, Rene," I say. "I'd like you to meet a friend of mine. This is Liza Librecz. She writes the—" *Owww!* Why is she stepping on my toe?

"I taught a class here a few weeks ago," Liza says. "Maybe you re-member?"

"I don't think so." He wrinkles his brow, confused.

"Let me refresh your memory." And linking her arm in his, she boldly drags him away.

"I was talking to him," Lilly Pulitzer says, frowning. "And she just . . ."

"Yeah. Liza's like that. I'm Julie Mueller, by the way." Extending my hand, I make a mental note to not slip and call her Lilly. "I don't think we've met."

"Deb Mundy." She purses her lips. "You're Michael's friend, aren't you? From long ago?"

So that's the cover, is it? "Something like that."

"He was talking about you at the last class. I mean, the second-to-last class. I wasn't here at the last one."

Chris passes by and proudly adds a spiced pear and Roquefort flan to the table. "The Crock-Pot pears," she declares. "Now he'll see what I was talking about."

When she goes, Deb hops right back onto the subject of Michael. "Are you two close?"

I'm not quite sure what to say since "close" has so many connotations. "Err . . ."

"The only reason I ask," she continues, fingering the pearls at her throat, "is that I've been playing matchmaker with him."

"Oh?"

"I'm a client of his, you see, and Carol's a friend of mine. We have children in the same class at Newton. Anyway, since her divorce she's gone through an awful ordeal." Lowering her voice and bending close, Deb whispers, "Eating disorder, you know. Hospitalized twice."

"I had no idea." I take a peek at Liza and D'Ours, who are facing each other, arms folded. "Anorexia?"

"Bulimia. She has a very unhealthy relationship with food, which is why this class is so good for her. Moderation and all that."

Moderation? What moderation? I could snarf down that tiramisu in one gulp.

"So, when Michael told me he'd won these classes, I had a brilliant idea. Carol and I could go, too, and that way I could get her together with Michael. He's such a super guy. I can't understand why he's still single."

Got a few hours? 'Cause I got a few theories.

"Turns out, my instincts were spot-on. They hit it off right away. They are the perfect pair. I'm so pleased for her."

"Me too." Never mind that the glass of champagne in my hand is about to be crushed. *Liza . . . get me out of here.*

"In fact," Deb continues, "they're out tonight and I wouldn't be surprised if he pops the question. Supposedly, he went down to the Cape last week to walk the beach and think about it, alone. Isn't that so romantic? Like something out of *Pride and Prejudice*. So Mr. Darcy."

The glass falls out of my hand and bounces on the carpet. "I'm so sorry," I say, bending down to mop it up before a waiter swoops in with a cloth. "You just caught me by surprise."

"Did I?" Deb holds out her arm and helps me up. "Well, then you caught *me* by surprise because Carol said Michael told you all about them. How did she put it? She said you two were as close as brother and sister, having grown up together. Is that true? Did you grow up together?"

"Everything okay over here?" It's Liza, eyes flashing, hair out to there, as if she just stuck her finger in a light socket. Behind her, D'Ours is glowering.

"I was just telling her about my matchmaking scheme," Deb chortles. "Did you know, Chef, that I brought two lovebirds together in your class?"

But D'Ours pays no attention. He's too busy heaving and panting at Liza, who mouths, "Michael and Carol?"

When I nod, she shakes her head. "I am definitely feeling sick to my stomach now," she says. "Obviously it's botulism."

"Oh, my," exclaims Deb. "Was it something you ate?"

"More like something she heard," barks D'Ours, the sinews in his neck standing out like twisted rods. "The *truth*."

Spinning around, Liza hisses, "How dare you? Listen, some of us don't have all day to reduce browned bones and broth into a Sauce Robert, did you ever think of that? Some of us have a life!"

D'Ours goes *Pfft*.

"Thanks to me, families can sit down to a healthy, balanced meal that's ready in under an hour."

"Under an hour." He sniffs. "As if that's cooking. Dog food, that's what takes under an hour. Open a can—voilà!"

"That's outrageous! Don't you think what he just said is outrageous, Julie?" Liza screeches.

I don't care. I just want to get out of here and away from any connection to Michael and Carol. It can't be true. He would have said something if he were going to propose to her. How could he not? Unless he didn't want to upset me, considering Mom's condition. Still, it doesn't make sense.

"I'll meet you outside," Liza says, brushing past me. "I'm feeling sicker every minute." Deb, now concerned that she might have eaten something bad, too, follows on her heels.

"Good. I'm glad they're gone," D'Ours says to me. "It was you I wanted to speak with, alone, anyway."

I keep an eye on Liza, who's been distracted by another glass of champagne. Some case of food poisoning. "I really should go. She's my friend, you know."

"Ah, don't bother about her. Her pride is hurt, but I will give her a call and patch things up."

"You will?"

"Sure. Why not?" He wiggles his head. "She may be the best example of why American cuisine is an oxymoron, but she is pretty and she has feist."

Feist. A new word.

"Though, perhaps you're right. Maybe this is a bad time and you're not ready to hear my idea about coming to work with me on the cooking show."

"You want me to work *with* you?" Momentarily, Liza and Michael fall from my thoughts. A new job away from TV news. Though that would probably mean publicity, right? Public relations, advance work. Was I ready to sell out my journalism career and do, *gulp*, PR?

"If you're interested, I will tell you. But you should know, this is very, um, shaky," he's saying. "My producers have given me no assurances that this show will go beyond the pilot stage or that, if it does, we will be picked up for more seasons. I am learning very fast that this business is touch and go. Up one day, down the next."

"Yes?" This might be the break I need to wean myself from TV journalism. "If it's public relations you're interested in, I think I could do it. I have lots of contacts across several markets and . . ."

"Public relations?" He arches his French eyebrow. "No. I want you to cook on the show . . . with me."

Is he joking? "I can't cook. I couldn't even roll out a piecrust or make chocolate sauce. I was the worst student you had."

"*Exactement!* That is why you are so ideal. You have experience in front of the camera and you are horrible." He said this by dropping the "h," as in *'orrible.* "Horrible at cooking. You are virtually without skill."

Now wait a minute, buddy, I want to say. That limeade pie didn't just make itself.

"You see," he goes on, leaning closer. "All these shows on The Food Channel are centered on chefs demonstrating how easy it is to make a steak au poivre. Pepper, some shallots in butter and cream, easy, no? And while, yes, I agree it is easy for them, it is not so easy for their viewers, no?"

"No," I agree, thinking, *What the hell is a steak au poivre?*

"So if I had you on the show fumbling and bumbling, turning up heat as you did with the chocolate sauce and making a total disaster, it would add some . . ."

"Comedy," I finish for him.

"And also education." He holds up a finger. "That is very important. People will recognize you. They will . . . how do you say . . ."

"Relate."

"And they will see that they, too, being bumblers and fumblers in the kitchen, can make steak au poivre, not just the expert like me. Plus, if it's your family obligations, you need not worry. I will require you go to California only two weeks at the most out of the month and whatever you're earning at your television station, I will more than double it."

This is stunning, a reversal of fortune. An unexpected swirl of events to play Jerry Lewis to his Dean Martin. A fumbling and bumbling assistant. It's so . . . *French.*

"But mostly," I say, "you want me for the comedy."

He shrugs. "*Oui.* So you will let me know?"

"By next week. First, I have to tie up a few loose ends."

Chapter Twenty-six

Sweets to the sweet: farewell!

—HAMLET, ACT V, SCENE 1

Several days before Mom's supposed to be released, Paul and I find a nursing home. Riverhead Elder Center. It's not ideal—it never is, when you have to put your mother's name down among many as just another anonymous person to be cared for—but it is better than the alternative: her going back to live with Dad.

Even I couldn't help her this soon after she's released from the hospital. There's too much "physical" work involved since Mom is still partially paralyzed and, well, not the lightest feather in the pillow.

"So much heavy lifting," Doria the social worker says, though we both know what she really means is that I would have to learn how to take care of my own mother's most private needs as if she were an infant. A 150-pound infant. "You've got to be trained yourself."

Indeed, I will be attending most of my mother's rehab sessions, learning how to feed her safely, helping her go to the bathroom, giving her a bath, checking her blood pressure, and administering various drugs once she's out of Riverhead. It's an exhausting assignment and my inner child is whining that I'm too young for this.

I know because I've been supervising some sessions already. The other day I was watching two orderlies help Mom out of the chair and found it so stressful I had to get up and walk away. So was seeing her try to take one step, one teeny tiny baby step, as she held on to the rails supported on either side by men strong enough to catch her if she fell—which she did, much to her discouragement.

During a particularly trying session when Mom is tired and fed up, Doria the social worker stops by and nods for us to go into the hall. "How's your mom?" she asks.

"Not good. She's getting discouraged and depressed."

Doria nods and brushes some lint off my shirt. "They've talked to you about depression, right?"

"Not really."

"It's a common complaint. Wouldn't you be depressed if you were her?" She juts her chin to the doorway where Mom, her right arm shaking, can't go on. "Keep an eye on that. You're not in any pain with a stroke, except here." She places her hand on her heart. "We have pills for that."

Doria's words come back to haunt me one afternoon when I'm hanging around looking at a magazine while a therapist gives Mom a reading test. The therapist points to a large word on the wall that says simply, SUN.

Mom squints and her mouth moves.

"Mmmm," Mom starts, bluffing. "Is it . . . man?"

I look up from my magazine, troubled. "She can't read?"

"That's what we're here to find out." The therapist purses her lips. "Not doing too good, Mrs. Mueller?"

"Not doing too well," Mom corrects. "Good is wrong."

The therapist slaps the pointer to the wall. "Come on, Betty. One more try. What's this say?"

Sun. It says sun. I'm practically out of my chair with agony.

"Can't do it," Mom says. "Oh, God, I can't read," she says, hanging her head as a lone tear drips down her cheek. Feebly she lifts her other hand, the "good hand" to wipe it away.

"Stop!" I yell, though I'm supposed to sit still. I know the rules. The therapist gives a sharp look to remind me. If I can't behave during these sessions, I will be asked to leave.

"That's my daughter," Mom mumbles. "She's a *good* girl."

I could say the same about Em during her first meeting with Mom since the stroke, a visit that proves to be a test of my abilities to simultaneously be the reassuring mother and unafraid daughter.

"Just remember," I tell Em as we pad down the familiar hallway of fourth-floor intensive care, "that your grandmother's still there, somewhere. It's a hardware problem, not a software issue."

Em, surprisingly tan considering Maine's tendency to be rainy and miserable, says, "Mom, please. Stroke. Brain damage. I get it. I'm fully prepared."

I don't know what happened to this kid during her brief stay in Maine, but she came back a woman, not the flighty flibbertigibbet who used to daydream her mornings away. Her suitcase returned neat and orderly, all items washed. She didn't forget anything, not even her cell phone, which she's constantly leaving at school or dropping in someone's car. And she has plans.

It stings to admit that this might have been Donald's doing. His psychiatric specialty is adolescents, after all, and from what little Em's described, he went out of his way to spend serious one-on-one time with her. They took the boat and explored a few islands, picked blueberries, and dived off rocks. He taught her how to water-ski and fish and, in between, he gently got to the bottom of her fears about college and her future.

Meanwhile, Em, being Betty Mueller's granddaughter, brought Angus to hand by imposing what he sorely needed—a schedule. Up at eight, dressed and outside by nine, swimming, lunch, reading, a hike around, dinner at six, bath by eight-thirty. In the beginning he held his breath and kicked his heels against her shins. In the end, he begged her not to go home.

Now I have this daughter, this strong, tall, beautiful woman, who is of the opinion that if she can take on a spoiled, hyperactive, indulged five-year-old for a week, she can take on the world. And I have an ex-husband who's finally seen the light and who wants his daughter to be more of a presence in his daily life.

We may not get what we want, when we want. But with a bit of perseverance and a lot of patience, we can get what we need.

So, emboldened by gifts of lime glacè and other "sweets," as my mother requested, I lead Em in to Mom's room. Mom is in a wheelchair, staring out the window, her left side slack, and doesn't turn when we enter. I can sense Em tensing with fear.

"Guess what?" I chirp, giving Em's hand a squeeze. "You're getting sprung soon. Dr. McKinley says one more MRI to make sure the bleeding's stopped and she'll let you go."

"That's swell." Mom picks at nothing on her lemon-yellow blouse. That blouse must be getting pretty rank by now. I should try to steal it for the wash, though I bet she won't let me take it off her. "Am I going to Green Forest?"

"No. Riverhead." She hasn't noticed Em is here.

"Aunt Charlotte will be disappointed. She doesn't know how to get there. It would be so much more convenient at Green Forest. Did you call?"

Em whispers, "Aunt Charlotte?"

This Aunt Charlotte thing has got to stop. The nurses tell me it's only her brain acting up, but it's gone on too long.

Finding that I'm naturally inclined to shout when my mother's like this, I bark, "Mother. You haven't said hello to Em. She's back from Maine."

"And I brought dessert like you asked." Em tentatively holds out the lime glacé. "How are you, Grandma?"

Mom swivels her good eye toward Em and breaks into a half smile of joy. "Emmaline! You're back. How was that naughty little Angus?"

See, this is what I don't get. As I set up the tray for lunch while Mom and Emmaline chat about the blueberries and Nadia's blubbery attempts at water skiing, I try to reconcile why one minute Mom's griping about Aunt Charlotte and the next she remembers Angus and that day when Nadia tried to learn how to skateboard.

"Emmaline tells me she's thinking of Vassar," Mom says, delighted. "Women's studies."

"Yes. Wouldn't that be wonderful?" Only the third most expensive school in the country, of course. The child always did have expensive taste.

Shaking out a fresh napkin and tucking it under Mom's chin, I wheel up a tray and present her with the array of gourmet treats. Puréed yams with ginger. Puréed broccoli with aged Parmesan. And, for dessert, the lime glacé with champagne from D'Ours's cookbook. A palate refresher, normally, but what the hell. I don't expect I'll be violating any Mt. Olive culinary standards.

Mom says, "You've bought a Cuisinart."

"I have."

"About time. Those machines are godsends."

I hand her the spoon and let her feed herself. She has trouble deciding which yummy Tupperware to start with, so I nudge the puréed yams in her direction.

"There's an opportunity . . . ," I begin, hesitating. "I've got a job offer."

Mom dips the spoon into the yams and then puts it down. "What kind of job offer?"

"It would be helping out on a cooking show." The way her brain works, I'll no doubt have to repeat this every day, so I should learn to keep it short. "It's with the chef who taught our dessert classes."

"D'Ours?"

Again I'm hopeful. Maybe she will get through this and be normal again someday. "That's right. He's getting his own show on The Food Channel: *D'Ours, D'Jour.*"

"What will you do?"

Em blurts, "She's going to cook. Can you believe it?"

Mom glances at Em in disbelief. "You're pulling my leg."

"No, I'm totally serious, Grandma. D'Ours thinks viewers will relate to Mom and do you know why?"

"Why?"

"Because she's so bad."

My mother's body convulses softly. It's laughter! When was the last time I saw my mother laugh? "Your mother's such a bad cook," she echoes. "It's funny because it's true."

"Not so fast, you two," I say, lifting Saran Wrap off the lime glacé. "Try this. It's from his cookbook."

"Do I dare?" Mom asks, playing up to Em.

"What have you got to lose?" Em says, and I wince. Tasteless, Em, tasteless.

But Mom doesn't mind. Shooting a finger at her, she says, "Right you are. I can't get much worse. Okay, I'll try it."

Dipping into the glacé, Mom tries a bit and nods. "Very good. You might not be so bad on that show as you think, Julie."

Actually, I think I've improved quite a bit, thank you very much. But no matter, there are more pressing issues to deal with today.

"The thing is, Mom," I say. "I'd have to be gone two weeks for every month to live in L.A."

Mom points the spoon at Em. "What about Emmaline?"

"Oh, I'm cool," Em volunteers. "Dad and I worked it all out and it's not like I'll have to change schools. Mom's more worried about you, Grandma."

"She is?" Her one eye goes wide. "That's silly. Go. Go." She shushes me with her good hand. "I don't need you."

"Yes, you do," I say. "Paul's not going to be around. He's heading back to Manhattan any day."

"I don't care. I have Alonzo. He'll take care of me while you're gone." Helping herself to another, larger spoonful of the glacé, she says, "Is that champagne?"

But I'm still processing the Alonzo bulletin. "Who's Alonzo?"

"Oh, he's a little Italian man. Very delightful. He's in room 304 and sometimes he comes down at night and sleeps in my bed."

"Holy shit," Em cries, immediately slapping her hand over her mouth. "I mean, holy *crow*."

"Really, Mom," I say, alarmed. "That's weird."

"Don't be so shocked. I like it. He's very warm."

"Would you excuse me?" I get up and take Em aside. "Watch her while I go out of the room. If she starts to choke, ring the buzzer."

Em nods and I fly out of there, burning carpet to hunt down this Alonzo character.

Nurse Kennedy is on duty coming out of 302. I pass her and go straight to 304, but the room is empty.

"Something I can help you with, Julie?" she asks. Kennedy's a striking woman in her late fifties with high cheekbones and a proud demeanor.

"My mother said this patient named Alonzo in 304's been coming into her bed at night. That's gotta stop."

Kennedy clicks a pen and tucks it in her breast pocket. "Your father asked me about him this morning and I told him there is no patient named Alonzo. It's the same thing with your Aunt Charlotte. Your mother has a head injury. I know she can seem normal at times, but at others she's not thinking clearly."

"Are you sure he's not real? Because she says he's . . ."

"Very warm." Kennedy smiles knowingly. "You're mother's a kick. Everyone thinks so."

Mom as a kick. Who knew?

Em's reading a magazine and Mom's on the phone when I return, her Tupperware dishes barely touched—except for the lime sherbet with champagne. That, she devoured.

"That Liza," Mom says, hanging up. "Such a pistol. I'll miss her. Say, do you think Mario can fit me in? My hair's a mess and I'm embarrassed to have your father see me like this."

I don't understand her. How can she care about something as silly as her hair when something as important as her brain keeps short-circuiting?

"I'm sure they'll have hairdressers at Riverhead. And then, before you know it, you'll be home and I'll drive you down to Mario's myself."

"Not if you take that job out in California." Mom's back to picking at her yellow blouse again. "You'll be gone for good."

So soon I have to explain this again. So *soon*. "I will not. It's two weeks out of every month. Dad can take care you. Or Em will drive you."

"No problem, Grandma."

"I dunno." She looks out the window, staring at nothing. "Be a sport and wheel me down to the gift shop, would ya? Lois took me earlier and I found the perfect gift for Emmaline's birthday."

I remind her that Em's birthday isn't until September.

Mom lifts her finger to her lips. "Shh. She's right there. Don't ruin the surprise."

"You two go," Em says. "I'll stay here and wait for my prezzy."

"Atta girl." And Mom pats Em's knee as I wheel her into the hallway. "You'll never believe what Lois and I found, Julie. Sapphire earrings. That's Emmaline's birthstone, you know. A single pearl and sapphire combination. Very adult. The kind of earring she'll be able to wear at a black-tie cocktail party. She's turning eighteen, you know."

Yap, yap, yap. For a woman who's half paralyzed, she sure can talk your ear off, I think as I punch the button for the elevator and we head to the first floor.

The gift shop is jam-packed with stuffed animals, a case of cut flowers, balloons, and clothes to make patients more comfortable—socks and wraps. There are only a few earrings and those are rather chintzy-looking crosses and fake pearls.

"Pearl and sapphire?" The volunteer at the counter acts impressed. "Don't I wish. Afraid not. That sounds more like something you'd find in a real jewelry store."

Mom is handling a brown bear with a big red heart that orders LOVE! "They don't have them," I tell her. "They never did."

"They did so. I saw them. I even pointed them out to Lois."

"Nope. Must have been something else. Either that or . . ." Or you're brain is playing tricks on you again, ". . . or someone bought them already."

"That must have been it. Too bad," Mom says as I wheel her out of the store and back to the elevator. "Aunt Charlotte agreed they'd be perfect for her. She used to have a pair exactly like that and they were lovely."

Aunt Charlotte is such a presence these days, even I'm beginning to think of her as flesh and blood.

"Don't you wish you could push me down those and be done with it?" she says when we pass the stairs. "One push and all our problems solved."

"Oh, come on, Mom. Stop talking like that. You're not a problem."

"Yes, I am."

But then she has to ride the elevator with a fat man's butt at eye level. This is no way for her to live, I think. She shouldn't have to put up with this or being wheeled everywhere, eating puréed food, unable to read or even take care of herself in the bathroom. Not her.

Just the other day she was weeding the garden and making peach cobblers. Where is that woman? Where did she go?

There is a tapping on my left hand. It's Mom.

"Don't worry, Julie. This, too, shall pass."

Chapter Twenty-seven

. . . good night, sweet friend:
Thy love ne'er alter till thy sweet life end!

—A MIDSUMMER NIGHT'S DREAM, ACT II, SCENE 2

For the sake of Mom (and Aunt Charlotte) I set up Paul and Liza by offering to take Paul out for a farewell beer at Bukowski's Tavern in Inman Square. Bukowski's is a dive that works at being a dive and hardly the place to meet a blind date. He'll never suspect.

But I'm wrong. As it turns out, wrong on a couple of levels.

"How's this? Is the white shirt, pressed jeans good enough?" he asks as we approach Bukowski's flaming dark door.

"Good enough for what?"

"Your old pal Liza Librecz. I know that's what you're up to. Mom's been after me about her, too, and with this being my last night in town it had to be a setup."

"Then why did you come?"

He shrugs. "It's for Mom and, hell, ninety-nine beers. With that kind of selection, I could be happy sitting across from Rosie O'Donnell."

Something about Paul's adolescent shrug, his lanky walk, and the youthful way he pushes back his graying hair reminds me of Michael. Two men who were playmates now grown up and single. I guess being a boy was so great, neither of them wanted to quit it.

Inside, the music is way too loud as we search for three empty stools at the bar. Murals of Charles Bukowski and Anaïs Nin line the walls to emphasize that this is a writer's bar for hard-drinking (not necessarily hard-working) writers.

Liza has happily claimed four. Two with her shoes. One with her scarf.

Four?

"Fancy meeting you here," she says, twirling around, playing innocent. "My what a surprise. And who is this handsome man?"

"And who is this stunning beauty? Wait. I know you. You're Julie's little friend all grown up," Paul exclaims, kissing her on either cheek.

What's up with these two? They're acting like old friends and yet it's been years since they've seen each other.

"Have a seat, Julie." Liza pushes Paul down on one and pats the other for me. "You make a decision about that Parisian snob's offer yet?"

"Not quite. I'm still thinking about it," I say. "Who are you saving the other seat for?"

"Because if you work for him, I swear to God our friendship is over. Unless he calls and asks me out. Then it's fine."

"He'll ask you out," I tell her. "He said he would. I think you really flipped his switch."

"That's not the question. The question is can he flip mine. And I think we both know what switch I'm talking about."

Paul taps her on the shoulder. "Excuse me. I hope you're not discussing another man in front of me, your so-called blind date. Who is this interloper?"

"My potential future boss, Rene D'Ours."

"Him?" Paul acts disgusted. "But he's all French and hairy—at least according to his cookbook photo."

"So are bichons frises and they're sorta cute in a furry football kind of way." Liza leans forward, trying to get the bartender's attention with a wave.

Again, I ask, "Who's the other seat for?"

The bartender slides down, cracks a couple of jokes, and asks us what we'll have. Paul asks Liza what she's drinking.

"Czechva," she shouts because, amazingly, the music's gotten even louder. "It's pretty good. I drank it when I was in Romania, the land of my people."

"That's right. You're a Gyspy, aren't you?" Paul sticks out his hand. "Read my palm, Gypsy."

Liza squints and holds it up to what little light there is. "It says you're going to meet a tall, dark, and handsome man."

"Oh. But I like the other kind."

What is going on with these two? It's as if I've stepped into a play and everyone has the script but me.

"And . . . ," Paul nudges.

"And," Liza says, "he's standing right behind your sister."

I've been set up.

Even before I turn or feel his hand on my shoulder, I know he's there.

"Hey!" Paul exclaims, hopping off the stool to give Michael's hand a vigorous shake and pat on the back. "How are you, man? Long time no see."

I glance sideways at Liza, who ever so slightly arches a brow. "You fink," I mouth.

"Never forget. I'm always one step ahead of you," she says.

Behind me, Paul is introducing Liza, though she needs no introduction. I'm being rude, keeping my back to him, but I don't dare turn around. Oh, cripes. This is so typical of Liza. Always a surprise. Always a scheme.

"And last, but certainly not least," Paul says, "Julie."

"Hi, Julie," Michael says.

Twirling around, I say levelly, "Hi."

He's let his hair go, just like he did at the Cape, and he's wearing a navy T-shirt that I complimented him on because it brought out the muscles in his shoulders. But it's that intense look of his, those dark brown eyes, that get me every time.

As much as I don't want to admit it, as much as I never wanted to admit it, I'm still in love.

"Say!" Paul holds up his watch. "Look at the time. Have you had dinner, Liza?"

"Why, no, I haven't," she replies with exaggerated enthusiasm. "Would you like to accompany me to the nearest quiet bistro before our eardrums explode?"

"That sounds grand. I assume, Michael, that you can take my sister home. Liza and I need to take separate cars since I have to get up in the morning for a very early flight."

Michael, never lifting his gaze, says, "That's fine."

"No problem," I add. "I'll take the bus."

"Do you want to tell me what I did wrong? Or are you going to leave me to guess for another thirty years?" Michael follows me outside to the humid August night. "Why haven't you returned my calls?"

I keep walking, confused and unsure what to do. Here, I'd gotten my life in order by squaring my mother away at a nursing home and arranging for Donald to take Em two weeks out of the month if necessary. I was this close to officially quitting my job at WBOS and saying yes to D'Ours now that there was no other reason to stay here because Michael was marrying Carol. I was about to take a huge risk for a new adventure . . .

. . . and suddenly he comes back.

"Please, Julie. At least give me a clue, because the last I knew we were on the Cape having a great time with great sex and then, yes, I know your mother fell ill, but it's something else since then. I can't understand it."

We've arrived at his BMW convertible, top down. "Can you take me home? 'Cause the bus sucks."

"I'd be glad to. But . . . let's go someplace. I'd really like to talk, just the two of us."

He means no Em. "Em's at a friend's house. We can talk there."

The drive home is excruciatingly tense until, unable to stand it anymore, I say, "I turned down Kirk's offer to join the national election team, you know."

Michael nods. "I gathered as much with your mother falling . . ."

"My decision had nothing to do with my mother." We're parked at a light on Mass. Ave. Students stroll the night sidewalks of Harvard Square, young and unencumbered, never realizing that the choices they take for granted—whom to sleep with, what to do with their days, even what to eat—will narrow and narrow until there's no choice at all. Only obligation.

"I didn't accept Kirk's offer," I say, "because of you."

The light changes and Michael idles for a second before accelerating. "Why me?"

"Exactly. I shouldn't have expected you'd understand, considering you're satisfied to be a loner. Though I guess that's changing, isn't it?"

He must not have heard that last jab, because he says, "Do you mean you turned down that incredible opportunity just because you thought we had a future?"

"Would you like for me to hammer it in granite?" I throw up my hands, as if I could throw off the feelings of embarrassment and anger. "Yes. There it is. After all those conversations we had about me having a crush on you when I was a kid and you searching for your true fucking love followed by your bursting into dessert class with an impulsive invitation to the Cape and then our weekend of wild, passionate sex, forgive me for thinking that maybe, just maybe, we had a future together."

Michael says, "But I . . ."

"And then," I add, almost hysterically, "we're driving back from the Cape and you pick up your messages and there's Carol—gorgeous Carol—murmuring in her sexy murmur."

"How did you hear . . ."

"So you don't deny it! You're just a lothario or a gigolo or one of those Os, aren't you, Michael? Good looks. Big Ivy League degree. Fancy German car. Slick job as a consultant."

I'm on a roll, a train thundering down the track that cannot be stopped.

"And now, I hear you and Carol are engaged. Engaged! What's wrong, did I fail the Cape Cod test? Was I so lousy in bed you decided, eh, Carol's better and you passed on curtain number two and went with curtain number one?"

"Geesh, Julie. Will you shut up! You're acting crazy. I am not engaged to Carol. Not even close."

He swings up our road speeding so fast I fear for the Hatchett twins next door, who might be out hopscotching, and zips it into a space in front of my house.

"You're not?" I say. "But you two did go out last Friday night, right?"

He bangs his head against the steering wheel. "Are you always this insanely jealous?"

"When a man I've been sleeping with goes out with another woman the next weekend? Yeah. I get mildly upset."

"Here's the thing with Carol. She's nothing. She's barely a friend. I feel sorry for her, okay? She's a lonely woman with a lot of personal problems and I've been trying to protect her privacy by not announcing them to the whole world."

"So, let me get this straight. No Carol."

"Right. No Carol." He smiles. "Feel better?"

I think about this. "Not exactly. Because you were still willing to let me go to D.C., as if you didn't care."

"What the hell do you want from me?" he says. "Did you want me to say, no, Julie, you may not fulfill your life's goals just because we had sex for twenty-four hours?"

"Yeah. Something along those lines."

"Then what was all that grief you gave me for telling Bledsoe to fuck himself? You looked like you were about to cry when you were recounting that. As if I ruined your whole life because I refused to answer some nosy corporate question Bledsoe had no business asking."

"That was different."

He shakes his head like this is a complicated mystery. "I don't get it. I try to go out of my way to be supportive of your career and then I'm shot down."

"Look, this is not Zeno's paradox, Michael. It's—"

"That's exactly what it is," he interjects. "During this entire argument, it's as if I've been running to keep up with you, but to do that I need to run a half more than I did before and then run half of that, etcetera, until I'm back where I started."

So *that's* Zeno's paradox. I never quite knew. "I was going to say, it's not a puzzle. It's love."

Michael says, "Love."

"Yes." Might as well get it out and over with. "I love you. I always have and I always will and if you didn't get the hint over our lobster dinner, you lunkhead, I am your true love. Not some little pixie you're going to meet down the road. Big ol' me."

With a quizzical expression, he says, "How do you know?"

"I just do. Sorry, there's no formula or a text you can consult for the exact specifications of a soul mate, but I'm it. And now I'm going to get out of the car and go upstairs and make a phone call I should have made days ago. Thanks for the lift."

With that, I get out and march across the street to my house, where I pick up the phone and call the number of Rene D'Ours.

Chapter Twenty-eight

Alas! poor world, what treasure hast thou lost!

—VENUS AND ADONIS

Lois and Teenie and Em promise to keep vigil over Mom while I'm in L.A. Still, I don't sleep well the night before. I'm too worried about all the responsibility I'm leaving behind and about the next crisis. Mom used to say once you had children you were never free, but this is worse than two a.m. feedings or staying up to make sure Em gets home.

This is my mother here. The only mother I'll ever have.

Therefore, on my way to the airport I make a last-minute decision to stop by Mt. Olive—a risky move since my flight leaves at nine-thirty and, considering Boston traffic, I'm cutting it close by slipping in right before visiting hours are over.

Dad has left and the nurses tell me they've changed Mom's sheets and given her a bath. "Nice and fresh," says Amy, a young LPN with a bouncy step and a bouncy brown ponytail as we head down the hall. "Your mom told me it reminded her of being a baby, all clean and fed and put to bed. Isn't that sweet?"

I feel a prickle and brush it off as nerves. Among other problems, I'm not a very good flier.

"Hi, Julie! How nice of you to wish me good night," Mom sing-songs as I tiptoe into the room to find her nestled amid sparkling white sheets tucked in good. She's sounding better than I've heard her since the stroke. Light and airy. Even her slurring has cleared up to some degree.

"Did you get the MRI results back yet?" It's almost eight. They might wait until the morning.

"I did! And all is well. No bleeding. They say I could be discharged as soon as tomorrow."

Great news and . . . not so great. This is exactly what I was worried about, that she'd be switched to the nursing home while I was in L.A. A month of waiting and, bing, as soon as I step on a plane they move her. Murphy's Law.

"That's it, I'm not going," I decide on the spot. "I'll call D'Ours and reschedule this taping for another time. No big—"

"Don't be silly. Your father's here. He can take care of me. He's my hero avenger, you know."

Yes, I think dully. Does he even know where the nursing home is?

Mom extends her soft, wrinkled hand and clutches mine. "He loves you, too, Julie. I know he doesn't show it, but he's so proud of you, of the way you've raised Em and kept a level head after the divorce. You should try talking to him more. He needs you."

"Yes, Mom. I will." I give her a squeeze.

"And, Julie? Thank you for all your hard work. You've helped more than I can say."

This is so not true. I did squat. Got her a so-so nursing home for which Paul is footing the bill because, having been out of work a month, I can barely afford to pay *my* mortgage. "That's nice of you, Mom, but I didn't do that much. There were other places besides Riverhead I wanted to get you in and it would have been ideal if I could have swung a private nurse. Maybe if this new job works out."

"Irrelevant," Mom says, yawning so loud it sounds like a vacuum-sealed can being opened.

"Why is it irrelevant?"

"Trust me."

"Okay, I trust you," I say, relaxing slightly. The MRI is good news. Tomorrow she'll be settled in a nursing home and begin a new course of rehab. This might work out after all.

Over the intercom comes the announcement that visiting hours are about over. "I gotta go, Mom. I love you."

"I love you, too," she says dreamily. "And don't forget, love abides."

Backing out of the room is hard. I don't want to leave her and yet . . . I can't wait to go. I'm torn between my desire to see L.A. and experience something completely different and my responsibilities to Mom and Em.

I have to remember what Em told me this afternoon: that quitting WBOS and joining up with D'Ours was actually good for her because it proved adventure didn't end just because you were a mother and over forty. You know, I think she was sincere, even if the line did sound like it was straight out of *The Feminine Mystique*.

That's what I'm thinking about, women's studies, as I ride the elevator to the garage floor, turn the corner, and run smack into Michael. And Carol.

Ah, yes. Miss Universe wreaks her final revenge. I knew I couldn't leave Mom without paying a price.

"Julie! What are you doing here?" Michael says as if my being in a hospital where my elderly mother practically lives is so unexpected.

Nodding upstairs, I say, "Mom. Remember?"

"I know. That's why I'm here. I wanted Carol to meet Betty before she left to go to the nursing home. You know how important Betty is to me and, and . . ." He's embarrassed at being caught trying to slip in right before visiting hours ended so he could introduce Carol to Mom without bumping into me. He's even stuttering. "I, I didn't . . ."

Carol shifts her feet and looks awkward. I give her a friendly finger wave.

"I mean," he says, "weren't *you* going to L.A. tonight?"

Paul must have told him. Or, less likely, Liza. "That's right. I am."

Carol says, "You know what? I really need to go to the little girls' room."

"One floor up, to your left," I say, directing her to the elevator, touched by her decency.

"I know what you're thinking. It's not what it seems," he says.

"Oh my God, that's like the beginning of a bad movie, Michael. Please. Don't treat me like a child. I get that you're playing Dr. Freud to her Dora," I say, attempting to wedge past him.

He stops me. "Can I take you to the airport? That way we could talk. There's so much—"

"Sorry, Michael," I interrupt. " 'But love that comes too late, / Like a remorseful pardon slowly carried, / To the great sender turns a sour offence."

"*All's Well That Ends Well.*" He grins. "That's a second Shakespearean reference. I'm impressed."

He should be. I spent five hours flipping through *The Oxford Complete Works of William Shakespeare* just for a moment like this.

Now to see if all that hype about the magic of Shakespeare's poetry is true.

When I get to the gate, I find I'm the last to board and the flight attendants give me a quick scolding.

"Under TSA guidelines," an attendant informs me, zipping my ticket through the machine, "we're to deny boarding to anyone who is five minutes late to the gate. In your case I'm making an exception because it's the last plane of the day."

"Thank you and I'm so sorry," I say sincerely. "I was saying good-bye to my mother, who's in the hospital."

She gives me a sympathetic smile. "That's okay, hon. Better hurry."

I rush to first class, where D'Ours's people have booked me a luscious seat for the cross-country flight. It's filled with businessmen, though, who seem none too pleased with me, the late boarder who's obviously held up traffic. Then I can't find a spot for my carry-on and nearly bump my elbow on the head of the guy in front of me when I try to squeeze my case into a tiny overheard space. It's a total disaster.

"I'll put this up front," an attendant says, taking my bag. "Meanwhile, why don't you sit down and I'll be back to get your drink order."

Slipping into the aisle seat, I clip on my belt and try to get comfortable. Next to me a paunchy man pretends to be sound asleep, his leg definitely trespassing into my territory. Oh, well, at least I made it. L.A., here I come. Leaning back in the leather chair and extending the footrest, I wonder, is the flight six hours or five?

The flight attendant who took my bag returns, my bag still in her grasp.

"Are you Julie Mueller?" she whispers so as not to wake the man next to me.

"Yes. Are you having trouble storing that? Because I think I can fit it under the seat in front of me."

She wiggles her finger. "Could you come with me, please?"

Mr. Paunch wakes up and gives me the evil eye.

"Is there a problem? Because I cannot get off the plane. If I miss this flight . . ."

"It's a phone call and it's very important," she whispers. "Do you mind?"

My heart leaps. It's Michael calling to tell me not to go! I knew he wouldn't let me leave. Though . . . it's not exactly great timing. They're about to close the doors. "I can't," I say. "I'll miss my plane."

"Please," the attendant presses. "I'll take your bag in case. Just come."

Goddammit. Why couldn't he have said something sooner? This is going to hold up the whole plane and everyone's going to hate me. And didn't the person who checked me in say this was the last flight of the day? D'Ours will be furious.

It's stunning, frankly, that Michael can pull this maneuver, what with all the regulations these days. He must have leaned on one of his political cronies to make some calls on his behalf.

At the gate where I checked in, a flight attendant waits, holding the phone.

"Do you know if there's another flight to L.A. tonight?" I ask. She might as well check while I'm talking to him. Why waste time? "I really need to be there by tomorrow morning."

The flight attendant just thrusts the receiver at me and says, "Here."

I get on and say, "Michael?"

"Is this Julie Mueller?"

It's the voice of a strange man sounding very formal and officious. It's not Michael at all.

I have an awful thought: not only that **Michael doesn't** care whether I go to California, but that the TSA *does*. They think I'm a terrorist or something because I was the last to board the plane. That's why they pulled me off. I'm going to be arrested and thrown in Guantánamo Bay!

"I'm Dr. Mori at Mt. Olive," he says. "Your father suggested I try to reach you before you take off."

Blackness circles the outer reaches of my vision. My focus seems to be limited to the white numbers on the black phone. "No," I hear myself say. "No . . . I've got to go."

"Your mother," he tries again, "seizure . . . five minutes ago . . . I happened to be on rounds, so I was there. There was no pain. . . . It was very fast, Julie . . . I'm so sorry. She's gone."

Which is when I drop the phone and slump into Michael's waiting arms.

For the next few minutes I simply survive as Michael transports me from the airport to the hospital. For the umpteenth time he recounts, at my request, how he was waiting for the elevator having just said good-bye to Mom when he heard the codes and figured out what was happening. He left Carol at the hospital and drove to Logan to find me while Mt. Olive's personnel put in an emergency call to security so he could be there when I got the awful news. And he made it—barely.

My one relief is knowing Mom was not alone when she died. Dad was there. Michael, too. And, oddly enough, Carol. Though, for all I know, she might be the Angel of Death. I will have to investigate that later.

Dr. Mori asks if I want to see Mom before she goes down to the morgue and I say, *Mom?* That's not my mother. My mother is elsewhere.

Isn't she?

Michael drops me off at home and arranges to get my car from Logan. I think he kisses me on the cheek and rubs my shoulders and tells me he's there for me at any hour, day or night. I dunno. It's all a blur. All I know is that I have to be strong and do what Mom would want me to do: comfort Dad.

I find my father in the kitchen searching for the telephone book to call the funeral home. For some reason, he's rummaging through the silverware drawer and won't stop until I hug him, his once sturdy chest now hollow and flabby in my arms.

"Mom called you her hero avenger," I say, trying to remember every glowing word she said about him.

"I know," he says. "I was there. I was the last person she was with."

As it should be. Those two always did have a special relationship with their own rules and rewards. Mom said I didn't understand it and she was right. I didn't and now I never will.

Dad and I stand there hugging silently and I'm surprised to feel this man of steel and concrete who's spent a lifetime in construction bear his weight against me. But then it hits me: This is how it's going to be from now on. My mother's not here to carry him. It'll have to be me.

"You sit down and have a cup of tea," I say, taking him to the couch. "Michael called Paul and he's on his way from New York. We'll take care of everything. I'll call Teenie." Who is probably by the phone waiting and ready, I suspect.

"There are papers in the freezer," he says. "There'll be instructions on her arrangements and who should get her jewelry."

"The freezer?"

"In case there was a fire. Your mother had a theory the freezer would protect them from getting burned."

Freezer burn, I think as I pick past the bags of frozen corn and peas, the almost empty carton of Hershey's chocolate chip. (Mom never could abide the teeny Ben & Jerry's tubs for $4.49.) There, behind the ice trays, among the many frozen leftovers and frosty bags of chicken parts, behind a roll of her famous icebox cake, is a double Ziploc bag containing folded white papers, an antique diamond pendant that was Nana's, and—lo and behold—a velvet box containing a pair of sapphire and pearl earrings marked as once belonging to Aunt Charlotte.

Now for Em.

I freeze—literally—my hand on the earrings Mom had "seen" in the hospital gift shop. Aunt Charlotte. Was Mom *really* talking to Aunt Charlotte? Charlotte didn't want her to go to Riverhead. Charlotte wanted Mom to be with *her.*

"Find 'em?" Dad calls out.

"Found them."

I pull out the bag and read the label that could have easily been for

MONDAY'S CASSEROLE or LAST SUMMER'S BEANS. In my mother's careful handwriting it is:

THE LAST WILL AND TESTAMENT
OF
ELIZABETH HENDRICKS MUELLER

And so it begins.

A take-charge energy comes over me in the days following. I am Miss Efficiency signing permission slips left and right to have my mother's body moved from one floor to another, to have the Eisenhower Bros., Inc., pick it up and cremate her remains.

While holding Em, whose sobs rack through my body, rippling against my ribs, I plan the funeral from first reading to exit hymn. A service Friday morning at Our Lady of Miracles with a reception afterward in the Parish House. Lois and Teenie can arrange the food. I'll make the dessert. All of it.

"How come you're not crying?" Em asks. "I can't stop. I miss her so much. I can't believe she's gone."

"She's not gone. She's right here." I tap my heart. "There."

Though, really, it's more like she's in my head nagging me to call my cousin Karen in Texas and tossing out half my menu suggestions. Already she's nixed the banana pudding as too hot for this weather. Why not use the icebox cake in the freezer? Better eat it up now, she tells me, before it goes stale.

With Paul by my side, his arm securely around me, we go to Eisenhower Bros. and retrieve the urn of Mom's ashes and yet another Ziploc bag, this one with her smooth platinum wedding band and worn diamond engagement ring. I want to clasp them to my chest and never let them go.

But I don't. I hand them to my brother. He is her child, too, and she loved him with all her might.

"If you give them to Scooter," I tell him in a mafioso way, "I will break your legs."

He shakes the rings onto his palm. "I remember being sick and sitting in her lap, playing with these." He coughs and looks away. "It's my earliest memory. I can still smell that perfume of hers."

"Chanel No. 5."

"Church perfume."

I give him a squeeze. "She loved you most of all."

"Don't . . ."

"It's okay. I'm not saying she didn't love me. She had her way."

At my car, Paul opens his door and stops. "Don't say that. Don't ever say that."

"Okay, Paul. Chill," I say, holding up my hands as truce.

"She was really proud of you, Julie, especially of how you've raised Em. Not that she isn't a great kid. Just that . . . it bothered her to see you held back because you had to mother Em alone. That's why she wanted you to get married again, so you could have someone to share the burden of parenting."

This is so counterintuitive to my opinion of Mom that Paul could easily be discussing a coworker on Wall Street or a neighbor. When we get in, I tell him, "If Mom wanted me to get married, it was because she was devastated to have a single mother for a daughter. She was a diehard traditionalist."

"You got that all wrong. Mom was really into your career."

"No, she wasn't. Just this summer she was going on and on about how much family time my career had stolen."

"Yeah? Then how come she died when she found out you had a new job possibility that could pay way more than you earned at WBOS and get you out of the news racket that you hated? She was fully aware she'd be a burden while you were in California." He reels back as if he'd just said something he shouldn't have.

"Are you saying Mom *killed* herself? For me?" Talk about guilt.

"All I'm saying is that I've read really sick people can let go when they want to. It's just a theory."

Chapter Twenty-nine

Sweet love, renew thy force; be it not said
Thy edge should blunter be than appetite.

—SONNET 56

"This is insane!" Paul spreads his arms at the mess in my kitchen.

White flour covers all the counters and there are squished raisins on the floor. A pot on the stove is lined with chocolate and another with vanilla custard. Lois, Em, and I have been chopping, mixing, whipping, and baking nonstop for two days and two nights, following with precise detail every direction in my mother's barnyard tin of recipe cards, which, I've discovered, are not just clippings from *Woman's Day*.

They're eternal links.

Links to her. And me. And Em and all the women in our family before us—thanks to Mom's neatly penciled notes on the side.

Some are recommendations (*"less sugar,—1 egg, too sweet*!). Some are memories (*Made for J's 10th b'day. Big hit.* Or: *Nana's—Straight from Germany. Authentic*!). Others are observations (*Good for parties. Finger food. Too much salt, drove Edgar Banks mad*).

No wonder she was so proud of them. I had no idea. If I'd known, we could have discussed her notes and maybe she'd have remembered more. This is the thing about death that's so aggravating; there are no second chances.

"Seriously," Paul is saying. "This is what an insane person would do." He steps over a butter wrapper (not thinking to pick it up, of course) and dips his finger into a bowl. "What is that?"

"Coconut ginger ice cream." I take a swig of Diet Coke and debate what to do next. The cream cheese tart with fresh blueberries and a raspberry glaze or the *Torta Caprese*. Think I'll do the tart since the cream cheese has been left out to soften.

"Since when did you learn how to do this?" he asks, watching me unwrap the cream cheese and mix it with cream, sugar, almond flavoring, and a touch of vanilla.

"According to Mom's notes, I've always been able to do it," I say over the whir of the mixer. "As a little girl, I used to make tiny pies next to her when she cooked. She'd give me jam and a toy rolling pin to flatten the dough."

"I don't remember that." He tries to taste the cream cheese filling and I slap his hand.

"Probably because you were at school. Then, once I got older, I stopped. Until these dessert classes. They brought it all back."

Slicing a lemon in half, I twist it over a juicer, pick out a couple of seeds, and dump in the juice.

"It smells like Mom's kitchen in here," he says, leaning against the counter. "It feels like Mom's . . ."

Here, I think, spooning the filling into the graham cracker crust.

He picks up the tin and squints at the rusted cow. "Where'd you get the recipe cards?"

"She gave them to me."

"Oh, yeah? When?"

I take a pint of blueberries out of the refrigerator and count back. "Sometime after my second class."

Paul steals a blueberry and says, "That was also in the article I read about people being able to determine when they died. It said they give away things beforehand, too. Personal items. Watches and jewelry and stuff. Even car crash victims who have no idea their days are numbered do that."

"Here," I say, handing him the berries. "Just cover the pie with them and put it in the refrigerator when you're done, okay?"

Paul acts like I've given him a nuclear bomb to defuse. "Where are you going?"

"To get the mail."

Then I go outside and sit on the back steps overlooking my mother's garden where, for the first time since she died, I give in and collapse in sobs.

Like most of the week before it, the funeral passes by in a blur and feels more like an overdue family reunion than what it is—a marking of my mother's passing. Aunts and uncles whom I haven't seen in years, distant cousins and their strange children, carpool in from Waltham, where they've got blocks of rooms at the Days Inn. We say over and over that we should have done this before. It's been too long!

Lois and Teenie come, as do Liza and Rene D'Ours, separately, of course, but still sizing up the other. Not sure it works, but I'll have to weigh that later. Donald arrives with his wife, Jillian, and Angus, who toddles after Em with eyes of love.

There are Mom's friends from church and from Meals-On-Wheels, crooked old ladies with limps and cackling laughs. Paul brings his girlfriend, Scooter, and Em brings Nadia. Even a few cronies from WBOS stop by: Arnie, Raldo, and interestingly enough, Valerie, back from D.C. and looking slightly more humble.

When Dad appears, he's late and sits in the back of the church wearing sunglasses. Like a rock star.

The only person missing is Michael, who came to the funeral with Carol and then left. He and I haven't spoken since his rescue at the airport. There have been nights this week when I've desperately wanted to call him, but my state is too fragile right now to tolerate yet more heartache. What I need is unconditional love—the kind mothers are famous for.

But maybe I should have called. When he was leaving the church, he slipped me the most wonderful note.

> *When everyone's gone, I'll stop by the cemetery and say farewell to Betty in my own way. She was my ersatz mother, my rock, the person who laid a foundation for me to grow and in many ways she meant more to me than my own. However, I don't want to detract from you and Paul. She's your <u>real</u> mother.*
>
> *There's not much I need to tell her except for something she's known forever:*
>
> *I love you. I always have.*

As I stand in the receiving line in the Parish Hall, Michael's note itches where I've secreted it in my bra. I want to pull it out and read it over and over to make sense of the words. I want to call him and ask, for the umpteenth time, what our future holds.

But I can't. To be the only daughter of a dead mother means, for a while, to be on display.

"Lovely service," Aunt Jean tells me, her gloved hands clasping mine. "Betty would have been so proud."

"Thank you. I hope so."

"Are you holding up okay? I know you two were very close."

In truth, Aunt Jean knows nothing. She is my father's sister and has not been on speaking terms with Mom since she refused to attend my parents' wedding.

"I'm holding up very well, Aunt Jean. I hope you'll have some food. We have so much."

"I saw that!" And off she goes to the groaning board loaded with turkey and ham, a roast beef and bread, cheese, lettuce, tomato, and condiments to make sandwiches. There is also a spinach lasagna for the vegetarians, courtesy of Em. And tons of dessert, courtesy of me.

My mother's friends brought Swedish meatballs in a Crock-Pot, chicken wings, fruit salad, a veggie tray, and some hideous pink aspic. All of them have been ignored in favor of Liza's contribution, a huge tray of smoked salmon with capers, sliced lemon, red onions, cream cheese, and bagels. Not a can of Cheez Whiz to be had.

Ignored, that is, after devouring what D'Ours brought on a silver platter: crackers, sliced cucumbers, hard-boiled eggs, and caviar one notch down from beluga.

"This is better than some weddings I've been to," Paul murmurs. "I can't wait to get out of this line so I can hit that table. Scooter was supposed to save me some caviar, but . . . where is she?"

I point to D'Ours, who is being accosted by a human lamppost.

Donald comes up and takes my hand, pausing for a bit before saying, "Grief is a necessary emotion, but kept unchecked it can turn into psychosis. If you're not aware of the symptoms, I can lend you a pamphlet."

"How nice of you to cheer me up."

"I'm a doctor, Julie, first and foremost."

Don't I know it.

Are my eyes deceiving me? Or is that Carol—*Michael's* Carol—slinking toward us in a handkerchief of black silk?

"Julie, I'm so, so, sorry." Carol gives Paul the once-over. "I had to come since I was—"

"There when she died," I say. "Yes. That's very thoughtful of you.

And thank you for that, by the way." Because what I said makes no sense, I add, "The more the merrier, I guess."

She smiles wryly, flicks Paul yet another glance, and whispers, "I know this isn't a good time, but at some point I'd like to clear up a persistent misunderstanding you might have about Michael." Turning to Paul again, she adds, "Or you could just ask him."

Ask Paul?

Paul shrugs and takes Carol's smooth hands as she goes on and on about my mother and how five minutes alone with her was enough to see what a fantastic woman she was. Even Scooter's on high alert, sticking out her neck and bugging her eyes.

Liza comes by a second time to pass me some salmon and get a closer look at Carol. "You know, there's something I never told you because I was held to secrecy, but now that she's died, I suppose that oath is off."

"Mom held you to an oath of secrecy?"

"Nothing big. Just those dessert classes. She was the one who put me up to it."

For a second, I have no idea what she's talking about. Put her up to what? Then I remember how this all started with Liza selling the tickets to Michael and Mom and fixing the church raffle so we both ended up in the class.

"Are you telling me Mom set me up with Michael?"

Wiping cracker crumbs off her fingers, she says, "That's right. Your mom threw in an extra five hundred bucks to seal the deal, too. Bet you'll never be able to pass through the church kitchen without wondering what that money bought."

So Mom wasn't lying when she told me those tickets cost her a lot of scratch. Still, it doesn't make sense. All those years of warning me to stay clear of Michael as a love-struck teenager and she goes out of her way to set me up with him decades later. Now, why would she have done something like that?

D'Ours is the last to stop in the line, assuring me, again, that the job's still mine if I want it and then that's it. We're done.

"I gotta wash up," Paul says, turning to go down the cobblestone hall. "Did you know shaking hands is the most germ-filled activity you can engage in? Worse than anonymous sex, from what I've read."

Outside the men's room door, I stop him. "Carol implied you know something about Michael you're not telling me."

"Not now, Julie. Bad enough the caviar's gone. There's hardly anything left of that salmon."

He's itching to get to that table, but I won't let him. I actually stand in front of the door and block his way. "Tell me."

"You mean, after meeting at Bukowski's Tavern and the drive home and the hospital and airport he still hasn't been straight?"

"Please, Paul. This is driving me crazy."

Checking to see no one's listening, he says, "Look. If anyone's to blame for you two not getting together sooner, it's me. My guess is that's what Carol wanted me to say. That I've been in the way."

This is confusing and makes no sense. "What?"

"I don't know if Michael ever told you about the time he came home from college and saw you in your shorts and tank top and . . ."

Rolling my hand for him to get on with it, I say, "Yeah, yeah. I know all this. So?"

"So, I wasn't too thrilled by that. I mean, you're my little sister and he's my best friend. He shouldn't have been checking you out like that."

"You mean, he really liked me back then?" I find this hard to believe, considering how he pushed me away when I threw myself at him at age seventeen.

"Didn't you see the way he looked at you? I don't know how much experience you've had with men—wait—I don't want to know. Maybe back then you didn't have any, but he was head over heels." Taking another breath, he says, "That guy loves you and always has."

"But he never told me."

"I don't know why. Everyone knew. Mom did, that's for sure. I don't know about Dad because . . . well, Dad didn't. I did. Our friends did. We'd tease him about robbing the cradle and jailbait. Though I didn't find it funny. I threatened to punch his lights out if he so much as laid a finger on you."

I'm giddy. I'm filled with joy. *Michael has always loved me.* He didn't just make that up years later to get my lobster.

"I'm really sorry. I should have realized when you two were having problems that my stupidity played a part." He thumbs the men's room. "Can I go now?"

"One more question. Michael wasn't afraid of you, not really. So what kept him from making a pass?"

"Who do you think? He was a full-grown man and you were her"—he pauses to fake a cough—"virgin daughter. Mom was on him like white on rice to keep away from you. Michael didn't care about crossing me, but he sure as hell cared about crossing Mom."

Mom and her bizarre codes of sexual conduct, I think, remembering how she pursed her lips when Nadia made that crack about virginity and Teenie confessed her affairs with the serviceman going off to World War II. My mother was open-minded in many ways, but not about sex.

"Look, Julie," Paul is saying, "I really have to go."

"Me too," I say, flying out the door, turning my back on my family, on Em and Lois and all the mourners, to find him before it's too late.

Michael doesn't show until the sun has sunk behind the trees, casting rays of subdued light across the gravestones. The ground over my mother's ashes, in the same plot where my father's body will be buried and where a space has been reserved for me, too, is covered with new dirt and strewn flowers—daisies, her favorite. She and I have been sitting here, yapping in what, for once, is a refreshingly one-sided conversation.

I understand now why she was so eager to get me into that dessert class with Michael. Because she was trying to make up for past misdeeds.

Here Michael and I had been meant for each other all along. Yet thanks to—as she once said herself—her silly Yankee notion that a relationship between a twenty-one-year-old man and a seventeen-year-old girl would end in some Shakespearean tragedy, she objected. Out of respect for her, Michael heeded her warnings and stayed away.

While I, reeling from my rejection at such a tender age, moved on, subconsciously fulfilling my mother's goals by dutifully graduating from college, finding a good job, and marrying a doctor—to disastrous results (except for Em, who is anything but a disaster).

Now, at last, we know the truth.

Seeing me sitting on a gravestone, Michael hesitates. In his arm is an ivy plant and it almost brings on a fresh burst of tears. How did he remember her unsuccessful campaign to plant the sloping bank in front of our house with ivy? That was her one wish—to have an ivy-covered house—and yet, despite her gardening savoir faire, she could never pull it off.

"It's English," he announces, holding up the plant. "To withstand the New England winters. I think it's called Twenty-eighth Street."

"So that's where she went wrong. She was always a sucker for the romantic Southern stuff," I say, sliding off Louis Marx's tombstone and walking toward him. Michael looks good in a light tweed jacket, gray T-shirt, jeans, and running shoes. As I get closer, I can tell he's searching my face to check my emotions.

His hand covers mine, warm and strong. "She was a kick," he says.

"That seems to be the general consensus. By the way . . . your letter." I pull it from my bra. "Did you mean what you said?"

"No," he says. "I was completely smashed and don't remember a word."

"I love you, too."

"Yes, I know you do. You've told me only a hundred times."

"You're so cocky. What you don't know is that I also know you've always loved me."

Wrapping his arms around my waist, he says, "Really? What gave you that idea?"

"For starters, all those girls you brought by the house. Never married one of them. Why? Then I got married, so you got married. Then I got divorced, and you got divorced. And then you moved back to Boston for no reason. Or maybe *I* was the reason."

"Little good it did me. You hated my guts for six years. All because I dared to trample on your journalistic integrity." There is a sarcastic tone to his voice, as if journalistic integrity is hardly worth denying happiness. He's right.

"I forgave you."

Michael opens his mouth to object, but I remind him that was his line.

"And now I find out from Paul that you loved me all along but that my sweet, wonderful mother cowed you into behaving yourself."

"So we're star-crossed, are we? Victims of bad timing and miscommunication. Very Shakespearean," he says. "Though, I suppose, we're the opposite of Benedick and Beatrice in that you and I, far from scorning true love, have been searching for it."

"When we didn't need to. When it was here all along."

"We could have gotten married young," he says. "Or, younger. We could have had children together, raised a family. But when you married Donald and got pregnant—"

"Not quite in that order," I correct.

"I was sure my true love had been taken away forever." Bringing me closer, he kisses my head lovingly. "Then you were free and I wasn't and then we burned so many years in a bitter, meaningless feud."

"Until my mother brought us back together."

"Thank God." Bending down to kiss me, he whispers, "I love you, Julie. I always have and always will. My only regret is it took us this long."

As I rest my head against his chest, I say, "I'm not sad we didn't get together sooner. I'm glad we found each other at last."

"After only thirty years?"

"Doesn't matter how long. The last words my mother said to me were 'love abides.' And I guess she was right because here you are and here she's not and yet my love for both of you is stronger than ever. Love lays waste time and death."

It's comforting, this thought that though parted, my mother and I will never really be separated.

Whenever I open her rusted barn recipe box, I will be swept back to her world, to her warm Harvest Gold kitchen with its reassuring smells of meat loaf and banana pudding. I will hear her voice remind me to go easy on the sugar and add vanilla to cake mixes for extra oomph. I will remember the stories of Aunt Charlotte's ugly china and Pokey the basset hound who lost his zing.

And I will feel her familiar hug reminding me that mothers may come and go, but their recipes—like all manifestations of true love—go on forever.

What is love? 'Tis not hereafter;
Present mirth has present laughter;
What's to come is still unsure:
In delay there lies no plenty;
Then come kiss me sweet and twenty,
Youth's a stuff will not endure.

—TWELFTH NIGHT, ACT II, SCENE 3

Acknowledgments

This book could not have been written without Dutton's inconceivable faith in me for which I am so very grateful. I am indebted to Brian Tart, Trena Keating, Lisa Johnson, Rachel Ekstrom and, especially, my talented editor, Julie Doughty, who worked relentlessly and thoroughly to give this book legs. Thank you, thank you. I am the luckiest author to have the support of this exemplary publishing house.

My agent and friend Heather Schroder at ICM went above and beyond her job description yet again by helping me hone and refine the concept and manuscript, reading it several times until she was satisfied. I am truly blessed.

In addition, I must acknowledge several excellent dessert cookbooks I consulted for inspiration. *Classic Stars Desserts* by Emily Luchetti (Chronicle Books) and *The Art of Dessert* by Ann Amernick (Wiley) were very helpful, as were Epicurious.com and my mother's own recipes, such as those for peach cobbler and gingerbread with lemon sauce. I have thrown in my own touches here and there in describing the dishes and most are edible. Except for the Roquefort flan. Not quite sure about that one. . . .

R.N. Chris Koonz and Karen George helped me with medical research and The Tarts—authors Nancy Martin, Harley Jane Kozak, Elaine Viets, Michele Martinez, and Margie—came to my rescue many, many times. They can come to your rescue, too, at *The Lipstick Chronicles*, a link for which can be found on my Web site at www.sarahstrohmeyer.com as can many recipes in this book.

My family—Charlie, Anna, and Sam—suffered through another year of my preoccupation and obsession as I went through draft after draft working late at night and skipping many ski races. Thank you for your patience, as always.

Finally, I cannot close out these acknowledgments without noting the cosmic wonder of my own childhood crush reappearing after nearly thirty years to remind a middle-aged woman of how there is no more powerful combination in the universe than young love on a hot summer night. Shakespeare knew that, of course, and now so do I.

ABOUT THE AUTHOR

Agatha Award–winning novelist Sarah Strohmeyer is the author of *The Sleeping Beauty Proposal*, *The Cinderella Pact*, *The Secret Lives of Fortunate Wives*, and the successful Bubbles series (*Bubbles All the Way*, *Bubbles Betrothed*, *Bubbles A Broad*, *Bubbles Ablaze*, *Bubbles in Trouble*, and *Bubbles Unbound*). She has worked as a journalist for numerous publications, including *The Plain Dealer* and the *Boston Globe*. She lives with her family outside Montpelier, Vermont.